Marquess of Mayhem

Sins and Scoundrels
Book Three

Scarlett Scott

Additional Dragonblade books by Author, Scarlett Scott

The Sins and Scoundrels Series
Duke of Depravity
Prince of Persuasion
Marquess of Mayhem

*** Please visit Dragonblade's website for a full list of books and authors. Sign up for Dragonblade's blog for sneak peeks, interviews, and more: ***
www.dragonbladepublishing.com

Returning to London scarred and bitter after his capture by Napoleon's forces, Morgan, Marquess of Searle, is hell-bent on vengeance against the man responsible for his imprisonment. He'll do anything to get what he wants, even if it means destroying an innocent in the process. There's just one problem. He's never met anyone like the woman he intends to use for his revenge.

Lady Leonora Forsythe has suffered enough awkward seasons. She longs to find a husband and make a family of her own. After the wickedly handsome Marquess of Searle ruins her, she has no intention of falling in love with the cold, distant stranger she's forced to wed. But it doesn't take long for her to realize there's far more to the marquess than she ever supposed. Or to hope she may be the one to heal his inner torment.

When Leonora is in Morgan's arms, reprisal is the last thing on his mind. With time running out and the truth looming, he must choose between the need for retribution and the fierce wife who unexpectedly owns his heart.

CHAPTER ONE

London, 1812

F ROM THE MOMENT Morgan, Marquess of Searle, discovered the true identity of the Spanish guerrillero responsible for his capture by French troops, he had set three objectives.

Objective one: sell out his commission and return to England before the Spaniard. *Accomplished.*

Objective two: ruin the bastard's sister so she would be forced to wed him. *In medias res.*

Objective three: make the rest of the Spaniard's life a living hell until he ended it on the field of honor. *A promise.*

Retribution was the sole thing on his mind when Morgan first saw Lady Leonora Forsythe. She was seated on the periphery of the ballroom, attended by a turban-wearing dowd with a wan complexion. The turban was obviously the lady's mother.

He'd been told Lady Leonora suffered an unfortunate limp, which precluded her from dancing. However, he had not been told she possessed the breathtaking beauty of an angel. The former did not deter him. He could easily guide her into a darkened alcove or an empty hall. Nor did the latter. Even angels were meant to fall.

Watching her, he sipped from his glass of punch. The stuff was sickening and sweet, and its only saving grace was in the bite of the spirits lacing it. When he imbibed, he preferred unsullied spirits. The sort that made him forget, if only for an evening. Sadly, not even a

1

drop of illicit Scottish whisky was to be had at the Kirkwood ball.

The man owned a gaming hell that served the best liquor in the land. Morgan would have expected better, but he supposed anything less than proper ballroom fare would have been frowned upon by the tittering lords and ladies who had assembled here this evening. Kirkwood's wife was a duke's daughter, and it would seem the festivities were his attempt to blur the boundaries between his world and the quality.

Morgan didn't give a damn for balls. He also didn't give a damn about the punch he was drinking or the room in which he stood, or the fact he was not imprisoned and being tortured by French soldiers who wanted answers he refused to give. His body, beneath the trappings of his evening finery, was marked with scars and burns, all testaments to his inability to ever give a damn about anything again.

Anything except making the Spaniard suffer, that was.

El Corazón Oscuro, the Dark Heart. Also known as the Earl of Rayne, half-brother to Lady Leonora. It was almost impossible to believe as he flicked his gaze over her, marveling at her white-blonde hair and skin pale enough to rival cream. But it was true. The blackest-hearted devil he had ever known and the lovely woman in the diaphanous silver gown shared blood.

And soon they would share one more connection.

Morgan's wrath.

But first, he needed an introduction.

Fortunately, he did not have far to look or long to wait, for his trusted friend and old comrade-at-arms Crispin, the Duke of Whitley, joined him by the next thudding beat of his heart. Revenge would soon be his. He could taste it, bitter and dark and delicious, upon his tongue. He could feel it in the surge, the pounding pulse of blood coursing through his veins, much as it had before a battle: fierce, fast, consuming.

It was a rush, and for the first time since his return to England, since he had been freed from captivity, he felt alive. So gloriously, viciously alive.

"Morgan." Crispin exchanged a stilted greeting with him, his bearing, his tone, and even his expression, stiff with guilt.

Much as it had been ever since their reunion.

Crispin had been with him on the Peninsula that fateful day, when *El Corazón Oscuro* had taken Morgan captive. The bleak, hideous, hateful day it had all begun...

But he would not think of that day now. Nor would he think of the torture that had ensued. For if he did, then the madness would come. And he could not entertain the madness today. Today, he must remain determined. Today, he must stay the course and keep the madness at bay.

He must begin his retribution. Imprisoned as he had been all those months, he had been given ample time to meticulously plan the foundation of his revenge. In the end, he had become so inured to even the beatings, that he would separate his mind from his body. His mind would wander while his body faced unimaginable cruelties and degradations. And in his mind, it was always London to which he returned, sweet revenge which he earned.

His heart sped up, pounding in his chest and in his ears.

But he could not give in here. He gulped down the rest of his punch to distract himself. "Tell me Kirkwood has something better than this swill hidden somewhere. Some misbegotten Scottish whisky, perhaps."

"Of course he does," Crispin returned, studying him with a gaze reminiscent of the manner in which one would survey a wild animal. A snarling fox, perhaps, with its fangs bared, about to decimate creatures smaller than himself. "But one does not partake of whisky at balls, Searle."

Morgan felt not so much like a snarling fox as a rampaging lion, hungry for blood. Too large and too angry and too voracious to be stopped.

"Balls would be so much less tedious if one did." A servant hovering nearby approached with a tray at the ready, whisking away his empty glass.

"I am glad to see you here, Morgan." Crispin paused. "My duchess has convinced me to play the role of the gentleman and indulge in the social whirl."

"Glad to see me at all, you mean to say." He cocked his head, considering his old friend, who had gone pale beneath his scrutiny.

Together, they had witnessed hell on earth. What he had endured on his own was a level beyond that, a tenth circle of hell, as it were. Inexplicable. And he would not lie. He envied Crispin for escaping as he had, with nothing but a sore head and a return voyage to London to take his seat as the heir. All while Morgan had lingered as a captive of first the guerrillas and then the French. All while he had been beaten and interrogated, while he had been humiliated and abused in vile fashion.

None of that had been Crispin's fault, it was true. Rather, it had been the fault of *El Corazón Oscuro*. Which was why he was standing here, in this ballroom, dressed as if he cared about waltzing and bowing and commenting upon the size of the gathering and the quality of the lords and ladies strutting about the room.

Peacocks, all of them.

But could he blame them, truly blame them? He had been a peacock once, too, after all. It had been only his time abroad and his years as a soldier that had rendered him any different. Those times had made him who he was today.

"Yes," Crispin said then. "I am damned glad to be seeing you at all. You have the way of it, precisely. I missed you, old friend. I...when I believed you gone..."

"But here I am," he interrupted quickly. Coldly, too. For truth be told, he could not bear any reminders. His overtaxed body and mind could not endure returns to what had happened. Even mere thoughts made him shake like a tree at the mercy of a violent wind.

He understood the problem was likely his and not anyone else's. It had taken him a solid fortnight upon his return to London before he could even leave his townhome. Before he could step a bloody foot out the goddamned front door. It had taken him just as long to understand what had befallen him as a soldier had changed him. It had changed him forever, and there would be no return to the Morgan he had been before.

There was only the hardened shell remaining now.

"Yes," Crispin echoed solemnly. "Here you are."

He said it as if the words were somehow untrue. And his friend was not wrong in this, for they were untrue, in part.

His attempt at a smile went flat. "War changes us."

"That day," Crispin began. "Your hand...I do not understand."

"The severed hand did not belong to me. Only the signet ring did," he bit out, for this was the last thing he wished to discuss ever, let alone at a ball in the midst of polite London society.

He understood Crispin's confusion. Though much of what had happened on that day in Spain remained mired in a part of his mind he had deliberately closed off, he could not suppress the image of one of *El Corazón Oscuro's* minions sliding his signet rink onto the pinky of one of the butchered French soldiers. The Spaniard had raised a deadly looking blade, and chopped the Frenchman's wrist with one swift blow.

The fallen soldier had not yet been dead, which had made the scene even more gruesome. Sometimes, Morgan still heard the poor bastard's scream in his nightmares.

"But the reason for what occurred," Crispin continued. "I am deuced glad *El Corazón Oscuro* left you whole, but—"

"I can assure you I am not whole," Morgan stayed him bitterly. "But I will not discuss this with you further, Cris. Not here. Not now."

Not ever.

Mere thoughts of what had happened made him lose control of his body. Already, a cold sweat broke out on his skin and his hands tremored.

Crispin's jaw ticked. "Then when, Morgan? You have been avoiding this dialogue ever since your return. You are my oldest and greatest friend. I thought you dead. I mourned you. Can you not imagine I would wish to revisit that day, to understand what occurred?"

What had occurred was that Morgan and Crispin had been ambushed by *El Corazón Oscuro*. Crispin had been left behind, and Morgan had been taken. It was as simple and as complicated as that. What came after that day…he could not think it. Could not face it.

He ground his molars with so much force his jaw ached. "Can you not imagine I would not wish to revisit that day, Cris? I have come here tonight in search of a wife, not to dwell upon the hells of war."

Crispin's brows shot upward. "You are seeking a wife?"

He well understood his friend's surprise. He had always sworn off the parson's mousetrap, having seen the damage such an institution could do to two people. His own sire and mother had been at daggers drawn for the entirety of their union. They had hated each other with a vicious vengeance. His father's wrath had run so deep he had refused to even share a roof with his mother.

But this was different, and he had a reason for seeking a wife. Not just any wife. One woman only. His eyes traveled once more to Lady Leonora. She possessed an icy, regal elegance. A beauty that took his breath. But she also had something else—a hesitance, perhaps. As if she were embarrassed of something. As if she were unsure of herself.

He could use her weakness to his advantage.

"I am contemplating marriage," he said, continuing to watch as the turban—still presumably the lady's mother—glanced in his direction and then began fluffing her skirts as if she were a hen in the house, ruffling her feathers. "Since my return, I have been visited by an affliction of sorts. I now possess a healthy respect for my own mortality, and the need to secure the line has risen within me, stronger than ever before."

The turban fixed a smile to her lips and appeared to surreptitiously deliver orders to Lady Leonora. Lady Leonora fidgeted her skirts, draping them over the limb he had noted her favoring earlier. Yes, there it was. Her infirmity was the source of the hesitancy he sensed.

Of course it would be. He imagined her sobriquet, Limping Leonora, would also be a great source of pain for her. She looked about the ballroom then, as if in search of someone. He willed her to look in his direction. To see him. But she did not.

"You are interested in Lady Leonora Forsythe?" Crispin asked quietly, dredging him from his inspection of the lady in question.

"Is she a familiar of yours?" he asked, hoping he had just found the solution to his problem, one which would enable him to accomplish objective number two with far greater ease.

Crispin studied him, his gaze intent. Searching. "She is, yes, through my lovely wife."

Crispin had gotten married whilst Morgan had been trapped on the Continent. Morgan had seen Crispin and his lovely duchess together on several occasions since his return, and the two exuded contentment and nauseating love with such disturbing devotion, he had been forced to excuse himself from their presence.

Mayhap here was something that would render Whitley's wife useful after all, and mitigate the suffering he had endured in having to witness their lovesick banter and mooning glances.

"Perhaps you can introduce us," Morgan suggested, a smile pulling at his lips for the first time this evening.

It was not a pleasant smile, and he knew it from the manner in which his friend stiffened and frowned. It was the smile of a predator about to snap his jaws upon his unsuspecting prey. Of the soldier who

7

slammed his bayonet into the gullet of his enemy before the other man could act. It was born of ugliness. Of relief and anticipation, of grim, satisfying victory.

He felt like the very devil about to descend upon the angelic Lady Leonora. But he had no place inside him for compunction any longer. It had been excised from his body by weeks of beatings. He had always taken the beatings, the pain. And he would take Lady Leonora now in the same way: without flinching.

She was to be his prize.

"I am not sure that is wise," Crispin said, his tone steeped in caution. "Lady Leonora is…delicate."

He stared right back at his friend, determination coursing through him as surely as blood in his veins. "I require an introduction to the lady."

"You intend to marry her?" Crispin asked then. "My wife will flay my hide if you dally with Lady Leonora and raise her hopes."

"Others have flayed my hide, Cris," he informed his friend bitterly. "Men with far greater determination to inflict pain than your duchess. Will you introduce me to Lady Leonora, or must I seek out another?"

Crispin exhaled on a reluctant sounding sigh, and Morgan knew he had won. "Very well. I shall introduce you. But if you hurt her in any fashion—"

"Lead the way," he interrupted curtly, returning his gaze once more to Lady Leonora. His future marchioness.

He knew in his heart and in his gut right then and there, he would hurt her. He would break her. He would use her, and he would not feel the slightest hint of guilt, for one day soon, *El Corazón Oscuro* would face him once more, man to man, and he would have his goddamn revenge.

FREDDY WAS MARRIED.

From her customary position at every social event, the resident wallflower seated on the outskirts of the ballroom, Leonora watched her dearest friend, Lady Frederica Kirkwood, smiling up at her dashing husband, Mr. Duncan Kirkwood. The evening's ball was a grand event, the societal debut of the married couple. Mr. Kirkwood—a gaming hell owner and illegitimate son of the Duke of Amberly—was determined to be respectable. And Amberly, who was in attendance this evening as well, had lent his aid to that cause.

Leonora was happy for her friend. So happy a sheen of tears blurred her vision as she watched the dark-haired Freddy and her golden-haired husband whirling about the ballroom. They made a striking pair, truly they did.

A spear of some indefinable emotion shot straight through her at the sight. She did not wish to believe it was envy, for she loved her friend, and Freddy deserved every happiness. She deserved a husband who was handsome and who gazed upon her with rapt adoration, quite as if she were the only female in all London, because Freddy was kind and noble and tenderhearted, and there was no finer lady to be found than she.

No, Leonora did not begrudge Freddy all the wondrous change her friend had experienced since marrying the man she loved. But some small and wicked part of Leonora wished that for once in her nine-and-twenty years, she would not be overlooked. That she would not be Limping Leonora, whom no gentleman wished to wed.

That she would have a husband of her own.

He did not even need to be as handsome as Mr. Kirkwood. Leonora did not fool herself about her matrimonial prospects. She was not a catch. Her dowry was paltry, and her half brother was the enigmatic Earl of Rayne, of half Spanish blood and notorious for his reclusive ways. He had not been seen in town for some years. Indeed, Leonora had only heard from her half brother occasionally in recent years, through sporadic letters sent from abroad. She knew nothing of his whereabouts beyond his presence on the Continent. To Leonora, Alessandro had always been a caring, affectionate brother, in spite of his absences. Naturally, however, the whispers about his madness did nothing to aid her cause of husband hunting. And neither did her advanced age or infirmity.

Surely, she could find someone, however. A gentleman of consideration and compassion, one who would not look upon her as a creature to be pitied and scorned but instead as a woman who might be his bride.

"Do sit up straighter, my dear," said Mama suddenly, breaking her customary silence. "He is looking upon you now."

"He?" Leonora stiffened and instinctively adjusted the fall of her gown, making certain no hint of her lame leg existed beneath the diaphanous silk crepe. She gave a hasty glance about the ballroom, but as far as she could see, they were surrounded by the standard cadre of glittering, tittering lords and ladies, and not a soul of them were paying any attention at all to Limping Leonora or her invalid mother on the border of the fete.

"Do not cast your eyes wildly about the room," Mama chastised, her lips scarcely moving as she pinned a smile in place and fanned her face with such slowness it had no effect at all.

She frowned at her mother. "Are you overheated?"

Mama made a sound of long-suffering. "If only I were not so often abed, struck low by my failing health, I could have taught you how to snare a husband. How do you think I wed His Grace? It was not by sitting in a corner."

Leonora's cheeks went hot with embarrassment. Though this was an old quarrel between herself and Mama, it was nevertheless a dagger whose blade had not dulled with time. It still had the power to cut deeply into her flesh, and it did each time.

She could have pointed out Mama had not suffered the burden of a lame leg.

Instead, she held her tongue as she always did, for it was easier. "Of course, Mama. I am sorry your health has affected you so, and that I have been a burden to you with my inability to make a match. If any gentleman would have me, I would already be a wife and mother, and you would not have to act the chaperone for me when you are unwell and would be better served to remain at home, resting."

Mama fanned herself again. "He has looked away now, but I do believe he and the Duke of Whitley are in conversation about you, my dear. Why, I dare not trust my own eyes, for no one has ever..."

Though her mother's words trailed away, Leonora knew what she had been about to say. *No one has ever shown an interest in you.* And it was true. Try as she might, none of the eligible gentlemen she met wished to wed her. They did not want a painfully shy, quiet wife who limped and could not join them in a minuet. They wanted diamonds of the first water.

She swallowed down a lump that had risen in her throat. "I am certain whoever it is you speak of now is not interested in me either. No one wishes to wed Limping Leonora, and I cannot blame them."

"I am sorry, my dear," Mama said in hushed tones. "I did not mean to suggest that at all. Any gentleman would be more than pleased to make you his wife. It is merely that the Marquess of Searle is newly returned from battle, and he is being lauded as a hero, with all the talk of his time in captivity and how he was able to escape at last by building himself a tunnel with nothing more than his bare hands and burrowing his way to freedom." She fanned herself vigorously as she concluded her rapt retelling of Searle's reputed heroics.

"The Marquess of Searle?" Everything inside her tensed, her voice emerging as a squeak.

Leonora had consumed every story written about him with great interest. The story of the manner in which he had escaped Napoleon's soldiers made for excellent reading. At first, she had been swept away by the romanticized accounts. Ladies swooned over the mere mention of his name, and a party was no longer fashionable unless the marquess was in attendance.

But that did not mean she was not terrified of the man. She had chanced to see him recently, at a musicale. His arresting green gaze had burned into hers, riveting her as the realization he had been watching her poured over her.

At the time, she had imagined he found her limp a curiosity. Or that he was bored. For though he had been dressed in the first stare of fashion, sporting a blue coat, fawn breeches which hugged his long, muscular legs to perfection, and a snowy cravat styled in the latest knots, he had also possessed an edge. He had seemed dangerous, as lethal as a blade.

But now, Mama claimed he was watching her once more, days later. Was one limping wallflower of sufficient interest for a gentleman like the Marquess of Searle? She could not believe so. Her hands trembled as they fisted her skirt. The material was cool and soft, ethereal as a cloud, but its opulence did not distract her now. She scarcely felt it against her palms and clenched fingers.

"Of course it is the Marquess of Searle," Mama admonished. "Who else? Good heavens, I do believe he intends to approach us. Are you sitting straight, dearest?"

Leonora slouched. "I do not want him to approach us, Mama."

Mama sent a look in her direction. "Sit straight, you vexing girl. No gentleman wishes to make the acquaintance of a lady who cannot even hold herself with proper deportment. Little wonder you have yet to wed."

Yes, little wonder indeed. She bit her lower lip and cast another, frantic look around the ballroom. The dancers whirled gaily about, another set winding down. She caught one more glimpse of Freddy, blindingly lovely as she traded partners and was opposite Mr. Kirkwood again.

And then, there he was, striding with purpose, his long, well-sculpted legs eating up the distance between where she sat in unobtrusive freedom and *him*. That gaze was fastened upon her, as if he could devour her with it. He had another gentleman at his side, the Duke of Whitley, and while Whitley was handsome in his own right, he did not command her attention. Not in the manner the marquess did.

Nay, the marquess was different. He stole the breath from her lungs and made her heart gallop, and not just because he was blessed with undeniable masculine beauty, from his dark hair to his slashing cheekbones. But because he was angry. There was a darkness raging inside him. She could sense it in the way he carried himself. His bearing was rigid, from shoulders to jaw, his countenance harsh, as if it had been frozen into joyless place. As if whatever horrors he had experienced at war had robbed him of any hint of softness.

"Do not bite your lip," Mama admonished lowly as the two gentlemen approached. "You are slouching."

"I am not slouching," she managed to grumble, drooping her shoulders. How she wished in that moment she were as invisible as she so often felt.

"Stand," Mama commanded her at last, rising from her chair like a ship about to set sail. "My head is beginning to ache, and I fear I am suffering from heart palpitations yet again, but if the marquess intends to court you, I shall endure all for your sake."

If one were to compile a list of Mama's ailments, it would prove longer than the Book of Genesis, Leonora was certain. But then she reminded herself Mama had made a great many sacrifices for her sake, and guilt instantly struck her for such an ungracious thought.

"Stand," Mama repeated, fanning herself as if she were in the midst of July heat rather than early spring, just after Easter.

Leonora considered remaining seated, but the thought of the Marquess of Searle hovering over her like a deity made her palms sweat. So, she rose, allowing herself a grimace as a twinge of pain radiated from her ankle upward. She had been seated for too long, and the old injury had stiffened as it tended to do.

"Smile," Mama commanded.

And Leonora would have, but she had lost the ability to think or breathe or speak. She did not even know she possessed a mouth at the moment, or lips with which to smile. All she knew was the Marquess of Searle stood before her.

"Lady Rayne," greeted the Duke of Whitley with flawless grace. "Lady Leonora. May I present to you, my lady, a cherished friend of mine, the Marquess of Searle?"

Leonora had not even glanced at Whitley. She was trapped in Searle's eyes, and at this proximity, they were not merely green. Flecks of cinnamon and gold striated the lush, verdant hue. His lashes were far too long for a man. And his intensity, the manner in which his gaze locked upon hers, sent a shiver straight through her, along with a shocking lick of heat.

For a moment, she could not move. She simply existed, a lowly creature pinned beneath the force of his stare, every part of her body humming with awareness until she tingled from the inside out. Sensations, so foreign and strange, radiated outward much like the ripples of a stone thrown into a lake's still surface. A strange feeling of finality struck her, as if this was the moment in her life from which all others would spring.

As if she would never be the same from now onward.

And then she realized a question had been posed to her, and she was exhibiting an appalling dearth of manners.

"Yes of course," she forced herself to say, still unable to look away from the marquess.

His brown hair was worn in glorious waves, longer than fashionable, yet the perfect foil for the harsh symmetry of his face. His countenance made no excuses for its blatant masculinity, and his nose was a slashing blade, his cheekbones high and sharp, his jaw a study in obstinacy, wide and harsh. The sole softness to be found was in his lips, which were well-molded and full. A cleft marked his proud chin, somehow tempering the severity, but his broad shoulders and tall, lean form held an air of command she had never seen on another gentleman.

He bowed with courtly elegance, his expression revealing nothing. "Lady Leonora, it is a pleasure to make your acquaintance at last."

At last, he'd said. Two words that signified so much. As if he had been anticipating this moment. Leonora could not help but feel as if she had, even without knowing it would ever happen. As if the Fates had destined this man, this meeting.

She swallowed and forced herself to maintain her composure, even as her heart continued to race. The Marquess of Searle was not just compelling and handsome, though he certainly was both, but being in his presence made her giddy and weak all at once. He affected her as no man ever had. Most gentleman bored her. Even when they ignored her, they did not hold her interest.

But this man...

He was different, and she knew it in a deep, primal part of herself. She felt it in the warmth washing over her, as if she basked in the benediction of a summer sun in the country. As if she were whole for the first time. As if she were not Limping Leonora but instead, someone of interest. Someone a gentleman would wish to be introduced to. As if she were a lady a gentleman would want to dance with and court.

This man, he was more dangerous than she had even initially supposed.

She forced herself to speak. "I am pleased to make your acquaintance as well, my lord."

Mama frowned at her, and she well knew why. Her voice sounded rusty and flat. She was incapable of flirting. She had never been seriously courted, aside from the odious Lord Robert Hurstly, who had courted her for a wager with the intent to cause her ruination. Her continued presence in the marriage mart was down to Mama's determination rather than to any hope a man would ask for her hand after all these years, though a husband and children of her own were all she longed for.

What would it be like to be looked upon with something other than pity, disinterest, or mild disgust? What would it be like to pretend, even for one evening, she too could be light and carefree, capable of gracefully gliding about a ballroom?

She stared at Searle, something at once awful and yet incredible happening inside her.

"We are honored by your presence, my lord," Mama said in a bright tone Leonora had never even heard. "Word of your bravery has been bandied about everywhere."

A coldness entered Searle's eyes, a rigidity seizing his bearing. "Thank you, my lady."

"It is a miracle Searle is here with us at all," the Duke of Whitley remarked, something in his expression and tone Leonora could not quite read.

"Would you care to dance, Lady Leonora?" the marquess asked suddenly then, and with such abruptness, even Leonora and her complete lack of experience with suitors was startled.

She wanted to tell Searle she did not dance. That she could not dance, and indeed never had in all the years since her debut.

But then it occurred to her that the reason she had not danced was not because she was incapable. She had taken lessons, and she knew all the steps, could even perform them, though she would never be graceful. No, she had never danced before because no one had ever asked her.

The knowledge sent a fresh emotion coursing through her, burning and fierce, part shame, part determination. She raised her chin. "I certainly would, my lord."

CHAPTER TWO

S HE HAD SAID *yes*. Morgan had been brusque and rude, nettled into action by references to his heroics and war. The need to escape had been so fierce, he had not stopped to question the wisdom of playing his card early.

He need not have been concerned. It was a different conundrum entirely facing him now. Morgan led Lady Leonora away from Crispin and the turban, astounded. He had taken his time, conducted his research well, and laid the foundation for his battle plan. Which was how he knew Lady Leonora never danced. Not once.

But she had accepted his invitation.

Now he could not help but to wonder why. He led her slowly, accommodating for the hesitance in her gait. In truth, her limp was scarcely noticeable, but he could tell the leg she favored pained her. She had grimaced upon standing, and her bearing had initially been stiff.

"Thank you for accepting my invitation, my lady," he said to her softly, because he knew he must say something.

He was meant to woo her, but it had been a long time—and a lifetime ago—since he had last attempted to charm any woman. There had been no need. No space in his mind or his life. There had been only war and then survival, and even now, dressed in his evening finery with Lady Leonora on his arm, he was still merely subsisting.

Surviving his current hell by creating a new one. A hell in which the Earl of Rayne and his glorious, innocent, unsuspecting sister, would join him. He supposed he ought to feel a needling of compunction. Instead, he felt only nothingness. A man did not survive the brutality he had suffered without being forever changed.

"Thank you for offering, my lord," she returned.

Her voice was husky and sweet, and it settled in his gut with the potent fire of whisky, wrapping around him like ivy. "You are the only lady in attendance I wish to dance with," he said, and it was true, even if his intentions were impure and cruel.

They established themselves on the dance floor, preparing for the next set to begin. Her lovely face was fraught with concern. Pinched. "It has been some time since I have danced, my lord. I fear I must warn you."

The trepidation in her tone gave him a moment of hesitation. "Are you certain you wish to—" But before he could complete his question, the music began.

He bowed to her formally, and she curtsied with an elegance he would not have expected and nary a hint of hesitation, though she did not dip as low as some.

Morgan linked hands with her. "Do you trust me?"

She inclined her head then. "My mind is not certain I ought to trust you, my lord, but something else within me says I should."

Foolish instinct. Foolish, foolish woman.

Victory washed over him. Already, she had made this battle into a decided rout.

"I find it always wise to trust one's instincts," he bit out, tamping down a swiftly accompanying wave of guilt.

A sad smile flirted with her lips for just a moment. "Perhaps not always."

Before he could reply, the dance had begun in earnest. It was a minuet, and he was heartily glad, as it granted him the opportunity to remain near to her without the necessity of trading partners. It was the dance of courtship, and he intended to use every rusty weapon of charm he could unearth to make her vulnerable to his seduction.

As they circled each other, he wondered what had happened to her, if the limb had been her burden from birth or if she had suffered an accident as a girl. And then he told himself her history did not matter.

The only part of Lady Leonora Forsythe which need interest him, was her kinship with her black-hearted, half-brother.

They left each other and then came back together again. His eyes clung to her, watching for any sign of weakness, and spying none. Not even her limp was in evidence as they performed the perfunctory steps. *One-two-three-four, one-two-three-four.* Her skirts swayed about her. A charming flush colored her pale cheeks, in stark contrast to her white-blonde hair.

Their hands met once more, and they circled each other, gazes meeting. Her eyes were an unusual shade of blue, a light periwinkle. They struck him. *She* struck him, like a physical blow to the chest.

She was a beauty. By God, she was breathtaking. And she danced like an angel.

Until she didn't.

As they parted and swirled about each other once more in the course of the dance, she stumbled, catching herself before she tripped. Stubbornly, she continued on, but he saw the pinched expression of pain on her countenance, noted the tightened knot of her otherwise generous mouth.

She was in pain.

Damn it, he intended to use her, not to humiliate her. A protective instinct surged within him, entirely unwanted. He did not know where it emerged from or why. All he knew was he did not want to see her suffer.

The music reunited them, hands linked.

"Do you need a respite, my lady?" he asked.

Her brows snapped together and her shoulders stiffened, her countenance growing determined. "No, though I thank you for your concern, my lord."

"My lady," he protested, uncertain where this vein of gentlemanly concern originated.

Her fingers tightened on his. She twirled about with him, not gliding but not allowing her painful limb to limit her. "I am perfectly capable of dancing, my lord."

The flash of pride in her gaze hit him. He wondered, then, at the reason for her never having danced.

"Of course, my lady," he reassured her to assuage her pride.

Why had she ordinarily kept stuck to her seat at such events? Was it because no man had ever gathered the courage to approach her blinding beauty and ask? Or was it because every man before him had been reluctant to ask because of her perceived infirmity?

The leg gave her pain, he could plainly see as much from her drawn mouth and the occasional grimace tightening her countenance. But she was determined to persevere, to force her mind to overpower any weakness.

And he could not help but to inwardly applaud her tenacity. Lady Leonora Forsythe continued to surprise him. If she had been emptyheaded or silly, if she had thrown herself at him in an effort to become his marchioness, if she had been anything other than what she seemed to be—an innocent beauty with a fierce determination—he would have already led her away from the dance and the ball with nary a prick of guilt.

Morgan would have convinced her to enter a darkened chamber or alcove with him. He would have lifted her skirts, his hand gliding beneath to touch her, from ankle to cunny. Christ, he would have ruined her already.

And he would have damn well enjoyed it.

Why was he tarrying? Why was he, even now, playing the noble courtier when all he needed to do was to convince her to escape from the ballroom and meet with him in private?

They worked their way back to each other, hands clasped, gazes meeting once more. Her face was more carefully devoid of expression this time, though her limp was growing a bit more noticeable.

"You dance beautifully, my lady," he praised, rather than inquiring after her welfare once more, something he could sense she would not wish.

Her face reflected her astonishment for a brief moment, before a flush stole over her pale cheeks. Damnation, she stole his breath. She was like a fae creature walking among mere mortals. Too beautiful to be real. He tried and failed to find any physical resemblance to her evil-bastard-of-a-brother. If only she had looked like the dark-haired, dark-hearted one, *El Corazón Oscuro*. It would have rendered what he must do so bloody much easier.

"I dance beautifully for a lame-legged spinster, you mean to say, my lord," she responded tartly. "You need not sound surprised. I am as capable of dancing as I am of walking. Unfortunately, my weak limb does not wish to allow me to cultivate grace, regardless of how much I would prefer it."

Devil take it, he was mucking this up badly. His dubious reputation as a war hero aside, he was aware of the manner in which most ladies viewed him. He was handsome. There was no reason why his overtures ought to be failing so abysmally.

Except he had underestimated Lady Leonora.

He forced a charming grin to his lips, recalling some of the old Morgan. The devil-may-care man who had been a silver-tongued rogue, carefree and unabashed in his pursuit of skirt. The original Morgan, before war had carved him out and left him a hollow shell.

"I said precisely what I intended, my lady," he parried smoothly. "You dance beautifully, and I consider myself fortunate indeed to have the loveliest lady in attendance as my partner."

They parted once more, circling each other and winding their way through the dance floor before coming together for a final turn. This time, when their hands clasped, her gaze was bright and glistening.

"Thank you, my lord," was all she said.

And he knew then and there, he would win.

He would have this woman however he wanted. Sadly, the capitulation left him feeling as numb as ever. Not even a shred of relief or satisfaction could sweep aside the deadness within.

The dance ended, and he bowed to her as she dipped into a perfect curtsy, the concentration on her expression revealing how much control she exerted. He offered her his arm and began leading her slowly back to the turban.

Here was his chance, and he needed to seize it.

"I want to get to know you better, my lady," he told her quietly. "I confess, you intrigue me in a way no other lady has."

"In the manner of a spinster—"

"In the manner of a beautiful woman," he corrected, not wishing to hear her disparage herself once more.

Because, though he had sought her out with impure motives, he could not help but to suspect the old Morgan would have been enamored of her, intrigued by her. The man he had once been would have noticed her on the periphery of the ball, and he would have been determined to win her. But his reasons would have been pure and true.

She swallowed, keeping her face averted when he would have dearly loved to search her gaze and take a guess at her emotions, her vulnerability.

"Was this dance the product of a wager, my lord?" she asked at last. "You would not be the first, though I must admit, you are the gentleman who has brought the most charm along with him for the duty."

A sharp pang, something akin to regret mingled with anger, struck him in the chest then. Others had used her for a lark or to line their pockets with some betting, book-won gold. The notion made him sick twofold: one, that she had suffered such thoughtless and careless attentions when she was so clearly deserving of far more; and two, that he was no better than the nameless, faceless bastards who had transgressed against her.

He stopped them, well on the outskirts of the ballroom floor, but far enough away from her mother, they could still speak with candor. For he needed her to know. He needed it with a ferocity that threatened to tear him apart, and he neither understood it nor could avoid it.

He faced her, falling into her light-blue eyes. "I did not dance with you because of a wager, Lady Leonora. I danced with you because I have been watching you from afar, and I had become desperate to make your acquaintance. When my old friend, the Duke of Whitley, mentioned he was an acquaintance of yours, I could not stop myself."

She searched his gaze, and he knew not for what. It wasn't just her beauty that made him ache as he gazed down at her upturned face. Nor was it the sure knowledge he had found the one woman who would be able to help him achieve the revenge he so desperately needed.

He was a man broken, and in that moment on the outskirts of the Kirkwood ball, he found himself within the glittering depths of Lady Leonora Forsythe's eyes. Her scent wafted to him then, gentle and sweet.

Or, at least, he found the version of himself he had been forced to become, vicious and merciless, even against the innocent. He would destroy this delicate flower, and he would do so without compunction. She could not possibly hold a candle to the blinding force of rage swirling within him.

She raised an imperious, ice-blonde brow. "My lord, you are the most eligible bachelor in London, a war hero freshly returned from rescuing yourself from Boney's soldiers, horridly handsome, and here I am, a spinster firmly on the shelf, nine-and-twenty and suffering from the aftereffects of the limb I broke as a girl."

Her impassioned speech answered one of his many questions. She had suffered a bone break as a girl, and that was the reason for her pain. Likely, it had never healed with proper care. He had seen more than his fair share of broken bones on the field of battle, and he knew all too well how difficult recovery was, ofttimes impossible given the grim panorama of war.

"My lady," he returned with equal passion, merely one that originated from a vastly different source. "I have no wish to be the most eligible bachelor in London, and I most certainly am not a war hero. Nor are you anything less than the loveliest woman I have ever seen."

Everything he had uttered was true. The only impurity was in his motivation and in his goals. But he could not allow himself to feel guilt over his intentions. Lady Leonora was his enemy. She was the sister of the man who had singlehandedly caused Morgan's imprisonment with his rash, stubborn, stupid posturing.

For a moment, he wished she was turnip-faced, or a bitter harridan, or an arrogant wench. Anything other than the humble, timid, gloriously beautiful lady who had lived her entire life on the periphery of everyone else's.

But he could not change her any more than he could change himself. And he could not quench the burning need within him, the raging fire, with anything other than her complete sacrifice.

"You pay me a great compliment, my lord," she said then, disrupting his inner war.

Enemy, he reminded himself with lethal force. *This woman is your enemy as surely as her brother.*

He would not be weak. With great effort, he summoned up a Lothario's smile. She was the sort of woman he could not cozen into meeting him in a darkened alcove or an abandoned chamber, and he realized that now. He would have to woo her in a different manner—

first a few shots fired, then retreat, and then the final charge.

"The compliment is all mine, Lady Leonora," he assured her, forcing his gaze to seek out the turban, who watched their interchange with unabashed maternal curiosity and calculation.

The mother would not be a hindrance to his cause, at least. She had already decided he was the matrimonial prize her daughter required to save her from spinsterhood. How wrong she was. He was no prize. If anything, he was a curse.

"More words," Lady Leonora said, giving him another start.

His gaze snapped back to hers. "I beg your pardon, my lady?"

"You offer me words, my lord," she elaborated, giving him a half-smile that made him want to crush her mouth with his. "But I find the greatest indication of anyone's true intentions is through action alone. The tongue tends to be the easiest muscle in one's body to use, does it not?"

Bloody hell. He would like to use his tongue. Upon her.

He swallowed against a sudden rush of lust caused by Lady Leonora indicating she preferred action to words and referencing her tongue. By all that was holy, he would show her action, and he would show her the manner in which he preferred to use his tongue against her. There would be no words. Only deeds.

"Perhaps you are correct, Lady Leonora," he said softly. "But I dare not keep you from Lady Rayne any longer. I would not wish to tarry with you overly long and cause any hint of scandal to attach itself to your name."

What rot. In truth, he had every intention of causing her scandal. Of forcing her to wed him by compromising her so thoroughly she had no other option save becoming his marchioness. But not now. Not quite yet. First, he needed to convince her his intentions were pure and true. He would wait for the right moment to strike.

"Yes," she said, her tone growing subdued, her expression freezing, becoming guarded once more. "Of course, my lord."

He guided her in the direction of her mother, a new plan formulating in his mind. After all, there had to be a manner in which he could draw her to his side sooner rather than later. He only needed to be wise and to play his cards like a proper gambler.

"DID HE SAY anything else?" Mama prodded.

A lengthy span of time had passed between the Marquess of Searle returning Leonora to her mother's side and now. In that time, she had watched him dance with no less than three other ladies. All of them had been debutantes, younger and more beautiful than she. One of them, Lady Sarah Bolingbroke, was the toast of the Season. A diamond of the first water. She was everything Leonora was not, dark-haired and regal, elegant and graceful, beautiful, sought after…not suffering from a limp.

Of course, everything he had said had been mere flummery.

Why would it be anything else? Why would the Marquess of Searle, the most sought-after bachelor in London, be interested in a spinster who could scarcely manage one minuet without embarrassing herself?

"Leonora?" Mama asked once more, reminding her of her silence.

The Marquess of Searle robbed her of thought. It was as if he had entered her realm and lit all the candles and lamps within, only to flood the chambers with water thereafter.

"He said nothing," she lied flatly.

In truth, he had spoken empty promises. Precisely what one would expect of a handsome man who had all London kneeling at his feet. He was a hero unparalleled. He had defeated the French menace with nothing but his own bare hands and determination. He had saved himself.

And for one enchanted dance, she had dreamed he was the saving grace of her as well.

Now she knew differently. He was the same as every other gentleman.

"It did not seem like it was nothing," Mama added. "You were engaged in conversation for quite some time following the minuet. It seemed, at the very least, promising."

Leonora closed her eyes for a moment as she inhaled deeply. Her mother had been pressing her for additional details from the moment Lord Searle had bowed and taken his leave. She supposed she could not blame Mama, for no gentleman had shown such an interest in her in some time, not since that horrid wager. When she opened her eyes at last, Mama was watching her with an odd expression.

She sighed. "I am sorry to disappoint you. His lordship was courteous and kind, but I cannot help but to feel he only danced with me and exchanged pleasantries out of some sense of duty. Perhaps an obligation to exert a kindness toward an unfortunate—"

"Do not," Mama interrupted, "suggest you are cause for charity, because you most assuredly are not. You are the daughter of the Earl of Rayne, and you are beautiful."

And she also had an errant half-brother who was the subject of scurrilous gossip and her limp, which could not be hidden, to say nothing of her advancing years. But she could not fault Alessandro for the latter, only the former. His letters had grown increasingly sparse, and she missed him dearly.

She scanned the dancers, searching for Searle's tall, commanding form against her will. Irritation pricked at her, both for the manner in which she had so easily fallen prey to his charms and for the way she still looked for him even now. The way her eyes traveled through the throng of revelers, as if drawn to their home. All these years of hoping for a husband, and how easily she was felled by the silver tongue of one man.

Meanwhile, he was either amusing himself at her expense, or he had been lying to her when he had claimed he had not asked her to dance as the result of a wager. Tears of humiliation stung her eyes.

"But I *am* a cause for charity," she told Mama. "I have no suitors, and I shall never have a husband of my own."

How her heart ached when she said the last, for though it was a fear that had lived within her for the last few years, this was the first time she admitted it aloud. Doing so heightened the veracity of her trepidation.

Her failure was utter and complete. She would never have children, which she wanted with such desperation the desire had become a blazing, all-consuming force within her. For what man would want the burden of a wife who was the laughingstock of polite society?

"Hush now," Mama scolded quietly, her frown immense. "I will hear nothing more."

Leonora pressed her lips together, holding back the sobs that threatened to come. How foolish of her to be so affected by one dance with a gentleman she scarcely knew. What was it about the Marquess of Searle that pierced her flesh and went straight to her heart, to all the dark places she tried to pretend she did not possess?

"Excuse me, Mama," she forced past the lump in her throat. Her face felt as if it were aflame, and her eyes watered and burned. Despair was a weight in her stomach. She needed to flee. To collect herself. "I require a moment to myself."

"Leonora," her mother protested.

But she did not care to hear more. Ignoring the ache in her leg as she stood, she fled from her mother's side and from the ballroom with as much grace as she could muster. She made her painstaking way from the chamber, cursing her leg for the pain radiating through her.

In the several visits she had made to Freddy, they had always met within a cheerful salon, and Leonora made her way there now. The din of the ballroom faded farther away with each step, until at last she entered the privacy of the chamber she sought. Wall sconces were lit,

"Sit," he ordered.

She sat. Or perhaps it would be more accurate to say her knees buckled. One moment, she was helplessly falling into his handsome countenance and the next, her bottom hit the cushioned bench. For a breath, they remained frozen as they were, his hands upon her, his thumbs setting her alight as they traced circles over her bare flesh.

"You cannot linger here, my lord," she managed to summon the sensibility to say.

After all, even if her wits were addled and her body responded to him far too easily, she did have a mind that functioned quite well whenever she was not in Searle's intoxicating presence. And this—being alone with the marquess and allowing him to touch her so intimately—was wrong. If they were discovered, the rapidly disintegrating and eternally slim chances she had of ever making a match would disappear entirely.

"I can do whatever pleases me," he told her lowly, his gaze intense. "And right now, it pleases me to see to your wellbeing."

"I can see to my own wellbeing," she argued. "It is unseemly for you to be here, taking liberties with my person. I could be ruined, or you could be forced to the altar."

His expression turned grim. "I have been forced enough in this lifetime, my lady. No one will ever force me to do anything again. I do what I wish, when I wish, and anyone who dares to oppose me can go to Hades."

She swallowed against a fresh tide of tumult. Her heart ached for this man, so beautiful and yet so broken. The horrors of war and his imprisonment surely haunted him, much in the same fashion as her old injury. She would have the lingering pain and the limp to remind her forever. His reminders were internal, scars and wounds she could not see.

It seemed she was being given a glimpse of the real Searle. That he was not the polished, poised gentleman who had whirled her about the ballroom earlier, but instead, the man who spoke in a velvet voice wrapped in razors. A man whose eyes reflected the grim realities of what he had faced.

A man who seemed haunted.

He sank to his knees before her.

Her heart leapt into her throat. "My lord, whatever are you doing?"

"Tending you." His hands settled upon her slippers. "With your permission, of course."

"My injury is an old one, Searle," she protested. Good heavens, he could not intend to lift her skirts. "There is nothing to be done for it now, though I thank you for the concern."

"What happened?" he asked gently.

"I was sliding down the bannister at Marchmont, our country estate, and I fell to the floor below." She paused, thinking of that long-ago day which had changed her life forever. Sometimes, in her sleep, she recalled the sensation of falling, the rush in her stomach, the fear clawing up her throat, and the brief sensation of weightlessness until the inevitable landing.

"Good God." His rigid jaw flexed.

"I landed on my feet rather than my head." She flashed him a smile of false brightness. "I will be forever thankful for that, even if the fall cursed me with this limp."

"Does the musculature in the affected limb grow tight and painful, my lady?" he asked.

His question surprised her, because it seemed as if he was not only concerned for her, but as if he may possess a knowledge of the aftereffects of injuries such as the one she had suffered. Perhaps his time as a soldier had taught him.

It was a matter of course that the muscles in her lame leg grew tight and burned, because her leg pained her and she accommodated for it. Excursions such as balls were particularly trying as they required her to be upon her feet for longer periods of time. Though this evening had been different. Ordinarily, she never danced.

"Yes," she admitted softly. "But you need not worry for me, my lord. I have a liniment I shall apply upon returning home this evening. A day of rest will help immeasurably as well."

A day of rest or five since her invitations to balls were growing sparser by the year. She had no new engagements for days. Not even a musicale, which she always found abominably boring.

"Which part of the limb did you break?" he asked, remaining where he was, upon his knees before her.

How disconcerting it was to have this large, strong, intimidating man humbling himself, intending to offer her aid. What a perplexing man he was, intent upon dancing with her and then dancing with a string of younger, more beautiful, more eligible ladies as if he had forgotten her existence. Only to seek her out once more.

"The lower half," she revealed, feeling awkward and breathless all at once. Anticipation and something else, something far more wicked and far more vexing, rose within her, vying for her attention. "The country physician was able to reset the bone, but I was a wayward child, and I did not allow it enough time to properly heal."

She had been desperate to flee from her bed, her leg immobilized by linen doused in camphor spirits, egg white, and lead acetate. And she had removed herself from her bed when no one had been attending to her, hobbling about her chamber in practice for the day she would be free. But the bandages upon her leg had not been firm enough to hold the bone in place enough and make the bone heal cleanly.

"I have seen similar cases." The rumble of his delicious baritone shook her from the past. "On the field of battle. Will you allow me, Lady Leonora?"

She was not certain what he was requesting permission for, but his hands had already found her ankles, curling naturally around them in a heated grip that left her swimming in far more than memories. His thumbs now paid court to her anklebones, rubbing slow, sensual circles over them in much the same fashion he had her collarbone.

She ought to tell him no. The denial was on her tongue. Leonora knew how dangerously near she treaded to utter and complete ruin. If they were discovered here alone…

What would change? Something inside her shifted, altering. As a girl, Leonora had been reckless and wild. As the woman who had been forced to live with the repercussions of the actions of her past, she had grown careful. Very careful. She was no longer the girl who slid down bannisters for the wind in her face and the sweet trill of rebellion down her spine.

She was no longer the girl who believed herself invincible. Who believed she would never fall. Mama had admonished her time and again. She had warned her against sliding down the bannister. But Marchmont Hall possessed a curving mahogany staircase that traveled through three stories. It had been irresistible. Perfect for sliding on her rump.

Until it hadn't been perfect any longer, and neither had she.

"My lady?" persisted the marquess, the man whose hands had already begun to glide up her calves in unison.

For some reason, she did not see any need to inform him she possessed only one infirm leg and not two. For some reason, she did not move away or tell him to keep his large, warm hands and knowing touch to himself.

Instead, she sighed. A complicit sigh. Her body was wanton, and so was she, but she was also tired. Tired of being Limping Leonora, of living her life for propriety only to spend an eternity on the edge of the living. It was as if she inhabited a Purgatory of her own making. Here and now, in this moment, she was willing to toss her caution aside for the first time in years.

But this man was no banister slide.

"It is the left one, my lord," she told him, but her voice was breathless, and he did not seem to hear her.

When his long, strong fingers began to expertly knead her flesh, she forgot to care.

He discovered muscles she had not known she possessed, aching muscles, tight muscles. Muscles that relaxed beneath his gentle touch. He had not lifted the hem of her gown or petticoat and chemise. Instead, he had simply slid his hands beneath them, maintaining her modesty except for two inescapable facts.

One: he was touching her limbs.

Two: the heat of his caresses through her stockings told her he had removed his gloves beneath her skirts before beginning.

And while she was enumerating facts, she had another to add to her list: her entire body felt as if it belonged to another. The juncture of her thighs pulsed and ached. Her breasts tingled. Her mouth was dry. Her heart thumped with relentless persistence.

Tenderly, he worked his way up her calves to her knees. She could not be certain if it was the soothing effect of his massage or the manner in which his proximity and touch ravaged her senses, but her bad leg did not even ache. She felt as if she could dance a dozen minuets as long as she was in the Marquess of Searle's arms.

Throughout his ministrations, he had not taken his gaze from her. Those vibrant orbs scorched her, pinning her to the settee, making her incapable of both the ability and the desire to preserve her reputation and flee.

"Your countenance has relaxed, my lady," he observed, satisfaction underscoring the deep rumble of his voice. "You no longer have a vee between your lovely brows."

He thought her eyebrows lovely?

Her cheeks burned, and she wanted to look away, to shield herself from his probing stare, but she could not. "It feels much better, thank you, my lord."

Both limbs felt better. *She* felt better. And her cheeks went hotter still at the realization, for she was being an unseemly wretch. She was spoiling her reputation. Ruining herself with each moment she lingered. It had taken her a long time to once again heed the call of the forbidden, but she was listening. She could not stop.

His expression did not change. He remained fierce and intense, his jaw hard and angular, his mouth set in an uncompromising line. There was precious little charm in him now, but he needed none to lure her closer to his dangerous flame.

"I am sorry the dance pained you," he said at last. "It was not my intention."

His words warmed her even further. "My old injury is not your fault."

His caresses traveled higher, reaching her knees, his long fingers dipping into the hollows there. "Nevertheless, I ought to have been more considerate."

Suddenly, she recalled the sight of him dancing with Lady Sarah, ethereal with her golden hair and lustrous beauty. Her fingers tightened in her skirts, twisting the soft fabric. "You were paying me a kindness, my lord. We both know no one truly wishes to dance with someone like me."

"Every gentleman in London would be fortunate indeed if he could dance with someone like you, Lady Leonora." He massaged back down her calves once more rather than traveling higher.

How she wished she could believe him, for she possessed common sense and the distinct, bitter memory of every disappointing year since her comeout. She longed for him to skim past her garters and connect with bare flesh. "Experience suggests otherwise, my lord."

Before he could respond, the door to the chamber opened. A chorus of gasps and exclamations of her name intruded. Her shocked gaze settled upon the threshold where Freddy, Mr. Kirkwood, her mother, and the Duke and Duchess of Whitley stood. The countenances staring back at her were reflections of astonishment. It was clear no one had expected her to be within, a gentleman for company.

No one expected her *worthy* of ruination. How grim.

All the voices sounded at once, rushing over each other, some demanding, others outraged.

"Leonora? Are you injured?"

"Good God, Searle, have you lost your bloody mind?"

"Everyone get inside," Mr. Kirkwood issued the last directive, his tone one which brooked no opposition. "If we linger here, we are only doomed to draw a crowd and that is the last mistake any of us can afford to make."

Their unexpected audience filtered into the chamber. Mr. Kirkwood closed the door and turned to face them, his expression one of concern as he eyed Leonora. "My lady, are you well?"

She wet her dry lips, acutely aware the Marquess of Searle had yet to remove his hands from her person. He clasped her now instead of massaging, almost in a possessive grip. As if he feared relinquishing her.

It made no sense.

"I am perfectly fine," she reassured her host and the rest of the assemblage which had gathered to witness her ignominy. Mama gaped at her, her expression a marriage-minded mother's eerie confluence of delight and concern. "Lord Searle escorted me here because my leg gave out, and I could not walk unaided."

The instant the falsehood left her lips, she wondered at her reason for uttering it. To save him, she reasoned. To spare him the injustice of being forced to wed her and avoid her ruination. There was no need, after all. Thanks to Mr. Kirkwood's quick maneuvering, the only people within the chamber were all familiar and trusted to her.

The polite world need never know the Marquess of Searle's hands had been beneath her skirts. That his hands were still beneath her skirts, even now.

Why had he yet to remove them?

She could not think of a single explanation.

"None of that explains why Searle is making himself familiar with…" At a pointed look from Freddy, Mr. Kirkwood halted, rephrasing his words. "My lord, you have impugned the honor of a guest within my home. A guest who is dear to both myself and my wife. You must answer for this grave injustice."

"I will be more than happy to make Lady Leonora my wife," Searle said without hesitation, his voice booming clearly in the shocked silence of the chamber.

Everyone went quiet.

Leonora went still.

And the marquess's hands remained firm and strong upon her, unrelenting yet gentle. Surely, he did not mean to wed her?

His green gaze never wavered from hers, and what she saw burning in their vibrant depths shocked her. Determination. Solemnity. Promise.

"What if Lady Leonora does not wish to wed you?" Freddy demanded, stealing Leonora's attention with her outrage.

Freddy was the sister Leonora had never had. There was a question in her gaze, and Leonora knew she must answer it. She also knew she had not an inkling of the manner in which she should. In the end, she pressed her lips together and nodded.

"She may not have a choice, love," Mr. Kirkwood cautioned, giving Freddy a look of undisguised adoration.

"I am afraid that what Lady Leonora wants is immaterial," Mama said then, taking command of the chamber with a firm voice that belied the invalid she often was. "My lord, though you are kind to be concerned for my daughter's welfare, you have nevertheless placed her reputation in great danger. You will wed her as expediently as possible, and you will also remove your hands from her person at once."

With a wry grin, the marquess extracted his hands at last, and Leonora had to bite her lip to keep from protesting the loss of him.

"My lady," he said to Leonora alone, speaking quietly, his gaze riveted to her. "Will you do me the honor of becoming my wife?"

She swallowed. Nothing could have prepared her for this moment. For the Marquess of Searle, heralded hero, most sought after bachelor, more beautiful than she could even comprehend, proposing to marry her. How she wished he were proposing because of a true wish to marry her rather than out of a misplaced sense of duty.

"I will not be your obligation," she told him firmly. "But I do thank you for the offer. You pay me a great honor."

He remained where he was, upon his knees, his gaze as intense as ever. "I did not ask you to be my obligation, Lady Leonora, but to become my wife."

Hope and desire rose within her, warring with pride. From the moment she had taken her curtsy, she had wanted nothing more than to marry and start a family of her own. Perhaps here, at last, was her chance. It was not what she wanted. There was no romance or love between them, but there was something else...something physical and undeniable.

Perhaps it could be enough.

She inhaled slowly, never taking her eyes from Searle's. "Yes, I will be your wife."

His eyes closed for a brief moment, and the mask he wore dropped, revealing the man. He looked as if he had just been declared the victor of a bitter war.

What had she done?

And who, precisely, was the Marquess of Searle?

CHAPTER THREE

MORGAN'S SEED HAD been planted, and the Earl of Rayne was, at long last, returning to England. What the earl did not know—could not know—was he was already too late to save his darling sister.

Hours ago, in a ceremony attended by the Duke and Duchess of Whitley, the Kirkwoods, the dowager Lady Rayne, and Morgan's cousin, the Duke of Montrose, Lady Leonora had become the Marchioness of Searle. And Morgan had become exponentially nearer to gaining his retribution.

He watched her now as he introduced her to his domestics, this stranger who was his wife. Her lovely countenance was animated as she spoke to his housekeeper, Mrs. Arbuthnot. She was painfully beautiful and also kind, and the combination made his chest tight.

For the past few weeks, he had seen her on only a handful of occasions, deliberately keeping their interactions limited and few as the necessary preparations for their nuptials were underway. He had no wish to court her or get to know her better. Nor did he desire to make a connection with her that ran any deeper than the physical. She was his wife now, and he would bed her, but that was all. Anything else, and he ran the risk of developing a weakness for her.

Her worth to him was not in her compassion or her gentle beauty.

Her worth to him was in the suffering he could visit upon the bastard who had sent him to hell on earth. The scars on his flesh, hidden beneath the respectable trappings of a gentleman, burned in reminder.

"Mrs. Arbuthnot will see you to your apartments," he announced, the need to escape making him intervene. "I have other commitments which require my attention."

His new marchioness's gaze met his, her expression falling. "May I speak with you for a moment, my lord?"

He ground his jaw. "A moment and no longer, my lady."

Her frown had returned, that lone vee marring the otherwise smooth, creamy skin of her forehead. And her limping was more pronounced. The nature of the day had required a great deal of standing. More than she was probably accustomed to. He hated himself for making her frown as much as he hated himself for taking note of her wellbeing.

He escorted her deeper within Linley House, away from the prying eyes and ears of the servants who had gathered in preparation for their first arrival as husband and wife. It was a deuced old custom; one he should have eschewed as it would have garnered him the opportunity to leave immediately upon delivering his new marchioness to the doorstep.

"What is concerning you, my lady?" he demanded.

She flinched, presumably at the cold, emotionless tone of his voice. But she would do well to accustom herself to the man he truly was. War had robbed him of all softness. His compassion was as dead as his charm and his soul.

"It is merely that this is our wedding day, my lord," she said hesitantly. "I was hoping for the opportunity to spend some time with you, for us to get better acquainted."

Hope had no place in their marriage, and she would be wise to learn it now.

He flashed her a grim smile. "I married you out of necessity, my lady. Not because I wish to be your friend."

There was hurt in her eyes, but he refused to feel the slightest prick of guilt for being the cause. What had she expected of a forced marriage and a whirlwind, scarcely extant courtship? Did she imagine they would exchange kisses and declare their endless affection for each other?

"Of course not, my lord. I understand the situation in which we find ourselves completely." Sadness underscored her tone.

She was wrong about that, far more wrong than she could even guess. For she had no inkling of the true nature of the situation in which they found themselves. But she would. Soon enough.

"War has left me with precious little care for polite society," he told her, and that much was true.

While half the lords and ladies he knew had been at home, fretting over seating arrangements and new dance steps, he had been facing enemy bullets and being dragged across Spain by Boney's most vicious and depraved forces.

It was the wrong thing to say, and he knew it the moment her expression gentled. *Christ*, this woman was like a lamb who had been served up to a ravenous lion.

"Of course it has. I cannot fathom what you must have experienced, my lord."

There was a quaver in her voice that made him want to take her in his arms, carry her directly to his chamber, lay her upon his bed, and drive home inside her. How he longed to excise his grievances through the use of her willing, pliant flesh. But lust, too, was a weakness.

"You are correct, my lady," he said grimly. "You cannot. It would be best, therefore, if you do not even try."

Her eyes appeared brighter, glowing with emotion she did not bother to hide. "You showed me kindness that evening at the Kirkwood ball, and I do not think it was as rare as you would have me believe, Lord Searle. Believe me when I say, I understand better than anyone the need to show everyone around you one face while hiding your true face for only yourself. I have lived nearly all my life with the repercussions of youthful folly, and I have been met with more pity and disgust than most. But I have never allowed anyone to see how much that pity and disgust could break me."

There she went again, playing the angel to his devil. Hell, she even resembled an angel with her white-blonde hair and the silver tones of her gown. She was the loveliest woman he had ever seen, in a way that did not fail to make his breath still whenever he saw her.

But neither her beauty nor her innate benevolence would distract him from his true purpose. He was destined to be the mayhem in this woman's world. To ravage and shake and tear everything she thought she knew apart. Most of all, he was meant to tear apart the Earl of Rayne, limb by limb, bone by bone, sinew by sinew, until nothing remained.

And he would do it all with a smile until the day he faced Rayne on the field of honor and ended him.

The same smile he pinned upon his lips now. "Believe me when I say I am the last man you ought to feel sorry for, my lady. But please, do get yourself settled. As I said, I have other obligations requiring my attention. I shall return in a few hours."

He bowed, and then without waiting for her to protest, spun on his heel and left her behind as fast as he damn well could.

LEONORA JOLTED FROM sleep, blinking and disoriented.

For a moment, she expected the familiar canopy of her bed at Riverford House above her instead of the plaster, rose medallion staring down at her from the shadows. And that was when she recalled she would never again wake in her chamber at Riverford House. That she was no longer Lady Leonora Forsythe but instead, the Marchioness of Searle.

Leonora shivered and blinked, her gaze scanning her surroundings.

The remnants of a fire crackled in the grate, for it was unseasonably cold even by London's late spring standards. Her chamber here at Linley House was decorated sparsely. Mrs. Arbuthnot had kindly informed her that his lordship wished for her to outfit the chamber to her liking.

If only *his lordship* could have seen fit to relay that information himself, it would have made settling into her new home far easier. Instead, her husband had continued the trend of cold remoteness he had exhibited to her in the last few weeks of their madcap courtship, following what had happened at Freddy's ball. He had left her alone with his servants, disappearing with the promise of return.

Only he had not returned.

Not for dinner.

Not for the two hours following dinner she had spent in tedious frustration, reading a book and working herself into a dudgeon. Not as she readied for bed. And not as she had lain awake, staring at the same rose medallion until it had seemed to swirl before her eyes and come to life as a roaring dragon threatening to burn her alive.

She could not say his defection surprised her, for in the abbreviated amount of time she had known the Marquess of Searle, he had taught her to expect nothing from him. It almost seemed he had expended the only kindness he possessed when he had followed her to the salon and kneaded her tight muscles to ease her pain.

But his defection had hurt her. And infuriated her.

A knock stole through the silence of her chamber then, interrupting the pleasant cracklings of her fire. Firm and abrupt, the knock left her without question of who had come to pay her a call at this time of the evening...perhaps even early morning.

The Marquess of Searle had recalled he had a wife after all.

She frowned, a fresh surge of irritation rising within her, supplanting all else. Because she did not wish to remain abed in her nightclothes, waiting for him to come to her, she threw back her coverlets and rose. Her troublesome leg was extra stiff from all the time she had spent upon her feet during the course of the day, but she was determined. She found her discarded dressing gown, then thrust her arms into the sleeves before catching the belt around her waist and knotting it snugly.

If he wanted her, he would have to fight for her, she decided.

Mama had given her a stern talk about the grim realities awaiting her in the marriage bed. *It will give you pain the first time and the next few times as well. You must recall it is your duty. Close your eyes and think of the babes you will have to bless you after suffering your husband's attentions.*

Leonora made her painstaking way toward the door joining her chamber to Searle's. Her mother's words still filled her with trepidation, even though Freddy had reassured her she had nothing to fear in the marriage bed. Indeed, her dear friend had, with scarlet cheeks, confided she ought to find it...pleasurable.

She opened the latch on the door, pulling it toward her, and there he stood, the enigma she had married that morning. He was dressed in only a linen shirt and breeches, devoid of stockings and shoes, cravat and coat. His hair was mussed, his expression intent. The Marquess of Searle was every bit as much a stranger to her now as he had been the day he danced the minuet with her.

Nothing had changed.

And yet, everything had.

She was staring at her husband.

He gazed back at her, breaking the silence first. "I thought you were asleep, my lady."

It was not what she had expected him to say. "Why did you knock if you thought I was asleep?"

His expression remained unreadable, his countenance formed of ice. "Perhaps I hoped to wake you."

How insincere he sounded. How unfeeling and impenetrable. She longed to shake him. To tear him free of the inner bower he had retreated to from the moment he had asked her to become his wife.

For a man who had faced untold depravities and horrors at war, he was certainly cowardly when it came to facing the woman he had married.

"I think you hoped I was asleep so you would not have to see me again," she told him frankly, abandoning the care she had used when she had spoken to him earlier in the day.

"On the contrary." He reached between them, his fingers grazing her jaw. Just a glancing, gentle touch, but it made her heart leap, nonetheless. "You are all I wish to see."

"Pray, do not lie to me." She could not bear it.

No more false charm. No more flattery. The weakest part of her had wanted to believe him at Freddy's ball. The part of her that had hungered for a husband and a family of her own, for someone who would look upon her and not see a weakness but instead a great strength, had fooled her into believing the Marquess of Searle could be that man.

He had told her, over the course of the last few weeks, with each interaction, every word and deed, he was not the man she sought. He was, however, the man she had married, and the both of them needed to make their peace with their new situation.

"I am sorry to burden you with an infirm wife, my lord." She swallowed, summoning her arguments and her strength. Leonora had lived most of her life with the consequences of her limitations, but though she had long grown accustomed to them, she still remained resentful of their existence.

"You are not," he countered firmly, "my burden, but my prize."

When an odd assertion for him to make. She had never felt less like a prize than she did now, standing awkwardly before the man who had married her, more uncertain of herself than when she was seated at the periphery of the ballroom. At least when she could watch others enjoying themselves, she had ample distraction. So, too, the comfort of the familiar. But this was different, for she was the object of this enigmatic man's blistering attentions, and she had nowhere else to look. No other cause for diversion.

Nor had she ever been a wife before. Nothing about this day, this moment, this man, was comforting or familiar. He set her on edge. Made her feel as if she could not trust herself. Made her feel small.

"Surely not a prize." The smile on her lips was bitter, and she knew it. "I am certain you did not envision a wife who cannot walk unimpeded."

"You are the only wife I want," he said intently.

So intently, she believed him. But she could not shake the impression he was leaving something out, withholding something from her. If he wanted her for his wife, why did he remain so aloof? Was it the horrors he had faced as a soldier, which he had alluded to earlier in the day?

She inhaled slowly, trying to find her place. "I find that declaration difficult to believe indeed. But nevertheless, we are bound inextricably now. We must make the best of our circumstances."

"Not completely bound," he reminded her. His green eyes darkened. "Not yet."

Oh, he was a beautiful sight to behold, it was sure. The Marquess of Searle was a towering wall of a man, broad-shouldered and lean-hipped, dark hair styled in loose waves, face more handsome than any man deserved, mouth fashioned to make all women swoon.

But she would not be one of them. After all, he had married her and then disappeared. "Not ever if today is to be any indication of the future."

Dear heavens, was that her own voice?

She could scarcely credit it.

But she most certainly would not rescind it.

A slow and steady smile curved that sensual mouth. His eyes glittered in the low light. "Is that a challenge, Lady Searle?"

What was it about the manner in which his deep, seductive baritone called her *Lady Searle* that made her body hum with awareness?

She tipped up her chin, a newfound defiance surging through her. She would not grow weak for him. Not now. Not ever. Though their union had been founded in an avoidance of scandal rather than because of tender feelings, she would not be mistreated. She had wanted a husband and family of her own, yes, but not at the expense of her dignity.

"That is a *promise*, Lord Searle."

His expression shifted then, softening somehow. "I had previous engagements this evening, my lady."

"Engagements which could not have been moved to a day other than your wedding day?" she asked.

She knew theirs was an odd and hastened arrangement, but every bride deserved her husband's attention on the day she married. Most could expect a honeymoon. At the very least, a trip to a country estate. Instead, she had been rebuffed, foisted upon the kindly Mrs. Arbuthnot, whose pity had been apparent in every pinched line of her round visage.

A muscle in Leonora's calf chose that moment to tighten and spasm, causing pain to slice through her. She bit her lip to keep from crying out, but it was too late to recall her sudden inhalation.

"Your injury," he diagnosed grimly.

She flexed her foot, attempting to subdue her natural inclination to wince. "It is nothing."

"It is something," he countered, "else you would not have reacted in the manner you did."

"The limb is fine. I am well, and it is nothing." She had lied many times about the state of her leg over the years, and often the falsehood was spoken to assuage the guilt and concern of those surrounding her. This time, she offered up the fib to slake her own pride.

"Come, my lady." His countenance grew determined and hard, his jaw tense.

He took her hand in his and tugged her over the line separating them. She was now, undeniably, in his domain. Trespassing. Alone and in dishabille with the Marquess of Searle. The notion made her heart pound even if the rational part of her continued to resent him for his impromptu disappearance earlier that day.

It was almost impossible for her to realize, after a life spent according to the dictates of society and propriety, that she could be alone with this man, half-dressed, touching one another intimately, and no one would object. He was her husband, she reminded herself deliriously, even if he did not feel like he was.

Even if he did not behave as if he was.

Leonora told herself it was the distracted state in which she found herself, dogged by the leg cramp, disoriented by waking in a new chamber, left alone on her wedding day, her entire life as she knew it about to change forever...surely all these were reasons why she allowed the marquess to guide her to his bed.

Just her rump upon the edge, and even that felt like a betrayal of her own determination.

"Is it still paining you?" Searle asked, his beautiful face dipping low, so low their foreheads nearly brushed.

He took her breath. Made her forget all her reasons for not liking him and not trusting him. She had given herself a stern talking to whilst she had been left alone, in possession of ample time to sit with her thoughts and ruminate.

But this, Searle's mouth close enough to touch with hers, his hot breath fanning over her lips, sent all her wits and determination scattering like seeds tossed into a heavy wind.

"Is what still paining me?" she asked, searching his gaze, breathless.

"Your leg," he elaborated, his voice deep. Hard as his expression. Uncompromising and yet strangely tender as well. Seeking.

Once again, she could not shake the sensation this man was far more than he presented to the world around him.

She swallowed. The cramp, caused by overuse, had already subsided. But for some reason, Leonora wanted this man's hands upon her far more than she wanted to make that revelation.

"Yes," she lied.

He was in the bed within heartbeats. His hands settled upon her bare ankle, hard, large, firm, and hot. Claiming her, as if she were already his when she was in name but not in action. "With your permission, my lady, I will attempt to lessen your suffering as I did for you previously."

She almost laughed aloud at his unexpected reference to the day he had ruined her. And she could not help but to wonder now whether or not he had lessened her suffering or increased it by leading her to the brink of scandal and then wedding her. Perhaps it was a question that would only be resolved with time.

How irregular it was for him to seem concerned by her welfare, attuned to her discomfort, when he could not seem to show her a modicum of affection. He had not even given her a true smile, for the smile he had graced her with before leaving earlier in the day had been a wolf's smile.

"My lady?" he persisted. "May I?"

His hands had not moved.

"You may," she allowed, sternly reminding herself she could not—nay, *must not*—allow him any liberty beyond this until he earned it.

Unerringly, his fingers moved, finding the painful knot of her tight muscle. His thumbs pressed. She could not contain her sigh of relief. Nor did she miss the satisfied smile curving his lips as he cast a glance toward her.

"Improved?" he asked gently.

"Better," she allowed, frowning at her too-handsome husband and his too-pleased countenance. "You may stop, my lord."

"What if I do not wish to stop?" As he posed the wicked question, his hands moved higher, touching her left leg only, working her sore muscle. And here, at last, was the inkling of something else. Something deeper and darker than that which he had already deigned to show her.

She had overdone it today, between the ceremony and her seemingly endless preparations, not to mention the introductions that came later when she had arrived at Linley House. She was paying for the grandiosity of her presumption she could carry on without repercussions for one day. Just as he had been for the aftermath of her injudicious lack of propriety at Freddy's ball, the marquess was once again present to atone for her sins.

But then, thoughts of his absence returned once more, negating any gratitude blossoming within her toward him. She frowned. "If you do not wish to stop, you should not have abandoned your bride on the day you married her, Searle."

The immediate anguish of her cramp ameliorated, she caught his wrists and tugged his hands away from her willing and needy flesh. How could one man so thoroughly consume and confuse her? He was at the center of all her thoughts, and yet, to look upon him for too long was surely to get burned. Much like the sun.

"And if I assured you I could more than expiate my sins in other fashions?" he queried with deceptive calm, for his voice had taken on an edge.

A promise of the wicked.

She did not want to ask him to elaborate upon his question. Yet, she could think of nothing but his answer. "What fashions?"

His lips quirked higher, the smile delivering not just smug satisfaction now but sizzling with possibilities. She could not shake the restless feeling that had dogged her from the moment she had first seen the Marquess of Searle. That he was dangerous. More dangerous than she could comprehend.

And she had married him.

"With my lips," he drawled. Because she had yet to release his wrists—ever the fool, she—he turned his hands so the palms faced the ceiling and his fingers entwined with hers. "And tongue."

Leonora had never been kissed. Not even by Lord Robert. Her mouth tingled at the marquess's words. Anticipation licked through her, flaring down her spine and settling between her thighs. A strange, keening ache had begun to blossom there. She felt heavy and needy, and though she was an innocent, she knew what that pooling warmth meant.

Some years ago, she had discovered, whilst lying alone in bed one night, the sensation could be brought to a raging, pleasurable crescendo, and the heaviness and ache would only be satisfied by doing so. She knew she had been sinful, committing such an act of depravity, touching herself there, where her flesh was forbidden, but she had been unable to help herself.

And she had not stopped. She knew how she liked to be touched, what would make the pinnacle break over her like a wave hitting a shore and splitting into a thousand tiny, beautiful directions.

Even now, lying before her husband of one day, she could not suppress the thought of guiding his knowing hands to her, bringing him between her thighs. He could alleviate the pressure and the need. After all, he was the source of it. She felt quite sure.

"You must not," she found the strength to protest at last, shocked by her own vulgar urges.

His eyes glittered with an indefinable emotion, boring into hers with expert precision. He must have read something of her thoughts in her countenance, for his own expression changed, his lips parting, nostrils flaring. "Are you curious now?"

Curious, yes. But she must not allow her inner yearning to trump her determination to keep him firmly at bay. "I would have been curious if you had not fled the moment the introductions to your servants were completed. Now, I am afraid, I merely wish to find my bed and get some rest."

Her voice was a traitor, breathless and low, giving her away.

And Searle did not miss it, for his grin only deepened. "Liar," he charged softly. "Admit it. You are curious, regardless of my actions earlier today."

She shook her head, loathing herself for being so easily read, resenting him for being correct. Irritated with herself for the lack of resistance to this man. He was not the first handsome lord she had seen in all her years on the marriage mart. "No."

He raised her hands to his lips for a kiss, first one, then the other. "The truth, my lady. I begin to think there is far more to you than you have previously allowed me to see."

If that was the case, surely it was because he had not bothered to spend time with her over the handful of weeks following their ignominious display at Freddy's ball. They had waited for the banns to be read, and then they had wed. In the interim, he had taken her for a drive in his curricle once. He had paid a call lasting no longer than five minutes one afternoon, and he had danced with her at one more ball.

If he did not know her, the fault was his alone. She summoned all her courage to tell him so. "Perhaps you have not attempted to seek it."

"And perhaps I wish to do penance for the sin of failing to court you properly." His jaw was clenched.

"Do not forget the sin of failing to acquaint me with my new home." She could not resist reminding him tartly.

His eyebrows rose, dark arches inching up his otherwise flawless, high forehead. Every part of him was perfect, from his handsome face to his elegant air. She, on the other hand, was a limping spinster, surely a burden to him. The woman he had no doubt reluctantly taken as his wife.

But although she knew she ought to be grateful, he had made her his marchioness, and given her hope she may one day bear the children she so desperately longed to have, she could not seem to stop baiting him. Something had happened to her. She was changing. Altering. She was a new Leonora. The bravery slipping from her lips was perhaps foolhardy, but necessary.

For most of her life, she had been pitied and ostracized, and she had allowed it. She had sat on the periphery with Mama and her atrocious turbans, knowing no one would ever ask her to dance or seek her hand. But now, someone had.

Still, she was no longer the Leonora who waited on the edge of life, too tentative to live it. Even if having a husband was nothing like what she had imagined it would be for all those years of yearning and hoping. Rather, it was like living with a wild creature. She knew not what to expect. Knew not whether he would run at the slightest provocation, if he would allow her to pet him, if he would bite.

The notion tickled her sense of humor, and she could not quite squelch the sudden, inappropriate burst of laughter rising in her throat at the thought of the Marquess of Searle facing her like some feral wolf. It suited him so.

"You do indeed possess untold depths, my lady." His tone, like his gaze as it traveled over her from the roots of her hair to her toes in one scorching pass, was wry.

She tugged her hands free of his grasp and slid from his bed, her feet touching the luxurious softness of carpet. "Unfortunately, I also possess a strong need to get my rest. I am heartily glad you have returned this evening, my lord. Perhaps tomorrow we may begin again?"

He stared at her, a muscle in his jaw flexing.

Good heavens, he was so powerful and predatory. Leonine, really. Far more regal than a wolf. Yes, the exotic, hazardous beast seemed the perfect likeness.

Her lion, she thought foolishly. If only she might tame him.

"I bid you good evening, my lord," she said boldly into the silence he had yet to answer.

Thanks to Freddy, she knew her first night as a wife should have entailed far more than what had just occurred between them. But she was also painfully aware she needed to find her footing in this wilderness she was about to inhabit.

She swept from his chamber with as much grace as she could manage.

Just before the door latched behind her, she heard the unmistakable rumble of his voice.

"I bid you good evening as well, Leonora."

The sound of his deep, delicious voice saying her name haunted her all night long.

CHAPTER FOUR

"**D**EAREST LEONORA!"

Leonora smiled as she embraced her best friend back with just as much, unladylike exuberance. "Freddy!"

With the sudden wedding preparations on Leonora's part, and Freddy's own new marriage to keep her distracted, too much time had passed since they had been afforded the opportunity to chat alone. Freddy sounded and looked so pleased, happiness nearly radiating from her as Leonora took a step back. The salon her friend had turned into a writing area was cheerful and bold, and situated perfectly so the sun poured in through the bounty of windows on an opposite wall.

"Or shall I call you Marchioness now?" Freddy asked, grinning slyly. "You do look different, darling."

If misery had a look and it could be described as *different*, that would explain her friend's comment. Because one sennight into her marriage, Leonora had made a hideous, previously uncontemplated discovery; relieving herself of her spinster status and marrying an eligible *parti* had not fulfilled her as she had hoped it might.

Instead, it had left her confused, empty, and alone.

Contrary to her urging on their wedding night for them to begin again the next day, the following morning had dawned upon a Searle as cold and flatly emotionless as ever. He spoke few words to her. He breakfasted before she was awake and spent dinners at his club. His gaze was intense, but his moods impossible.

Most evenings, he did not return until she was already abed. Each night without fail, she heard him entering his chamber in the late hours of the morning, his heavy footfalls treading to the door adjoining their chambers. In the cool darkness, she waited as the portal opened and he stood there for an indeterminate span of time before closing it once more.

But she could not possibly share all that with her blissfully happy, utterly in love friend before they had even settled to take their tea. Leonora exhaled on a sigh, not wishing to unburden herself just yet. Perhaps not even at all. Freddy was like a summer breeze, shining and warm and abundant and sweet-scented. Leonora felt, in contrast, like a rasping, ravaging winter's wind, the sort that sucked all the moisture from one's lips and stung one's cheeks.

"I feel different," she offered with a noncommittal shrug. "But tell me about you, Freddy. It has been far, far too long."

Her friend pinned her with a shrewd, assessing look. "You look as if you have just slid your foot into your slipper and found it filled with treacle."

Had she been in a lighter mood, Leonora would have laughed at Freddy's witty observation. As it stood, her emotions hovered somewhere in the brackish vicinity between spontaneous laughter and a hideous bout of sniveling tears.

So, she forced a smile. "There is no treacle in my slipper, I assure you."

If there had been, it would have been a less trifling matter than the realization she had married a complete stranger, and that obtaining a husband felt rather like being gifted a prettily decorated box only to find it empty inside.

"And now you rather resemble a lady who has found dog offal in her slipper instead," Freddy countered, arching one dark brow as if to say she was not fooled by Leonora's reassurances.

"You are certainly laden with similitudes today, Freddy," she observed instead of responding to either of her friend's discreet inquiries into her wellbeing. "You look different as well. Radiant and happy, just as you deserve."

It was true, for her friend was a vibrant beauty on ordinary days. Today, however, she seemed to somehow shimmer with radiance. Perhaps it was her contentment. Perhaps love had softened her. Leonora still knew a pang in her heart whenever she thought of the manner in which Freddy and Mr. Kirkwood had gazed upon each other at their ball.

Had she truly been foolish enough to believe procuring herself a husband would provide her that same sense of comfort and joy? What a ninny she had been.

"Thank you." Freddy's smile turned secretive as her hand settled over her abdomen. "It is early, but I do think I may know the reason."

A riot of sensation burst inside her chest. Elation for Freddy. Longing for herself. Despair that the same thrilling announcement may never emerge from her own lips. Fear of what her life would mean, stretching before her, childless, with a husband who viewed her as a responsibility and nothing more.

"Oh, Freddy." This time, the smile on her mouth was not forced, for she wanted nothing but joy for her friend. "Are you *enceinte*?"

Freddy nodded, her eyes glistening with the hint of unshed tears. "I am. You shall be an auntie, and it is my greatest hope that you will soon have similar news for me. Our children could take their first steps together. Only think of how wonderful it would be. Is that the reason for your long face, Leonora? I know how very much you want babes of your own. But you have been married for only a week. It would be too soon for such a happy event to occur."

"It would also be too soon for a happy event to occur when a marriage has yet to be consummated," she observed dryly before she could think better of uttering confirmation of Freddy's fear she was unhappy.

Freddy's brows rose, her expression turning grave. "Pardon, dearest. I believe I misheard you. Of course you have...that is to say, you enjoyed a wedding night with Searle. Did you not?"

"Oh, Freddy." She surrendered her determination to keep her upset to herself. "He has not even attempted to kiss me."

"Not one kiss?" Freddy sounded shocked.

Leonora sighed again, a sudden twinge of pain forcing her to leverage all her weight onto the leg that had never been broken. "Nary a one."

Of course, Freddy took note of her discomfort.

"Forgive me, dearest," her friend said. "What have I been thinking, holding you here without a hint of proper manners? Sit, please do. Tea and biscuits should be here any moment now. I do hope you are staying for a nice, long visit. You *are* staying, are you not?"

Leonora had thought to visit Mama, as well, while making her first calls as the Marchioness of Searle. But Mama could read her as well as Freddy could, and Leonora had no wish to divulge the sad state of her marriage to more than one person today.

She allowed her friend to guide her to an overstuffed chair, where she happily took her seat. "I suppose I can stay for as long as you would like to have me here."

Just then, a servant arrived, bearing a tray of chocolate biscuits and tea. Freddy waited until the domestic had departed before pouring tea for Leonora, knowing just how she preferred it, and offering her two biscuits as well.

"Two biscuits?" Leonora frowned down at the delicious looking things, thinking of her waistline, which was frightfully responsive to sweets, and not in the manner she wished. "One should suffice."

"I am having three," Freddy said unrepentantly. "Duncan's chef is exquisite, recommended by the chef at his club. Every bit as talented, though blessedly possessed of a significantly smaller sense of his own magnificence. After your first bite, you will be cursing me for only offering you two, I promise."

Leonora bit into a biscuit, and she had to admit, it was buttery and decadent upon her palate. She chewed it thoughtfully before swallowing. "These are utterly delightful, Freddy. You are, once again, quite right."

"Duncan finds only the best," Freddy said with a smile.

"Of course he does," Leonora could not help but to observe. "He found you, after all."

Freddy flushed, taking a delicate sip of her tea. "One could say *I* found *him* after I trespassed at his club as I did."

"No matter which one of you is responsible, Freddy, you are both happy and in love, and I am so very overjoyed for you." And she was. She was incredibly delighted for her friend.

It filled her with warmth to see Freddy thriving. Mr. Kirkwood seemed the perfect foil for her, someone who understood and appreciated her mind and her novel writing, who could not just accept an unconventional lady but worship her as she deserved to be.

"But you are not happy," Freddy deduced.

Correctly, drat it all.

Leonora supposed it was inevitable she would have to admit the truth. She could not hide her feelings from her friend forever. She sighed for what had to be the third time since her arrival. "I am not happy," she admitted.

"Searle is not cruel to you, is he?" Freddy demanded, moving to the edge of her seat. Her expression had hardened, suggesting she would gladly take up the cudgels and use them upon Searle if need be.

So fierce and loyal, her friend. Leonora had never met another like Frederica Kirkwood. She was thankful to have found her and to count her an ally.

"No," she hastened to reassure her friend, and that much, at least, was true. "He is polite. Horridly so. He seems to resent me, in truth, and I fear the fault is mine for rebuffing him initially, in a moment of pique."

She flushed as she said the last, her cheeks stinging. For though she trusted Freddy implicitly, Leonora had never spoken about such matters as they pertained to herself. Not with anyone. Mama had advised her, and so had Freddy, but at that moment, she had yet to have a husband of her own. The warning words of her mother and her friend had been disparate, and they had seemed to apply to a future which Leonora could scarcely even contemplate.

"Have you expressed your interest to him?" Freddy asked.

"Of course not," Leonora said primly. "On our wedding day, he brought me to Linley House and left me after introducing me to the servants. I was not pleased with him, and I let him know as much upon his return."

Freddy nearly spat her tea. "You ought to have boxed his ears!"

"I was not certain what to expect of him. He is very much a stranger to me, and I have never had a husband before." She paused, her cheeks flaming with embarrassment. "I believe he may have been interested in consummating that evening. But when I told him he ought not to have left me and I needed my rest, it seemed to set the tone for the last week. He has been aloof and distant. I have been...existing."

"You were not wrong to tell him what you did," Freddy reassured her. "If he hurt your feelings, he should know. He should *want* to know. You are his wife, and it is in his best interest to please you in every way."

From the pink tinge to her friend's cheeks, Leonora could only surmise Mr. Kirkwood kept Freddy well pleased. Yet another twinge of envy pierced her. Oh, to have what Freddy and her Mr. Kirkwood had, love and passion and mutual respect.

"He is a difficult man to decipher," she admitted. "At times, I feel as if I shall suffocate beneath his stare, and other times, he is so cold, so remote. Sometimes, I cannot help but think he looks straight through me."

Freddy frowned. "I do know from Duncan, who has it from the Duke of Whitley, that Searle must have suffered a great deal when he was imprisoned. Perhaps that is the reason for his lordship's flux of moods."

Leonora had told herself as much. "How do you propose I express my interest to his lordship? Is not that task relegated to him? I had thought...if he wished...that is to say, I believed he would kiss me if he wished it."

"Your marriage was abrupt," her friend pointed out, frowning. "Perhaps Searle wishes to give you time to acclimate yourself to the notion of having a husband."

"Perhaps." But she was unconvinced. His aloofness had been concerning. At times, he seemed alight with intensity, as when his hands had been upon her. But he seemed equally capable of icing over, becoming detached.

He was a fortress she could not breach.

Impenetrable.

"What troubles you, dear heart?" Freddy asked then, clearly sensing Leonora's internal struggles.

"I fear I have made a great mistake," she admitted, suppressing a sob of despair. "I had hoped he would... I do not know—soften toward me. But each day, he has been polite yet removed, not even attempting to kiss me or to do anything more. It is almost as if he has given up on me already."

Freddy's lips thinned into a fine line of irritation. "First, you deserve nothing less than a husband who acknowledges you are the center of his day, the very driving force. Second, I saw the manner in which Searle touched you the evening he compromised you. I saw his expression. It was not the countenance of a man who is not helplessly, hopelessly attracted to you. Rather, it was the opposite."

Of course, Freddy would think so. She had always been her champion.

"I do not know what to do," she admitted, a new sense of help-lessness, mingling with despair, darkening her mood like a stain blotting an ivory skirt. "I want children, Freddy. I want our children to take their first steps together."

Her friend's expression turned determined. "Then the answer is simple, my dear. He is your husband, for fair or foul, and nothing shall change that now. If you want a babe of your own—and I know how much your heart aches for it—you must seduce your husband. I am afraid you have no other choice."

"BLOODY HELL," MORGAN growled, scowling down at the muck he had made of his ledgers.

Concentration was proving more difficult than ever before. Initial-ly, upon his return from the Continent and war, he had been unable to perform the smallest tasks without suffering from a crippling anxiety. He had hidden within the safe, familiar confines of Linley House, plotting his revenge against Rayne. He had slept in the bed of his youth because it had felt like where he belonged. Moving to the marquess's apartments had required time and adjustments and ample amounts of spirits, but he had managed.

The problem, however, was not his time at war or his days of imprisonment, nor was it his presence at Linley House, nor his usurping of the marquisate from his brother George—who would have been a far better man for the task than Morgan could ever hope to be. No, indeed. The problem, this time, lay elsewhere.

His wife.

The Marchioness of Searle was rotting his brain. That was what she was doing, and there was no other, more precise means of describing the perplexing trap in which he now found himself. The mere thought of her name was enough to make him burn. Four syllables, just as many vowels, and how it could encompass such flowering beauty in its mere utterance, he would never know.

Leonora.

Leonora of the flaxen hair, flashing blue eyes, delectable pink lips, prick-hardening curves, and the endless chorus of *no*. For one whole sennight—seven days, and he had counted them more than once because they seemed more like an eternity—his new wife had kept him at bay. She had yet to even allow him a kiss since he had left her on their wedding day, a departure which had been not just for his sake but hers as well.

Her bearing was eternally rigid, her expression whenever he was in her presence akin to a woman facing a phalanx of enemy soldiers about to pillage and plunder her home. As a result, he had spent most of his waking hours out of her presence. He returned in the evenings, hoping she might be awake, only to find her chamber enshrouded in darkness each time, echoing the silence of her refusal to allow him into her bed.

Though he was using her for his vengeance, he had no wish to take her by force. Therefore, he had bided his time. At first, he had been content to allow her to remain aloof. He feared he no longer had the skills of seduction within him, and he little knew how to be gentle in lovemaking after spending the last few years mired within savagery and battles to the death.

Part of him had been afraid he would hurt her, that the raging lust coursing through him whenever he saw her would somehow tear her apart. He had never bedded a virgin before, and it had been a long time since he had fucked anything other than his hand. The trulls following the army were not the game of chance he preferred to play, as he wanted to remain free of the pox.

And so, it had been years since he had made love to a woman. Since he had touched soft, silken skin, since he had kissed his way up the inside of a well-curved thigh. It had been so long, he groaned now, just thinking about Leonora, about her flesh smelling of sweet sunshine and spring flowers, of how warm and pliant her skin had been. He thought about wrapping his fist in the glorious cloud of her golden hair, holding her head still for the onslaught of his kiss.

It would have to happen soon, and not just because he hungered for her the same way he desired his next breath, his next meal, his next drink of water. Which he most assuredly did. But because his time was waning. He had a plan to set into motion, and that plan could not move forward until he had Leonora in his bed.

He expected the Earl of Rayne to reappear on England's shores, like the pestilence he was, any day now. That meant Morgan's time to consummate his marriage and set in place the makings of his ultimate revenge were long overdue. He needed to make Leonora his in every way.

He dipped his pen in the ink well, drawing off the excess from the tip before crossing out the mathematical errors he had made. He wondered if he was the problem, if his mind was the problem, and not just his distraction. All along, he had been the second son, the spare heir his father and mother had created before never speaking to each other without an intermediary again, duty to the title duly completed.

His father and George had both perished in the time Morgan had been away at war, his mother long before the both of them. Which meant, freshly returned from battle and imprisonment, he was the second son who had never imagined he would one day take up the reins of the Marquess of Searle, scrambling to find his footing on a deuced slippery slope. And now, though he wished he could be concerned with his estates as he ought, what he wanted more than anything was the Earl of Rayne facing him on the field of honor.

The victory would be hollow, and he already knew it. But the victory would be his, perhaps one manner in which he could reclaim what had been taken from him.

A light tap at the door disrupted his troubled musings, and he returned his pen to the ink well. "Enter."

His butler, Huell, appeared, unsmiling as ever. "My lord, Lady Searle has returned from her social calls."

At. Bloody. Last.

Clenching his jaw, he stood. "Thank you, Huell."

He had inquired after whether or not his wife had returned from her visit to Mrs. Duncan Kirkwood on no less than five separate occasions already. Finally, no doubt growing impatient with Morgan's repeated interruptions, Huell had taken it upon himself to keep Morgan apprised of his wife's whereabouts.

His butler bowed and retreated.

Morgan stalked into the main hall, irritated to discover it was already empty. All that remained was the sweet floral trail of her scent, the sole sign she had ever traversed the polished boards so recently. It lingered like a ghost.

But this time, he would not allow her to escape. This time, he would seek her out. Before his mind had even processed coherent thought, Morgan's feet were already eating up the space separating him from his wife. He took the last stairs two at a time, took the second-floor hall at a canter, and slipped into his apartments.

She was likely in her chamber, changing or perhaps preparing to attend to her correspondence. He had made a great effort not to force his presence upon her thus far in their fledgling marriage. But the time of exerting his patience and waiting had rapidly drawn to an end. He had no more freedom to be gracious. Leonora needed to face him, to understand she was his wife now, inextricably so.

He had been hoping she would soften. Perhaps even meet him halfway.

But he could not wait any longer. He had to act.

Morgan opened the door and crossed the threshold, stepping over the invisible line which had separated him from his wife for the last seven days. She was within, for he smelled the sweetness of her scent before he saw her, in the midst of changing her gown with the aid of her lady's maid.

Leonora froze when her gaze settled upon him, and so did the domestic assisting her.

"My lord," said his wife, her frosty tone proof he had yet to redeem himself in her eyes.

When she discovered the truth, he would be incapable of redeeming himself, so it was a moot point if she already found him hopeless.

"My lady." He bowed, sending a meaningful glance toward the woman tending her.

The lady's maid instantly curtsied and excused herself with such haste he was surprised she did not stumble over the hem of her gown.

He waited for the door to close completely before further advancing upon his wife. Upon his *scantily* clad wife. His gaze trailed over her form, savoring her, for she wore nothing more than a chemise and stockings. And as his gaze lingered over the delectable swell of her bosom, her nipples hardened into tight little buds that taunted him through her creamy linen. The pink tips were a tormenting silhouette beneath the gossamer fabric. His hands itched to grip the neckline and tear, exposing her to him. His mouth longed to suck.

Holy God, he could barely withstand the crushing weight of desire slamming into him. The mound between her legs was almost completely visible, another, equally alluring shadow his mouth and hands wanted to explore.

Leonora laced her fingers together, clasping them at her waist in a gesture he had already come to realize signified she was about to wage war. "What do you require of me, my lord?"

So many things.

So many deliciously wicked, filthy things.

Beginning with that sweet mouth of hers open to receive his…

Damnation. He forced his lust aside, willing his rampant erection to abate. Instead, he sought his voice. "The time has come, my lady."

Was it his imagination, or did her lips pinch? Did a small groove appear between her brows where none had previously existed?

She swallowed, and there was no mistaking the action. "For what has the time come, my lord?"

"Morgan," he corrected her. Initially, he had been concerned that urging her to refer to him by his Christian name would lull them both into a false sense of familiarity.

Now, he no longer cared. He was desperate to make her his. And not just because of his quest to gain revenge upon her half-brother, if he were brutally honest with himself. Rayne did not matter here.

Rather, the ferocity of his need for her was a force all its own. It was beating inside him like the pulse of a heart, and he could not deny it any longer. He wanted her. The woman he had married was beautiful and imperfect and caring and good. She was not afraid to defy him. She did not falter when it came to maintaining her pride, and neither did she falter when it came to living her life. She suffered from pain—he knew she must—and yet, she never complained. Nor did he note the slightest inclination of her feeling sorry for herself.

He wanted her body. He wanted her heart. He wanted her soul. Every part of her, all she had to give, but he somehow knew instinctively not even that would be enough. He was ravenous, starving, and only she could fill the void. He had to have her.

Now. Right bloody now.

"Morgan," she repeated softly. "I wish for you to consummate our marriage."

Damnation. He was going to spend in his breeches without even touching her. It had been madness to allow a week to pass. Madness to think waiting would enable him to control his raging impulse to claim her. He wanted inside her. Wanted to bury his cock inside her pink, slippery flesh and fill her with his seed.

To mark her as his.

Forever.

Four strides was all he required to reach her, and then, she was in his arms.

CHAPTER FIVE

FREDDY HAD TOLD her to seduce Searle, and Leonora was sure she had not meant for her to merely blurt the words *I wish for you to consummate our marriage*. But she did not have long to wait to discover whether or not her embarrassing attempt at swaying her new husband had been successful. Because he was upon her.

There was really no other way to explain it. His hands were everywhere, a hot brand through her chemise, beginning at her waist, cupping her breasts, molding her bottom. He swept over her, leaving a trail of longing in his wake. As he touched her, his gaze traveled over her as well, scouring her flesh as surely as his touch.

The silence was heady, heavy. Somehow, his lack of words heightened the moment, making her every sense sing. Her breasts felt full and achy, the mound between her thighs throbbed and pulsed. She could smell the earthy scent of him, the bergamot of his tea lacing his breath. She had never been so aware of her body, so aware of her own need to be pleasured. Of another person's capacity to fulfill that desperate longing.

He found her breasts again, cupping one, then rolling her nipple between his thumb and forefinger through the barrier of her chemise. When a gasp tore from her, he increased the pressure.

"Tell me if I hurt you," he rasped.

His words took her by surprise, sending confusion skittering through her, along with a small tremor of alarm and a trill of something else, anticipation. His touch was firm but not rough. Pleasure tinged with an edge, just as he was. This man was dangerous, as she had thought all along, and she…she *liked* it.

Craved it, in fact.

He pinched her nipples harder, then rubbed lazy, soothing circles over them with his thumbs. His eyes scorched her, the amber flecks alive and alight. He dipped his head toward her, running the blade of his nose along hers and inhaling deeply, as if she were something delicious he wanted to savor. But still, he did not kiss her.

His breath fell hot upon her lips, and she licked them, eager for this small part of him she could have. It shocked her to realize she was every bit as ravenous for Searle as he seemed for her.

He pinched again, until a small moan left her. And then he rubbed his lower lip along hers. Nothing more. "You like this."

It was a statement, not a question. Because he could read her better than she could even understand herself. Pleasure and yearning were not new to her, but this—her reaction to the marquess and the way he seemed to anticipate what she wanted before she could even ask—took her by storm.

She swallowed. "Yes."

A low sound, part growl, part groan, rumbled from deep within his broad chest. "You want this."

Good heavens, yes. She wanted what he was doing and more. How odd it seemed, how incredibly awakening, for this beautiful man in his fully-clothed elegance, scarcely touching her, and yet so thoroughly consuming her. And he had still yet to kiss her.

Leonora nodded because she did not think she could speak. Her hands had landed upon his shoulders somehow in the aftermath of his seductive aggression, and her fingers tensed upon him now. He was warm, so very warm.

He released her nipples and caught her lower lip between his teeth, delivering a nip that stung yet was somehow tender at the same time. "You are mine, Leonora. No matter what happens. Regardless of what is to come beyond these walls and beyond this moment. You are mine forever."

Yes, she was his now. It had not felt that way over the last week they had spent at daggers drawn, circling each other like duelists, afraid to make the first move. But it felt that way now, with him surrounding her with his hands on her body and...

He stepped into her, pressing his hard body against her softness. She felt something long and thick through the layers between them, and she knew what it was, what it meant, for Freddy had explained a great deal more to her mere hours before. He raked his teeth down her neck, and her head fell back of its own accord, desperate for whatever ravishment he would give. Teeth and lips and tongue. He sucked at her throat, beneath her ear, then lower, once more at the place where her shoulder met her neck. These were places she had never bothered to touch herself, skin that had never clamored to be touched until this man.

"Mine," he said, finding her collarbone and biting. "Say the words, Leonora."

When she hesitated, he bit again. Harder this time, and she was sure it would leave a mark. She did not care.

"I am yours," she managed, breathless.

"Yes, you are." His voice was dark and resonating, and it made something inside her flutter and then burst wide open.

Her leg pained her, but she was helpless to stop the reckless desire coursing through her. She would stand here with him all day, his mouth and hands upon her, his body burning into hers. She never wanted it to end, except she did. She wanted more. She wanted to be closer. She wanted nothing between them but skin.

The first time she had touched herself, she had not dared to do so directly. Rather, she had used her nightdress as a barrier to keep her shame from drowning her. In time, she had realized her nightdress was not necessary and that everything felt so much better without its encumbrance. She had no doubt Searle's body and caresses would only be enhanced by the same removal of limitations.

But just as the thought hit her, so, too, did an undulating tide of pain from her injury, radiating up her leg. She shifted again, attempting to remove all weight from it when he stilled.

Perhaps he sensed her movement and knew what it meant without needing to ask. Perhaps he was carried away by her declaration. She would never know. But he had suddenly taken her up in his arms, and he was carrying her in the wrong direction. Not toward the beckoning invitation of her bed, but to his own chamber.

"Searle," she protested, flushed and needy and confused.

He ignored her and kept walking.

Her arms locked around his neck, and she could not help but to admire his profile. How strong his jaw was and set at a determined angle. His cravat was not tied with a fop's love of intricate knots and falls, but simplistically instead, revealing far more of his neck than gentlemen ordinarily allowed.

She wanted to bite him there as he had done to her. To sink her teeth into his flesh. To make him as wild and mindless as he had made her, with nothing more than a few simple touches and a wicked mouth. She ought to be ashamed of herself, shocked by her own reactions. What periphery-dwelling, lame-legged spinster entertained such beastly cravings?

"I want you in *my* bed," he told her, staring straight ahead as he carted her over the threshold and into his territory as if she weighed nothing.

Yes.

She thought she said the word aloud, agreeing with him, for there was suddenly no place she would rather be. But she could not be sure, because he had once again rattled her senses, addling her wits.

He was a strong man to carry her thus, for she was no willowy miss. With his broad body and lean strength, she had no doubt it would have been difficult indeed for the enemy to take him prisoner. He would have fought viciously. The notion gave her a shiver, for she wondered again how much he had suffered. What had happened to him?

He looked down at her, a slight frown marring the flesh between his brows. "Cold?"

For a moment, she was reminded of the first evening she had made his acquaintance, when he had descended upon Freddy's private salon and had tended to her, ordering her about in clipped, one-word sentences. She wondered if he was always looking after the wellbeing of others. He hardly seemed the sort of man to be possessed of a caretaking nature. Perhaps it was ingrained in him from his time spent at war.

"No," she answered, awash in sensation, in emotion, in *him*.

The Marquess of Searle affected her as she had not even known was possible. Her gaze dipped to his mouth, and how she wished to feel it upon hers, hard and hot as she somehow knew it would be.

But before she could act upon her restless urgings, he had deposited her on her feet alongside his bed.

"Certain?" he asked.

For a beat, she wondered what he was asking her. Her mind was filled with thoughts of the immense, beautifully carved bed at her side. With what would happen. With his mouth.

"I am not cold," she said at last, her mind returning.

"Good." His hand found the heavy chignon keeping her wild curls tamed, his fingers spearing through it until he held her tight, angling her face toward his.

He lowered his head.

At long last, his lips connected with hers. It was a kiss.

Her first kiss.

And it was more than she had dared to dream a kiss could be, not just a meeting of the mouths but an onslaught. It was as if he stood at the brink of damnation, a hellfire in eternity, and kissing her was the only act that would keep him from the flames. He kissed her long and hard, demanding, coaxing, his lips working over hers, his tongue finding the seam and sliding inside to tangle with hers.

She tasted his tea in truth now, the sweetness of sugar upon her tongue and the dark truth of something else, him. *Searle.* His kiss tore her apart and then put her back together again. It was bruising and harsh, yet powerful and tender. She would never be the same.

But as quickly as it had begun, the conflagration ended. His mouth lifted from hers, and there was a sound of denial in the air. A protest. Hers? His? She could not be sure. All she could do was blink, attempting to find her purchase in a world torn desperately asunder. Her lips tingled. And she wanted more.

"Your chemise," he said roughly, releasing his hold on her as her body cried out in protest. "I want you to remove it for me."

His wicked directive stole her breath, and she hesitated, fear and shame threatening, attempting to crowd the desire from her mind and body. She had a lame leg. Her hips were too full, her belly too rounded, her bottom far too large. No man had wanted her since her comeout. Why would this one be any different?

"Please," he added.

This lone word, this torn and ragged and desperate sounding word, was what tipped the scales for her. Her hands fisted in the linen of her chemise, and with one effortless tug, she had it over her head, sending it sailing somewhere behind her. It landed, she knew not where, with a hushed whisper, but all thoughts of the garment and anything that was not the Marquess of Searle fled her at the look of blatant need that came over his face.

Beneath his gaze, she felt…transformed. She felt as if she were someone different than Limping Leonora. As if she were beautiful and desirable. She arched her back and inhaled as his eyes raked her form, and she told herself she would not cover her imperfections. She would not hide anything from him. She was herself, and she was horridly flawed, but she was also the woman he had wed.

His forever, just as he had said.

"My God," he gritted. His gaze was pure fire as it skated over her curves, lingering on her breasts, lowering to the mound between her thighs, sliding down her limbs. "You are the most beautiful woman I have ever seen."

She would have laughed and flushed had any other gentleman made such a proclamation, for she would have known it flattery at best and falsehood at worse. But this man—this strange and perplexing and delicious man she had married—was different. His charm was sparse. He was cool and remote, vexing and confusing, harsh and unrepentant. He was a sharp blade that could cut deep.

And so, when he uttered those words—when the Marquess of Searle told her she was the most beautiful woman he had ever seen—she believed him.

Freddy's directives returned to her then. *Make him weak for you. Gentlemen like to be touched.*

Because she felt bold, and because she felt beautiful, and because nothing about either her marriage to Searle or this seduction in the midst of the day had been expected, she decided to dare. For the first time, the wallflower was ready to break free of her mold. The periphery of life could go to perdition for all she cared.

She wanted action. Touch. Passion. She wanted everything she had never had.

"I want to see you," she told him.

MORGAN INHALED SHARPLY against a sudden burst of violent need. Leonora stood before him, entirely nude. *Lord God*, she was a vision to behold. Better than he had imagined, and he had spent every night since seeing her for the first time, imagining her whilst stroking his cock.

She was all creamy curves and sweet pink perfection, a mouth-watering marriage of the innocent and the wicked, the musky perfume of her desire redolent in the air, mingling with the floral notes of her fragrance. He had never wanted another woman—or another damned thing for that matter—more.

He clawed at his clothing like the wild beast he was, tearing open the knot of his cravat. She did not need to tell him twice. He stripped off his jacket and waistcoat. Flung the linen of his neck cloth to the floor. His shoes and stockings were next, then he undid the fall of his breeches, tugging them down.

He paused before removing the final garment shielding him from her—his shirt. His back was a macabre mural of lash marks, and burn scars marred his chest. One of his captors had taken great joy in stubbing the glowing tips of his cigars upon Morgan's flesh in an effort to get him to reveal privileged information about the movement of English troops. Others had preferred whipping him while he was tied to a post as if he were no better than a mule.

Morgan did not wish to horrify or disgust her, and he had no way of knowing how she would react. No one had ever seen them but him and the doctor who had tended his infected wounds when he had finally escaped and made his way back to English forces. Instead of removing his shirt, he caught her waist in his hands, marveling at the silken smoothness of her flesh. So soft. So lush.

So his.

And then he took her mouth again. He kissed her with all his desperation and need, his burning desire. He could kiss this woman forever and never have enough of her lips yielding to his, of the husky sounds of surrender emerging from her throat. He lifted her and settled her gently on the center of his bed, nudging her thighs apart and settling between them as he joined her.

He rocked against her wet heat, against the gentle swell of her cunny as he deepened the kiss, his tongue sinking inside the way he longed to plunge deep within her. She was slick, so soaked for him, his cock glided over her folds.

My God, she was a revelation. This desire between them was something he had not anticipated, and it was potent and raw and real. Though he had fantasized about bedding her, he had never once imagined she could surpass the wickedness his mind had cooked. That she would want him as much as he wanted her. That she would be brazen and bold in her passion, her body so responsive, he feared all he need do was stroke her pearl once before she would explode.

He kissed his way down her neck, finding her collarbone, exploring the roundness of her shoulder before sinking his teeth into her. She made another husky sound of desire, so he soothed the perfect skin he had just marked and then bit again. This one would leave a mark he would see tomorrow when he stripped her bare and bedded her again. He liked the notion of seeing the evidence of himself upon her flesh. It made his prick harden even more.

She cried out in earnest, hips swiveling against him in an effort to bring her swollen flesh into greater contact with him. He had been right about her on the day of their wedding. She was curious. Curious and hungry, and he would give her what she wanted.

His fingers dipped into her folds, connecting with the engorged bud he sought. He bit back a moan as he kissed his way to her lush breasts. Damnation, she felt good. Too good. He sucked a nipple into his mouth, then caught it in his teeth and tugged. Then the other. She grew restless beneath him, her breath coming in faster pants that told him she was on the edge.

He hummed his approval and flicked a tongue over one distended nipple. "Spend for me," he commanded, and then he increased the pressure over her pearl.

She did. Oh, how she did. When she came, she was even more splendid, a goddess come to life, her white-blonde curls a halo about her face, her cheeks rosy, mouth open, eyes closed. Her back arched, her breasts like ripe offerings just for him, all for him. He worked her until the tremors rocking her subsided, admiring the sight of her coming undone, of his hand buried in her golden curls, of her thrusting shamelessly against him.

Barely holding his own desire in check, he raised his fingers, glistening with her juices, to his lips and sucked them clean. Tomorrow, perhaps even later, he would take his time and would make her spend on his tongue. For now, he was not going to last, and he would have to satisfy himself with this sweet taste of her instead.

Her eyes were upon him, shocked and dazed, glazed with pleasure, her cheeks tinged pink. He expected her to protest. To offer some maidenly shock. It had been so long since he had been with a woman—and then never an innocent lady like her—that he had no inkling of what would make her swoon. He was acting upon instinct alone, driven by his raging lust.

"Your shirt," she said, her fine-boned fingers snagging in the fabric, tugging it.

She surprised him, not just by the demand in her tone but by the request itself.

"I have scars," he bit out.

"I have a lame leg," she countered.

"You are perfection," he said, meaning it. She was glorious, lovely, and he knew a moment of guilt at claiming her with such bitterness in his heart, such rancor and murderous rage in his blood. The ugliness festering inside him should not dare touch the woman beneath him.

But he had gone too far to stop, and she was his wife. Moreover, he felt quite certain he would burn alive if he could not sink inside her.

"Please?" she asked softly. "Trust me with yourself, as I have entrusted myself to you."

Hell and damnation, what was he to do with such an angel?

He knew what he ought to do, set her free. Grant her an annulment. Send her on her merry way before he hurt her. Before his quest for revenge left her sullied and stole her innocence and banished all the kindness and goodness from her.

He also knew what he was going to do, take her. Seal both their fates. Make certain she would never forget she was his wife.

He caught fistfuls of his shirt and yanked it over his head. Her hands were upon him before he could stop her, caressing, soothing. The sensation of her small, soft hands upon him proved his undoing.

He did not care if she was disgusted by his scarred hide. Blood was roaring through him. Desire was heavy and hot, sliding down his spine, radiating through him, driving him relentlessly forward. He reached between them once more, stroking her, and she was as wet and responsive as ever.

Morgan gripped his cock, guiding it to her entrance as he lowered himself over her, taking her lips in another kiss. He could not even warn her this would hurt. Could not form more words. All he could do was feel and need and take.

He plunged his tongue into the velvety recesses of her mouth at the same time as he breached her. One slow thrust of his hips, and he was partially inside her, the tip of his shaft bathed in her heat. The animal in him screamed to thrust all the way. To sink home, to take her relentlessly and hard and deep. But he reined himself in, exerting so much control, beads of sweat rolled down his neck. One more slow, agonizing thrust, and he met the barrier of her innocence.

His to claim.

Forever his.

The knowledge was so potent, so thrilling, sending a great rush of possession surging through him, that he lost his ability to stop. He sank deeper as she stiffened beneath him, the only sign he had caused her pain. Still kissing her, he returned to her pearl, rubbing over it in slow, steady circles until she relaxed. One more thrust, and he was all the way home, seated as deep as he could be.

And she was tight. God, was she tight, milking his cock as her body adjusted to him. She was close to spending once more. He could sense it in the small jolts rippling through her and the sounds in her throat, the small moans he swallowed with his frenzied kisses. His body took on a will of its own, his hips undulating in steady, shallow thrusts. He could not stay still. She felt too good, sucking him inside her, clenching on him, bringing him closer to his own release.

She came again, shaking beneath him, contracting on his prick with such force, he knew he could not last much longer, even as he wanted to prolong this. He wanted to stay inside her forever. But his hips were moving, and he was taking her harder and faster than he wanted. Faster and faster as she made sweet, breathy sounds of her own helpless lust, her hips rocking against his, meeting him thrust for thrust.

Warmth rolled down his spine and his ballocks tightened. Rocking against her, he emptied himself. Bedding a woman had never felt so satisfying, as if it completed him.

"Damn," he groaned, trailing kisses down her neck, burying his face against her elegant throat. The oath was torn from him, and he knew he should suppress it, for she was a lady, but his emotions were so violent and visceral, nothing else would do. "Leonora, you feel so good. So bloody, bloody good."

Her hands were on his shoulders, fingers pressed into the blades, clutching him to her. "So do you."

She still clenched him hard as the last of his climax rippled through him. Reluctantly, he slid from her cunny and rolled to his back, his body more sated and replete than he could ever recall. He lay there, staring at the plaster work on the ceiling, a medallion of acanthus leaves that had become so familiar to him as to cease existing, not truly seeing anything, breathless and mindless.

He ought to be gloating. He ought to be celebrating the latest step in his mission of vengeance. But his bed was rumpled, and the air smelled of fucking, and Leonora's perfume, and all he could think about instead was when he could be inside her again. She had been a virgin, after all. Her blood was smeared upon his cock, mingling with the remnants of his seed.

Several hours from now? Tonight? Tomorrow morning?

Pray God it could be soon.

Leonora rolled toward him then, startling him by cuddling into his body as if she were a cat seeking comfort and warmth, her arm going around him. Her show of tenderness made him hold his body still and rigid. He did not want her trust or her pity. He wanted her body, and his ability to enact retribution upon her evil kin. He wanted to meet the Earl of Rayne at dawn and send him to hell as he deserved.

But then she did another thing he least expected.

She pressed a kiss to his chest, directly above his frantically thudding heart. "You are beautiful, my lord."

He felt the imprint of her lips upon his skin as if it had marked him as surely as the fiery end of a Frenchman's cigar.

CHAPTER SIX

Leonora woke to the sounds of terror and misery. A low, masculine cry, half groan, half growl, rattled through the stillness of the chamber. The sun had set, blanketing her surroundings in darkness, and for a moment, she was not even certain of her surroundings. Riverford House? Nay, not the chamber she had inhabited for so long; it was as gone to her now as her childhood.

Remembrance and awareness returned to her all at once. She was at Linley House, in the marquess's bedchamber. In *his* bed. The soreness between her thighs forced her to recall in exquisite detail what had passed between them hours earlier. After he had made love to her and brought her body to such an astounding pinnacle, she must have fallen asleep, and heavens knew for how long.

She could not even discern the time of day given the lack of light, and neither could she determine the source of the sound.

Until she heard it again, and she realized it was coming from alongside her in the bed.

"No! Do not touch me." This time, Searle's words were clear, unmistakable as his voice. *"Ne pas. Ne pas!"*

He began thrashing then, his breathing deep and harsh. Another strangled cry emerged from his throat.

Dear God, the marquess must be suffering from a nightmare. And if he was speaking in French, it was a possibility his mind had returned him to the source of his torment. That he believed himself once more in Spain, the captive of Boney's forces.

The urge to calm and console him was instant and instinctive.

"Searle." Tentatively, she reached in the direction of his voice. Her hand met with cold, clammy flesh that trembled beneath her touch.

And then a hand clasped around her wrist in a manacle grip, and she was propelled onto her back, trapped beneath a heavy, strong body. Powerful thighs trapped her hips, pinning her to the bed, and he did the same with her wrists, clasping both and holding them over her head. His chest pressed against her naked breasts with thinly veiled force.

His breathing was even more ragged and desperate, hot on her face and neck. Something cold and wet dripped upon her cheek, and she wondered if it was somehow, impossibly, a tear. And then, at his mercy, something else occurred to her. Something horrible.

It was possible he was out of his mind. Possible he would hurt her.

"Morgan." His name was torn from her, all she could manage in her sudden fear. "Morgan, it is Leonora."

"Leonora," he exhaled her name, as if it were a prayer. A shudder ripped through him, and she felt it from her thighs to her breast. "Leonora?"

"Yes." How she wished she could touch him. Comfort him. Caress him. But he had not released her wrists. "It is me, my lord. You were having a nightmare, I fear. Will you not release me, if you please?"

"Jesus." He released her instantly, his voice laden with remorse. His forehead tipped to hers, resting there, his breath fanning hotly over her lips as he seemed to struggle to regain his composure. "I am so sorry. Have I hurt you, Leonora?"

He had momentarily stolen the breath from her, and her wrists smarted from the force of his grip, but she was more concerned with his wellbeing than her own. Freed, her hands found their way to his bare back. Tentatively, gently, as if he were a beast, she could not be certain would bite, she caressed him, her fingers finding the ridges of his scars mingling with the smooth, velvet heat of his unmarked flesh.

"You did not hurt me, Morgan," she assured him softly, his name feeling right on her tongue for the first time.

Even after the shocking intimacies they had shared when he had made love to her, calling him thus had felt foreign and wrong. But he seemed more reachable to her now, in this rare moment of vulnerability, than he had ever been before. Here was her first glimpse of his humanity, of the suffering dwelling within him that no doubt caused the cold aloofness he showed the world and herself most of the time.

"Damn it to hell, I did not intend to fall asleep," he gritted, attempting to move away from her.

But when he would have gone, she held him still, trapping him with her body. She wrapped her legs around his lean hips, crushing him tightly in her arms. "Do not move away from me. Please, let me give you comfort."

He stiffened, and it was as if he had turned to stone. She could not be certain which version of the Marquess of Searle frightened her more, the battle-weary soldier defending himself in his slumber or the icy-cold stranger she had wed. Hours earlier, when he had been kissing her, when he had been inside her body, he had been someone else still, and now she feared she would never reclaim that man. The man who had kissed her as if her lips were the most decadent sweet he had ever tasted. The man who had made her experience such glorious rushes of pleasure, the likes of which she had never imagined possible.

"I do not need your comfort, madam," he all but spat, his head jerking up, severing the connection between them but not tearing away from her entirely.

Not yet.

"I think you are wrong," she told him boldly. "I think you do, Searle. I think you need me very much."

"This." His hand cupped the space between her legs. "I need your cunny, wife. Do not delude yourself that I need anything more from you."

His words hurt more than his manhandling of her had, but she knew they emerged as a defense. The Marquess of Searle may be her husband of only one week, but it had not taken her long to discover he was a proud man. He never showed a hint of either weakness or tender emotion, and she did not fool herself it was because he was incapable. Rather, he did not *wish* to show anyone else his true defenselessness. He had been a prisoner, after all, and he would have been at the mercy of his captors.

"Then take comfort in me as you must," she told him through the darkness, still tenderly stroking his back and all the puckered evidence of how very helpless he had once been. Her heart ached for the wounded warrior within him, the man whose outer scars had healed but who bore far more painful inner wounds that continued to ruin him.

"This is not comfort," he growled, his fingers delving deeper into her, finding the bud of flesh that even now, longed for his touch. "This is fucking, Leonora. I do not require your pity or your softness or your gentle bloody touches after I have nearly broken you in two with my own bare hands. Do you understand?"

Yes, she understood. She understood him better now than she had ever before. He was ashamed of himself, frightened he had hurt her, or that he *would* hurt her, terrified of his own weakness. But she could not help but to feel she was meant to be his second chance. Filled with a boldness she could scarcely credit as her own, she slid her hands from his back to his neck and then higher still, her fingers sinking into his thick, silken hair.

She cupped his head, wondering at what mayhem could possibly be rioting within his mind, trapped inside the lean, angry elegance of this beautiful stranger she had wed. "I am yours, Searle," she whispered into the inky silence curtaining them.

It was as if they were the only two people who existed in the world. There was nothing but the demons of his past and the rawness of their bare, imperfect bodies pressed together. There was nothing but untamed desire and the raging need to be one. If she could heal him, if she could offer up herself as sacrifice, she gladly would. And she would enjoy it, for he set her aflame with the wanton fires of the wicked, and she wanted nothing more than to scorch in them.

"Yes," he growled, his chest pressed so tightly to her breasts she felt the vibration of it. "You are mine, aren't you? What a curious thing you are, urging me to bed you after I have just taken your maidenhead and then hurt you."

Self-derision underscored his every word.

"You did not hurt me," she denied. *Not with your hands*, she added silently. *But I understand. I understand you. Let me in.* "Perhaps you do not wish for comfort from me, my lord. But you do want something else, do you not? You want what is yours."

His breathing grew harsher, and she felt the exact moment what she had said settled upon him, for he grew hard and thick against her inner thigh. "It is too soon," he said. "You must be sore."

He had tended to her with a bowl and cloth at some point in the hazy aftermath of their lovemaking earlier, washing away the blood and soothing her swollen flesh. She felt bruised but in a delicious way. Even as he murmured the denial, he rocked against her, pressing that huge, demanding staff into her skin in a crude imitation of what he would do to her next.

And she did not know what was wrong with her, or if anything was wrong with her—indeed, perhaps it was only natural to feel this way toward one's husband—but she wanted everything he would do to her. She wanted him to give himself to her, to enter her, to lose himself inside her once more.

But still, she sensed a hesitancy in him. Perhaps she could never erase the memories haunting him or the terror dogging him, but she did know she could give him one thing he wanted.

She could give him herself.

Gentlemen like to be touched.

Freddy's advice echoed in her mind again as her left hand abandoned his hair in favor of sliding down his well-muscled body to touch him. Nothing could have prepared her for the first sensation of him in her hand, smooth and soft and hot, yet firm and beautifully formed. How impossible it seemed to think this thick length had been within her. Little wonder she was sore. Why, if she had felt how immense this part of him was before, she would have been fearful indeed.

But now, she ached for him again, the need pulsing within her, blossoming, blotting out the lingering pain. Instinct driving her, the combination of the darkness and the wildness of him, the danger still tingling through her veins, she gripped him hard. With her other hand, she tugged on his hair, grabbing a fistful.

"Tell me what you need, Searle," she urged. Her voice was throaty. Not her own. Indeed, she scarcely recognized herself.

"You tell me, wife," he said darkly, increasing the pressure on her until she was sure she would lose all control. "Tell me what I need."

A long finger sank inside her before she could even say a word. This invasion was unexpected, but it was…oh, it was so very good. He worked that finger deeper, so deep inside her she was on edge, writhing against him, wanting him to stop and yet wanting him to go on forever at the same time.

"Me," she whispered, tugging his head down to hers, rejoicing when he allowed it. When his lips were so close to hers, she could taste him. "You need me."

But she had fooled herself if she had believed the Marquess of Searle would allow her a victory over him. "Not all of you." A second finger joined the first, sliding in wetly, for she was ready for him. "Just your cunny. This is all I need from you. This cunny is mine, is it not, wife?"

His fingers curled within her, finding a place that was deliriously sensitive. She cried out, arching against that knowing hand. "Yes."

"Say it, damn you." His order was low, guttural, as if it emerged from some dark place inside him.

She knew it was the place where his fear dwelled. The place where his tortured memories lived. She rode his hand, and she stroked him, and her body arched up instinctively to meet and welcome his.

"My cunny is yours," she told him at last, the indecent, improper words burning her tongue. But she said them because she knew it was what he wanted to hear. And because she wanted to please him. Because she was going to heal him. She was going to make this man whole again. And she wanted him. Oh, how she wanted him.

"Yes," he said. "Are you certain you're not sore?"

Not too sore for what she wanted. "Certain."

That quickly, his fingers were gone, and in their place was the thick, solid length of him sliding home. Sliding deep.

He felt so good, so right. She kissed him, and he kissed her back, their tongues tangling. He thrust in, then out, then in again. This time was different than the last. He did not hold back. She suspected it was not just because she was no longer a virgin, but because he had lost his ability to control himself.

Because he needed her, and not in this one, simple sense as he claimed. No indeed, he needed all of her, her heart, her patience, her desire to understand him.

The yearning to love another, which had waned over the years, but which she had never been able to blot out completely, rose strong. If she had to fall in love with anyone, she thought as Morgan brought her once more to the heights of pleasure and she exploded into a fine, shimmery mist of stars, why not her husband? Why not this man? Why not the Marquess of Searle?

His kiss turned harder, almost bruising. When his fingers upon her bud set her free for the second time, he lost himself simultaneously, burying himself to the hilt, his seed pouring into her as her body convulsed all around him, welcoming him, embracing him.

And she knew, in that breathless moment in the darkness, awash in sensation, her husband's body heavy atop hers...she knew she was home. That this man, flawed and dark and dangerous and bitter and scarred, was hers in the very same way she was his.

No realization had ever been more beautiful, nor more welcomed.

Yes, she was home.

The Marquess of Searle was hers.

MORGAN WOKE WITH a thudding head and a stinging sense of guilt in his gut, just as if he had spent the previous day drinking and wenching himself to oblivion. Only, he had not done anything of the sort. Or, rather, he had done no drinking but he had done more than his fair share of wenching. Oddly, the wenching had been of the proper sort. With his wife.

Early morning light pierced his chamber as remembrance washed over him.

He had not just consummated his marriage the previous afternoon after his wife had returned from making her calls—and like an utter savage, he could admit to himself if no one else—but he had then fallen asleep with her in his bed. And he had been plagued by the same nightmares that had been terrorizing him since his return with unpredictable efficacy.

Sometimes, he would go weeks without suffering a bout. Other times, he would become helplessly caught in the throes of them, unable to sleep for days on end for fear of reliving what had happened to him in Spain. Last night, after he had bedded his wife for the first time and fallen into a sated stupor, he had found slumber only for the dreams to return with an aggression that had provoked him beyond reason.

Trapped in the darkness of his demons, he had not realized who the presence alongside him was until he was already straddling Leonora beneath him, pinning her wrists over her head. It had been a shameful moment of weakness. An embarrassing display of his inability to control not just the memories of what had happened to him but his mind since he had returned to England as a free man.

More signs he would never break free of the chains binding him.

Exhaling on a sigh of disgust aimed at himself alone, he rolled to his side to find she was still here. Still in his bed, her white-blonde curls fanned over a pillow, her face in sweet, angelic repose. The bedclothes had sagged to reveal one ripe, luscious breast.

All he wanted to do was suck that nipple deep into his mouth, roll her onto her back, and take her again, just as he had once more in the night.

But he was more lucid now than he had been in the blackest hours of the early morning, neither light nor rational thinking between them, and he knew she could not sustain another round. Not when she had just been bedded for the first time the day before. And she deserved more, this luscious, giving beauty he had made his. He was using her for revenge, using her body for his own gratification, and she was asking for nothing in return.

Part of him wanted to wake her with a kiss, the sort of sweet peck lovers might share, laden with promise but free of pressure. But such a kiss would be indicative of a weak man. Of a man who did not intend to use her as his means for vengeance. And so, he rolled away from her, left the bed, and quietly stalked across the chamber to complete his morning ablutions and dress himself.

He left her without a backward glance.

"MY LADY."

Leonora jolted awake, blinking at the hazy, sideways apparition hovering over her. It took a moment for her sleepy eyes to settle, for her mind to regain an awareness of her own body. She was lying on her stomach, face buried in a soft pillow that smelled like the marquess. She was even sorer now than she had been the previous night, the place between her legs tingling with a newfound awareness. Her mouth was open, and she was horrified to discover she had been drooling into her husband's pillow.

On a moan partially wrought from embarrassment and partially from all the sore muscles in her body crying out in protest when she moved, she swiped at the wetness on the corner of her lips. Moving was painful. She was tired, and she felt so lovely precisely where she was, buried within the luxurious bed linens.

"My lady?" Hill, her lady's maid, prodded again in a tentative voice.

Leonora turned her head slightly, so Hill's face was visible. She did not think herself capable of speech at the moment. "Mmm?"

It occurred to her then, to wonder why her lady's maid was here in Searle's chamber, and furthermore, to wonder where her husband was. Leonora was alone in his massive bed. Stifling a yawn, she stretched like a lazy cat sunning itself on a summer day.

And promptly realized she was nude.

Her cheeks heated.

"My lady, his lordship directed me to come here to you," Hill said calmly, as though Leonora was not lying about in her husband's bed, the rumpled bedclothes and her dishabille shameful evidence of what she had spent yesterday afternoon and evening doing.

Dear heavens, they had not even taken dinner. What must the servants think of her? What must Hill think of her?

"His lordship also indicated you would wish a bath, which I have drawn for you and perfumed with your favorite scent."

A warm bath did sound divine, but there remained a great deal of questions which had gone unanswered.

Namely, where was his lordship? How long had she slept? When could she kiss him again?

With great effort, she forced her seemingly boneless body into a sitting position, holding the covers to her breasts as if they were a shield. Of course, she had been unclothed before her lady's maid on innumerable occasions, but somehow this time seemed different.

It seemed wicked, even if it was not. Well, perhaps some of it had been wicked...

Her cheeks flamed all over again. "Where is his lordship, Hill?"

"I cannot say, my lady." Hill's countenance was expressionless as ever. "He sent for a carriage some time ago."

The news pierced the delirious fog of lovemaking that had infected in her mind. Here she was, mooning over him, lolling about in his bed, and he had gone without so much as a word. Somehow, she had imagined today would be different than all the others that had come before it as the Marchioness of Searle.

But he had risen from her side, left quietly while she slept, and had already broken his fast and departed. Perhaps, she consoled herself, he had left a note. After all, he had directed Hill to find her here and draw her a bath.

"Did the marquess leave a missive behind for me?" she dared to ask, half afraid to hear the answer.

"No, my lady, his lordship did not." Hill held up her dressing gown. "May I escort you to your bath now?"

Disappointment pricked her, mingling with hurt. Of course he had not. He had simply taken her maidenhead, availed himself of her body, and gone about his day as if nothing life altering had occurred. As if he had not spent the night bringing her the sort of pleasure she had not dreamed existed until now. As if he had not held her and kissed her, as if he had not been inside her, his touch so sure and powerful she could almost feel it upon her still. As if he had not left his mark upon her, a small bruise from his mouth she could see upon the curve of her left shoulder.

Why had she been foolish enough to believe one night would be enough to thaw the ice he wore around his heart? He had warned her what he wanted from her, had he not?

And it was not her heart. Not her at all. The solace he found in losing himself in her body—that was what he wanted from her. That was all he was willing to give.

Swallowing against a sudden surge of tears, she nodded at her lady's maid. She must look a disaster this morning, lying abed as if she were a harlot, her curls tangled and twisted about her, wearing love bites and nothing else.

"Yes, Hill," she managed. "I am ready for my bath."

It would seem she would have to wage war with her husband if she wanted to break through his defenses. And she would have ample time to plot whilst she scrubbed all traces of him from her skin.

CHAPTER SEVEN

MORGAN STRODE TO his study upon his return to Linley House, nettled by his inconvenient attraction to his wife, which seemed to grow more boundless by the hour. He had fled that morning to be removed from her and the temptation she presented. But meeting his ne'er do well cousin, the Duke of Montrose, had not provided sufficient distraction. Neither had a bout of sparring with him. Monty possessed one hell of a punch, and Morgan's jaw was still ringing with the pain of the blow he had suffered.

However, neither that nor the subsequent round of indolence they indulged in at the Duke's Bastard seemed to do a damned thing to keep Morgan from thinking about his marchioness. He had been sporting a most inconvenient state of hardness for the entirety of the day, and though he had been doing his best to distract himself, he had discovered not even the dissolute companionship of Monty was enough to make him stop recalling how delicious it had felt to sink home inside Leonora for the first time.

Not even the painful fact he could ill afford to develop tender emotions toward her seemed to matter one whit to his body. The sounds she made, the responsiveness of her lush body, the shameless way she had followed his lead…

"Damnation," he muttered to himself, slamming his study door with more force then necessary.

What was it about her?

In his old life, before he had purchased his commission and gone to war on the Continent, no woman had ever interested him the way Leonora did. This infatuation he had developed for his wife was ludicrous. Monty had urged him to take a mistress, and it was likely the only bit of advice he should have ever taken from his rakehell cousin. If he had, maybe he would not be so overwrought at this moment. So overwrought, in fact, he almost failed to see the blur of movement racing across the carpet and tucking itself beneath his desk. Almost, but not quite.

His frown and his black mood both growing, he stalked around the corner of his desk and peered beneath. Two bulging, warm brown eyes blinked at him. He caught sight of a pink tongue. Clipped ears.

By God, there was a bloody dog in his study. Beneath his desk. And a skittish one at that.

How in the name of Hades had a dog managed to find its way here?

The answer hit him in the same fashion the mere thought of his wife did, as a wallop straight to the chest. A visceral reaction he could neither like nor relinquish. There could be only one person who would dare to secret a mutt within his territory.

A mutt who, by the smell of things, had already desecrated said territory with a most impolite deposit. He had only been gone for mere hours, damn it all.

Growling, he turned and stalked from the room.

He located his butler first. "Huell," he all but roared. "Have you any inkling of how a creature has managed to find its way into my study?"

Huell paled, the only indication he possessed a pulse. "There was an unfortunate incident in the kitchens. A small family of mice was recently discovered but eradicated instantaneously. It is possible one of the miscreants managed to escape."

"Not a mouse," he corrected, feeling grim. "A canine, Huell. A bloody dog with two ears and a tail and a slavering mouth and a foul stench. It is in my study."

Huell blinked, his color leaching even further. "Forgive me, my lord. I do not know how such an event could have occurred. Shall I have it removed?"

Yes, Morgan wanted to snap.

But then, for a brief moment, those huge brown eyes returned to him, and he could not seem to form the word. Instead, he demanded something else of his butler. "Where might I find the Marchioness of Searle?"

"As you indicated your intention of dining at your club this evening, her ladyship is taking her dinner at the moment."

"Excellent." He stalked in the direction of the dining room.

"My lord, what shall be done with the canine?" Huell called after him.

"See that it is fed and walked," he called over his shoulder. "And send a maid round to see to the mess the little devil has made upon the carpet."

Morgan did not stop until he discovered his quarry at last, finishing her dinner alone with a sole footman standing sentinel. She should have seemed a pitiful figure, dining by herself, but she was ever the regal, icy picture of beauty. She was a splinter lodged deep into his chest, and he could not seem to remove her, though she continued to make him bleed.

She had never been meant to be his torture, damn it, and that he allowed her to assume the role now, albeit against his will, infuriated him almost as much as being dragged halfway through Spain by a ragtag band of guerrilla soldiers had.

"You are dismissed," he told the footman without bothering to glance in the fellow's direction.

Being a wise man, the servant fled.

Leonora's gaze settled upon Morgan, her expression placid and unconcerned. She was dressed to perfection, her glorious hair in a chignon with ringlets framing her angelic face. Her gown was a deep, claret red, offsetting her porcelain skin and her bright eyes and sultry lips. She personified the fusion of the palely beautiful wallflower he had first met with the lush, unbridled wanton who had set his body aflame last night. A perfect fallen angel. *His* fallen angel, and he would torment her more than she could ever imagine before he was finished.

But for now, he was struck anew by the force of her loveliness. If he had been a painter, he would have been driven to capture her on canvas, thus, this moment, innocence and seduction all at once. The odd, unwanted thought she ought to be wearing the Searle rubies at her throat and ears hit him then, leaving him momentarily bereft. He envisioned her wearing nothing but the glittering gems, and his mouth went dry.

"Lady Searle." He addressed her formally, because she was staring at him expectantly, and everything inside him was a confusing riot. He could not look upon her now without recalling the exquisite taste of her upon his tongue, without recalling how she had gripped him, without hearing the sudden throatiness in her voice when she had said *my cunny is yours.*

Sweet Lord. He could not think of one single thing to say beyond her name. Why had he sought her out anyway? Why did he stand before her now? His mind had been robbed of everything but a sudden, gripping appreciation for this woman.

"Lord Searle." She lifted her fork to her lips, and damn him if he was not envious of the silver tines of that utensil. "Have you dined?"

"Yes." Rather, he had imbibed. The Duke's Bastard possessed a legendary chef, but he and Monty had been too intent upon the priceless whisky cache to bother themselves with *velouté.*

"Then why, may I ask, are you here?" she queried calmly.

So calmly, he was certain he had misheard her. He stood there for a full minute at least, gazing upon her as if seeing her for the first time.

And then he realized she, the half-sister of the man who had nearly gotten him killed, the woman who was to be his implement of revenge, his wife of one sennight, was asking him why he was standing in his own goddamned dining room.

He swallowed, recalling his rage, a far more fitting armor than lust. Recalling, quite belatedly, his reason for being here. The bloody dog. He would show her. Surely Huell could not have removed the creature already.

He sketched an elegant, ironic bow and held out his hand. "Come with me, my lady."

She chewed slowly before raising a snowy napkin to her lips and gently dabbing. "I beg your pardon, my lord. As you can see, I am currently otherwise engaged."

"The chicken fricassee can go to hell for all I care."

Appearing singularly unconcerned, she took another bite of her dinner. For some entirely inexplicable reason, watching Leonora eat made him harder than a fire poker. There he stood, watching her lips, mollified by a glimpse of her pretty pink tongue glancing over the seam of her mouth. Imagining taking that mouth and ravaging it with his own.

This would not do.

She had planted an interloper in his territory, and now he could not even think of anything but kissing her. Taking her in his arms, swiping away the china and cutlery, and settling her rump upon the table linens. Making her his feast. Licking her to submission as he should have last night. As he would have had he not been so lost in his need of her that he had been driven to a near desperate state.

No, by God, this would not do at all.

"I am rather enjoying the chicken fricassee, Searle," his wife said with a bright smile, bringing another bite of the dish to her lips.

"There is a mongrel in my study, my lady," he gritted. "And unless my nose is mistaken, I believe it has befouled the carpet."

She took her blessed time chewing before swallowing slowly, then taking a sip of her wine as he looked on, impotent and furious. One more delicate dab of the linen square to the corner of her lips. And then she licked them.

His cock twitched.

"Julius Caesar," she said calmly.

He stared at her, confounded, and said the first thing that came to mind. "Hamlet."

His lovely wife's brows knitted into the perfect frown. "Hamlet is a dreadful name for your new dog, Searle."

What the devil?

He blinked, his rancor momentarily melting away. This woman confused him. Confounded him. "I thought we were naming Shakespeare's plays. I most assuredly do *not* have a dog."

She forked up another bite of chicken, closing her eyes as if in ecstasy. "My heavens, you have my gratitude for hiring Monsieur Talleyrand as chef. This is exquisite."

He forced all unwanted lust aside, grinding his molars together and taking a deep breath.

"Perhaps you did not hear me, so I shall elucidate, my lady," he said, trying again. "I do not have a dog."

"Correction, Searle." She gave him a benign smile that somehow served to spur his lust anew. "You do have a dog now, and his name is Julius Caesar."

Perhaps he had married a Bedlamite. She shared blood with the Earl of Rayne, after all, and if anyone's blood was tainted with madness, it was that sinister bastard. Regardless, he was hovering over his wife as if he were an uninvited guest, watching her eat dinner. He ought to sit in the presence of a lady, and he knew it, but somehow could not force himself to do so.

Meanwhile, there was a creature running wild in his study, shitting all over his carpet and lord knew what else. The creature had been obtained by her; he had no doubt. And she had named it the most ludicrous name in the history of canine-kind.

"I do not have a dog," he corrected her grimly. "I have an infesta-tion. A trespasser. An unwanted hairy, slavering beast who is ruining my study as we speak."

"Dogs are great sources of comfort," she said simply.

And all the heat within him turned to ice. Fiery ice. The need to obliterate and destroy, the hunger for retribution that had never been far from his mind, rose, strong and ravaging and voracious.

"We have been through this unwarranted and unwelcome subject before, my lady." He slammed his palms down on the table with so much force the china upon it clinked and jumped. And then, he lowered his head until they were eye to eye. "I do not require comfort, madam."

Damn her, she had not even flinched. She stared at him, her ex-pression as placid as the lake at Westmore Manor, his country seat. Her white-blonde hair and effortless grace, coupled with her determi-nation to remain unperturbed, made her seem all the more ethereal.

And he was all the more determined to break her.

"Yes," she argued with him, her tone calm and measured. Almost mild. Certainly mellifluous. "You do, my lord."

"Do not begin to imagine you have any inkling of what I need," he growled, his hands fisted on the table.

Because what he needed had nothing to do with a canine interlop-er and everything to do with her. He wanted to pummel something. To smash and destroy. To shock her. Perhaps even to frighten her. What he wanted more than anything was to wreck, to ruin her until she was as blackened and dead on the inside as he was, like the remnants of a fire in the grate, nothing but ash.

"You are suffering from nightmares, my lord." She raised a brow, then returned her attention to her plate, as if she had said everything she needed to say.

Yes, he suffered, as would any man who had endured what he had, at the mercy of an enemy that had proved incredibly merciless. He had been abused in more ways than he wished to ever acknowledge or relive. The indignities he had suffered still had the power to make him retch.

But that was neither here nor there.

How the devil could she sit there and be so calm when he was raging? The calmer she remained, the more irate he became. He would never, for as long as he suffered the indignity of walking the earth, understand the beautiful creature before him. Nor the power she had over him. The power to make him weak. To make him forget his every reason for making her his in the first place.

"I am suffering from nothing, and I do not want or need the dog. I demand you have it removed from my study." He pounded his fists in punctuation.

"You are suffering from something, Searle." She forked up another bite of chicken, chewing it as if she hadn't a care. As if she were facing him over a dinner party rather than after having thrown down the gauntlet. "He does have a name, you know. Julius Caesar is yours, and I will not be requesting his removal."

To perdition with her and this canine nonsense, and this Julius bloody Caesar which had shat itself in Morgan's study. Which had cowered beneath his desk. Which had been removed by the clever and careful Huell, a man who may not always approve of Morgan, but who was blessed with the capacity to perform his duties effortlessly and without asking a single question.

"I am suffering from a wife who does not know her place," he countered. "Come with me, and I shall show you where you belong."

Her lips compressed. "I belong here, finishing my dinner. You, my lord, belong in your study, tending to Julius Caesar before he makes a complete muddle of your carpet. Though from what I understand, the precious little fellow already knows how to behave properly. Perhaps you terrified him and that is the reason for his lapse of propriety."

Had she just referred to a mutt shitting on his study Aubusson as a *lapse of propriety?* Yes, the minx damn well had.

Her continued poise stretched him to the brink. He rounded the elaborately carved table—a relic of his mother's, and a table his father had subsequently refused to dine at—wanting no more barriers between them. No more table, no more linens, no more china and chicken fricassee. No more pretense.

She was being cool and aloof, and he did not like it, damn it. Not one whit. Her eyes widened, brows arched in surprise as he caught her elbows and lifted her from her chair with scarcely any effort. The chair in question toppled over behind her under the swiftness of his action.

"I do not want your mutt," he informed her coldly.

"Julius Caesar is not my mutt," she corrected him, unassailable as ever. "He is yours."

"A lofty name for a furred creature who stinks and hides beneath my desk," he snapped. And then, the temptation to touch her face proved too great to resist. His fingers rested upon her soft, smooth chin, tipping it up. Tilting her waiting, delicious mouth toward his. "Furthermore, I do not now, nor have I ever desired, a creature to tend to."

"Perhaps not," A lone, neat brow rose, taunting him. "But perhaps you may long for companionship. Dogs are very loyal creatures, quite comforting, or so I am told by Freddy."

Jealousy surged through him, bitter and sharp and stinging. He did not like the way it felt. His brows snapped together as he pinned her with his most ferocious frown. "Who the devil is Freddy?" he growled.

Whoever the fellow was, Morgan would make him swallow his teeth. At the very least, he would leave the bastard wishing he had never importuned the Marchioness of Searle. *Devil take it*, was Freddy a former suitor of hers? His ears were growing hotter by the moment as he contemplated all the possible reasons for his wife being acquaint-ed with a cursed *Freddy* who fancied he could speak on behalf of all canines.

She flushed, and by God, the delicious pink tinge swept over her cheeks, down her throat, and all across her delectable décolletage. She resembled nothing in that moment so much as a confection he would devour in small bites.

Christ, he could consume her whole. Lift her skirts...would the sainted Freddy perform any of those feats? He rather doubted it. If Freddy even so much as dared, Morgan would plant him a facer so vicious that it would send him into next Wednesday.

"Freddy is Lady Frederica Isling, mayhap better known to you as Mrs. Duncan Kirkwood." Her frown overtook her entire face then, anchoring the corners of her lush lips into a perfect frown, leaving her looking joyless and empty and ferocious all at once.

His foolish jealousy dissipated with the suddenness of a summer thunderstorm chased by the sun. It would seem the bloodlust he had felt toward the mysterious Freddy was wholly unwarranted. Oddly, his chest felt lighter.

He cleared his throat. "Indeed. Pray explain why you had occasion to discuss canines with Mrs. Kirkwood."

Her countenance softened. "Do not fear, my lord. I did not divulge your nightmares to Freddy."

Irritation thundered through him once more, replacing the relief. "I do not have nightmares."

It was a lie, and they both knew it. But he detested this weakness within him, a frailty he could not shake or control. He stared at her, daring her to contradict him.

To his relief, she did not. Instead, she rose at last. "If you do not want Julius Caesar, I will keep him for myself. I never had a pet dog of my own, though I wholeheartedly longed for one. Mama's constitution did not allow such a possibility, for she claims they make her sneeze. She finds furred creatures grotesque, you know. Even felines."

The memory of those brown eyes returned to him once more.

Sad, pathetic little pup, really. And what ailed him was he saw himself in it.

"Where did you find the mongrel?" he asked in spite of himself.

She smiled as if he had pleased her, and he felt the effects of that sweet quirk of her lips in a place where he was supposed to feel nothing, his heart.

"The Duchess of Whitley aided me," she said softly. "Her Grace has recently acquired a pug for His Grace."

"You accomplished all this while I was gone today?"

"Yes." Her smile deepened, and for the first time, he spied a charming dimple in her right cheek. "For you."

For him.

Her words took him aback. No one had done something for him in…he could not even recall how long it had been. Surely one of his nurses or his old governesses had shown him kindness, but that was a long time ago now, and if they had, he could not recall it. He knew without a doubt neither his mother nor his father ever had. They had been too preoccupied with venting their mutual hatred upon each other that there had been little room for anyone else in their lives. Especially not their sons, reminders of the bloodless sense of duty which had drawn them together in matrimony.

"But it would seem you are displeased with Julius Caesar, and that was not my intention," she continued. "I shall see him returned if you would prefer, my lord."

Brown, blinking eyes taunted him.

"A ridiculous name for a dog," he said instead of answering her, offering her his arm to escort her from the dining room.

Her hand slid neatly into the crook of his elbow, as if that was where it had always been meant to sit. As if their bodies had each been fashioned for the other. "You may call him Caesar instead, if you prefer, my lord."

He made a noncommittal sound in his throat. It would seem the mutt was staying after all. "We shall see, madam."

CHAPTER EIGHT

"THERE YOU ARE, my lady." Hill finished brushing out Leonora's curls. "Is there anything else I can do for you this evening?"

"Thank you, Hill." Leonora, seated before a looking glass in her dressing area, contemplated her reflection. She wore nothing beneath her dressing gown but a nightdress so fine it was transparent, and she felt as if she were entirely nude, her body acutely conscious Searle would soon make his evening visit. "That will be all."

Hill quietly slipped from the chamber, leaving her alone with her thoughts.

Not much time had passed since her husband's return that evening and his subsequent discovery of her little furred gift for him. She had been distraught when she had taken tea with Freddy for the second time in as many days, but fortunately, the Duchess of Whitley had been present.

Though she had not revealed to the other ladies that Searle had suffered a nightmare, they had instantly noted her morose countenance. And, as lady friends were wont to do, they dug for the source. It did not take them long to realize precisely who was to blame. While she had related to them her husband's cool nature and easily changeable moods, she had, just as she had promised him, kept the marquess's nightmares to herself. However, the duchess, whose own husband had fought alongside Searle in Spain, relayed Whitley's joy in the dog she had recently acquired for his companionship. Whitley took the adorable pug everywhere, according to the duchess.

The seed of an idea had instantly been planted within Leonora, and it took root when the duchess casually mentioned there remained a lone male from the litter which the duchess had taken under her wing, but who could not be kept with his sister, who Whitley had grown such a fondness for.

Leonora had instantly known what she must do. And when she had taken one look at the sweet brown eyes of Julius Caesar, she had known no heart, regardless of how hardened and withered it may be, could resist the innocent allure of a puppy. She had not quite anticipated the violence of his displeasure, but she was pleased with herself for remaining firm.

She was slowly growing to understand how best to approach the man she now called husband. Extraordinarily slowly, perhaps, but she did consider it a victory, albeit a minor one, that her clash with him at dinner had ended not just with him choosing to keep little Caesar on his own, but with him escorting her from the dining room and spending an hour with her and the pup in the drawing room.

The Duke and Duchess of Whitley had already taught Caesar a fair number of tricks. Searle's delight at the pup offering up his paw upon command had not been feigned. Indeed, it had been so real, so sudden, the sting of tears had burned her eyes, and she had been forced to blink rapidly to dispel them, lest he see them fall.

A subtle knock sounded at the door joining their chambers.

So subtle, in fact, Leonora almost failed to hear it. Rather the opposite of the brusque manner in which he had stormed into her chamber the day before, as if he were an invading army, intent upon conquering. And conquer her, he had. Oh, how he had.

Her cheeks warmed, her body tingling in pleasant remembrance and delighted anticipation. "Enter," she called.

The door opened to reveal him, the magnificently handsome, utterly vexing enigma who was somehow hers. He wore a dressing gown belted at the waist, firm calves and bare feet peeking from beneath the hem. She had never imagined a gentleman's feet could interest her, nor his bare limbs. But when it came to the Marquess of Searle, everything interested her.

Far more than was decent.

"Good evening, my lord," she greeted him hesitantly, an odd, unwanted shyness falling over her now that they were alone again, with precious few layers between them and space that decreased upon each confident stride of his long legs.

"Good evening, Leonora," he said in return, a slight smile curving his well-molded mouth.

Her name in the decadent rumble of his deep baritone sent a frisson down her spine as he stopped before her. The delicious scent of his cologne hit her senses next. And then she drank in the beauty of the sharp, masculine angles of his face. He exuded a dark, dangerous elegance this evening, his aloof air once more firmly in place. She could not shake the impression he was half lord, half weapon. If he were a blade, he could slice her cleanly in two, and she would still somehow revel in her own destruction.

Understanding hit her, not with the subtlety of a butterfly's wings, gently beating in the air, but with the trampling rage of a stallion gone wild, intent upon galloping over everything in its path.

She was a fool for this man.

Leonora wet her suddenly dry lips with her tongue. Anticipation and nervousness warred within her. She wanted to say something. He was staring at her with an expression of anticipation. Indeed, it was her turn to offer something to their dialogue. And yet, her mind failed her. It was empty. Cavernous.

Shaken.

"I have something for you," he said into the silence, taking her by surprise.

His words startled her tongue into belatedly functioning. "I do not require a gift, Searle. The gift I gave you this evening was intended for your comfort alone, not with the hope you would reciprocate."

His smile deepened, fine lines appearing alongside his vibrant eyes that suggested while he no longer smiled readily now, he had done so enough in his past for his happiness to have left its mark upon his skin. "No one has given me a gift in as long as I can recall. It was remiss of me not to thank you for your consideration."

Leonora blinked, wondering if her ears had deceived her. If she was delusional. Had the Marquess of Searle developed a fever? She barely thwarted the urge to press her fingers to his brow and ascertain whether or not it was hot to the touch.

He laughed before she could respond, the sound laden with bitterness. "You need not look so surprised by my gratitude, my dear. I behaved in an abominable, ungentlemanly fashion to you earlier, and I know it."

How very confusing he was. Though he had not offered an apology, she supposed this was Searle's version of one. Very well, since they were dabbling in the art of honesty, she would meet him halfway.

"You left me this morning." On a rush, she said the words. Not in an accusatory tone, but a mere stating of fact. "And you did not return until dinner. Your abrupt departure was more ungentlemanly than your reaction to Julius Caesar."

His lips thinned, his jaw clenching.

She had displeased him with her honesty, but she did not regret it.

"I had matters which required my attention."

"The same matters which required your attention on the day of our wedding?" she could not resist asking.

For the first time, it occurred to her that he may have a mistress. That she may be sharing him with another woman without even knowing it. The notion made her stomach clench and her mouth go dry. Of course, she ought to have expected it before now. In their circle, it was not just customary but expected for a gentleman to have a wife and a mistress at once.

The wife was forced to pretend the other woman did not exist. Mama had warned her. After all, her father had kept at least as many mistresses as wives. Her brother Alessandro's Spanish mother had been Father's mistress before becoming his third wife. Mama had been his fifth.

"Come," Searle demanded then, cutting through her concerns by gently clasping her elbow and guiding her to stand before the looking glass she had so recently abandoned.

He stood behind her, exuding heat and his own potent magnetism at her back. She stared at their reflections wordlessly, taking him in first, tall, strong, and so handsome, she ached. Their gazes met. His hands settled upon her waist, anchoring her there, drawing her snugly back against his body.

"What are you doing?" she asked, cursing the breathlessness in her voice. The hardness of his shaft was unmistakable, a ridge prodding the curve of her lower back. He had not answered her question, and her weakness for him nettled her.

Was this his means of avoidance? His way of distracting her so she could forget the questions crowding her mind? And curse her, why was she allowing him to succeed?

His gaze challenged hers in the glass. "What do you think I am doing, wife?"

"Distracting me," she answered without hesitation.

A grin kicked up the corners of his mouth. "Is it working, darling?"

Darling.

Oh, how she hated the simmering, sinful burst of longing that lone word sent though her. If she had thought him a blade, she was wrong. This man was a cavalry sword, mowing down anything in his path without mercy.

But how sweetly he mowed.

And neither was she certain she wished for his mercy in this particular circumstance.

"Of course it is working," she answered honestly. Her own tone held a note of flirtation she had not even known she possessed. "You are a handsome devil, and you know it."

"Am I?" His head dipped, that divine mouth of his pressing a kiss to the whorl of her ear.

"Yes," she whispered, for his hands had roamed from her waist, sliding over the dressing gown until he cupped her breasts.

His fingers tightened, grasping her with the same debilitating confidence he had visited upon her the previous night. He bit her ear gently, then kissed behind it, his tongue tracing over the shallow dip. "Tell me. How am I distracting you?"

She shivered, her knees going weak. A twinge of pain rocked through her leg, but she ignored it. "You know."

"But what if I do not know?" he countered.

He pinched her nipples through the silk of her wrapper and nightdress. Between her thighs, her flesh pulsed and throbbed with awareness, with possibility. Yes, indeed. No mercy was preferable.

"Touching me," she admitted at last. "Kissing me. Standing so near I can feel you pressed against me. I cannot think with your hands or your lips upon my body, and you know it."

"I do now, sweet Leonie." He kissed down her throat, finding the curve where her shoulder and neck met. And there, he bit into her skin with more tender ferocity.

This, too, would leave a mark. Another love bite to add to her collection. Traces of him she could wear upon her skin. This should not thrill her. Perhaps something was wrong with her to feel such a desperate need for him.

To want him as much as she did.

But she would not worry about any of that now. She was like a drunkard, but lost in desire rather than liquor, eager for her next taste of passion. Of whatever he would show her, whatever he would give her.

"No one has ever called me Leonie," she said as his thumbs and forefingers rolled her nipples. *Dear heavens*, how weak he made her. His tongue flitted against her racing pulse, his fingers working their magic.

"Do you like it?" he asked, tugging at her nipples once more.

She was not even certain what he referred to—his lovemaking, his diminutive for her name, the way he felt against her—but the answer was the same regardless. "Yes. Yes, of course I do."

"It seems somehow fitting, for you are now my lioness," he said, murmuring against her bare skin, against the flat blade of her collarbone. "I do not have a mistress. Was that your question before I began...*distracting* you?"

Relief swelled within her, along with a great, bursting tide of want, which she had been keeping at bay until now. She relaxed, her head falling back upon his shoulder, the admission escaping her. "Yes."

He nipped her overly sensitized flesh as he gave her nipples another delicious pinch. "Do you want your gift now, darling?"

She wanted anything. Everything. Him, his touch, his mouth, his lips, his cock...good heavens, she was awash in sensation, lost. Helpless, her desire overcoming everything.

She stared at their reflections in the glass, a fresh wave of heat overtaking her. The flesh between her thighs was already wet without him even needing to touch her there. "You need not give me a gift because I gave you Caesar. My intention was to please you, not to cozen you into gifting me something in return."

"This gift has nothing to do with the hound," he said coolly, but she did not think she mistook the hint of fondness in his voice when he referred to Caesar. "Indeed, I am remiss in not offering it sooner, as it is something which should have been done on our wedding night, in accordance with familial tradition."

She thought she knew why he had not offered it on their wedding night—first, he had been absent, and then she had been reluctant to allow a wedding night at all to a new husband who had disappeared on the day of their nuptials. But she felt no guilt as she continued to meet his assessing gaze in the glass. Only curiosity. What sort of gift could it be? He had nothing in his hands save her body.

He withdrew his touch, and she almost protested aloud at the loss of him. But she held her tongue, wishing to cling to whatever shred of dignity yet remaining her own, and watched his hands disappear from sight. The rustling of his dressing gown broke the silence that had fallen between them as she presumed, he delved into a pocket secreted in the robe.

His countenance was grave when he extracted something glittering and shining with red and gold. A necklace, she realized, as he settled it upon her neck and fastened the clasp at her nape.

But not just any necklace. This piece was heavy, cold where it settled upon her skin. Fashioned of thick golden flowers with ruby cabochons at their centers, its grand statement was a massive golden bloom bearing an equally large, faceted ruby nestled amongst its petals. She stared in awe at the magnificent piece, stunned by the extravagance of his gift.

"It is the Searle rubies," he said softly. "A fitting gift now that you are the Marchioness."

She swallowed, a tremor passing through her at not just the opulence of the gift but the meaning behind it. How incredible a gesture it seemed, coming from this austere man who kept himself so closely guarded. "I cannot possibly accept such an extravagance," she said, raising a hand to gently stroke the intricately fashioned golden flowers and the immense ruby at the centerpiece in spite of herself.

It was the most stunning necklace she had ever seen, and it seemed to fit upon her neck as if fashioned for that very purpose. *Good heavens,* she did not even particularly care for jewelry, but this piece was so lovely, she could not help but to admire it.

"You can accept it, and you will," Searle countered, his tone brooking no opposition. "These belonged to my mother before you, though my father had them reset into this necklace after her death. I confess I cannot fault him for his choice even if I do not like his reasons. She never did care to wear them anyhow. Do they please you?"

Of course they pleased her. How could they not? But there was a story there, hovering in the air, going untold, and she wanted answers. Why had his father reset the necklace after his mother's death? Had the former marquess been too morose, so swept up in his grief he had lashed out against a family heirloom?

It seemed unlikely.

Through his reflection in the glass, she noted the frown gathering at her husband's brows and compressing his sensual lips. This necklace troubled him, she thought. Or perhaps not the necklace itself, but the details behind it.

"It is lovely, my lord," she said softly, realizing belatedly her fingers were still stroking the painstaking craftsmanship evident in the golden flowers.

Now that he had told her they were the Searle family rubies, she knew they were traditionally kept by the marchioness. She could not deny the gift, and neither was it a true gift either, but in contrast, more of an expectation. A burden, perhaps. She wondered again at the story he had not offered to share, the reason why his father had seen the rubies placed in an entirely new setting following the death of his mother. Therein, perhaps, lay the true burden.

"You do not like it," he said flatly.

"I love the necklace." Her disavowal came instantly, without thought. But neither could her curiosity be squelched. "Why did your father have it reset?"

"He despised my mother as one would a mortal enemy. She had chosen the setting for the stones herself, having them reworked into something more suited to her taste from the original piece, and he did not wish to be reminded of her in any fashion."

Her eyes sought his in the glass. This admission seemed torn from him, but she was grateful he had given it to her. "Why did he despise her?"

His lips took on a sardonic twist. "Theirs was an arranged marriage. My mother loved another. My father loved only himself. They wedded to suit their families. He needed her dowry, and her family wished to secure a tract of largely untillable marshland."

"It seems an untenable trade," she offered lamely. From his tone and the precious, little information he had shared regarding either of his parents, she could only assume he had not been privileged enough to possess a happy childhood.

Though her mother had been her father's fifth wife, Papa had been kind and loving toward Leonora. Her parents' marriage had not possessed any rancor, though Mama had been a good two decades Papa's junior.

"Far more untenable than one would suppose, given the exchange." Her husband's deep voice interrupted her ruminations once more. So, too, his touch, for his fingers were upon the central ruby in the necklace now, stroking as he spoke. "She hated him as well, so do not think her an innocent. The fire and anger between them burned brightly on both their parts."

"Your mother and father lived in enmity for the entirety of their union?" she asked, though she knew he likely did not wish to speak of his distant past any more than he wished to discuss his far more recent one.

"They lived in bitter hatred," he said calmly. "Enmity seems far too polite a descriptor."

She wondered now if part of the reason for his detached manner lay in his childhood, as well. Surely a home in which two people hated each other with such ferocity could not be a happy home for that couple's children.

"It must have been difficult for you," she said softly, treading with care. Her eyes met his in the glass, and she held her breath, awaiting his reaction.

"Do not fret for me, madam." His tone was cool. "There is no difficulty I cannot face."

She believed his assertion. The Marquess of Searle was a strong man, a living, breathing fortress. But she wanted inside his walls. "Still, a child ought not to bear the weight of his parents' quarrels."

"I had my brother," he said then, his fingers gliding over the necklace before he settled his entire hand there, cupping her throat gently. "We provided each other with comfort, of sorts."

She knew from Mama—who possessed an almost uncanny ability to recite Debrett's—Searle's elder brother had died shortly after their father's death. But this was Searle's first reference to his brother. Progress, perhaps.

"You and your brother enjoyed a friendship, then?" she asked, prodding him because she knew she must. He would give her crumbs when she longed for a laden table.

"We did. George was a good man. A gentleman." Searle paused, his jaw clenching. "He made an excellent marquess. I was not raised to the task, though Father loved to remind me of my duties to the line, often in the form of a switch. The old marquess was adept at caning. Perhaps it was one of the reasons my mother hated him so. I expect he may have exercised his anger upon her as well. I do recall seeing bruises upon her that her lady's maid attempted to cover with powder. As a lad, I thought her clumsy. As a man, I have wondered."

A chill swept through her at the thought of not just what Searle had endured but what his mother had possibly, also. And here, at last, was a revelation from him, but a horrifying, heartbreaking one all the same. "I am sorry, my lord. Sorry for the loss of your brother and the suffering of your past."

His smile was grim, his hand tightening slightly on her throat. Just a subtle flex, enough to remind her how very much she was at his mercy. "As we have already established, I do not want your sympathy."

She knew precisely what he wanted from her, and the flesh between her thighs was slick and aching with the same want. But she longed for more from her husband than just passion. She also wanted to know him. To dismantle his defenses.

"Whether or not you want it matters naught," she told him, resolute. "You have it. I am your wife, my lord. It is my duty to concern myself with you."

"No," he said, dipping his head to press a kiss to the left side of her neck. His hand remained on the opposite side, his warmth seeping into her flesh. "It is not your duty to concern yourself with me. Your duties are to bear my children and refrain from cuckolding or embarrassing me publicly. But that is not enough for you, is it? Caring for others is merely in your nature, is it not, my sweet Leonie?" He kissed his way to her ear, sending a trill straight through her. "You are an angel. So perfect, so sweet, caring when you should not, giving when you ought to keep for yourself. You are so good, wife. Too good. *Far* too good."

His words seemed somehow couched in warning. But she could not question them now, not when his mouth was moving over her bare skin, and his left hand had found her thigh, caressing her there. She struggled to maintain control of her faculties as he wreaked havoc upon her ability to both think and resist him.

Because why would she resist this gorgeous, breathtaking man? Why would she want anything other than his complete domination of her body, his annihilation of her defenses in every way?

The Marquess of Searle was her weakness. He was cold and dark and bitter, scarred and mysterious and remote, and yet, he called to her more than any man ever had. It was not merely that he was her husband. Another could have sufficed for the role. She had wanted children of her own, and that was all. But this man was different. He crawled beneath her skin and made his home somewhere within the fragile boundaries of her heart.

"I am not an angel," she told him, "and you do not expect enough of your wife if your only requirements consist of no embarrassment and no cuckolding. While it may be useful to convey, I have no wish of committing either of those sins against you, I do feel compelled to suggest my position in your life is far more useful than the duties you have mentioned."

His hand found the knot at the belt on her dressing gown, plucking it open. The twain ends of her wrapper fell apart, revealing her transparent nightgown. In the looking glass, she saw herself as she supposed Searle may, unbound, white-blonde hair, full lips, wide eyes, breasts too heavy and round, nipples poking through the fabric, a soft belly, and the shadow of the apex of her thighs. Where she hungered for him most.

"I would agree on the last, darling." His breath was hot in her ear as he spoke. "I do have far more useful tasks for you in mind."

His gaze was unyielding in the glass, holding her captive, sending a fresh blossom of want straight to her core. She knew what he wanted. Desire altered his expression. Never had she been looked upon with such aggressive possession. The man staring back at her did not just want her. He wanted to devour her.

And she wanted nothing more. Her breath hitched in her throat, her pulse pounding. "What tasks, my lord?"

He pressed a hot kiss to her ear then, enough for her to sense the need building within him, a fire to match the one already burning inside her.

"Is your leg paining you, Leonie?" he asked, taking her by surprise with his thought for her comfort.

The diminutive still felt strange, almost as if it belonged to some-one else, yet somehow *right*. Once again, he was an enigma to her, this man who was cold and aloof yet oddly concerned for her wellbeing.

Telling her he did not want her sympathy yet caressing her, holding her throat and yet kissing her ear. He was the juxtaposition of hard and soft.

But she did not require his comfort. Not now, for she bore most of her weight on her uninjured, right limb, helping to alleviate the stiffness and aches. It was a crutch, of sorts, and she used it often. Over the years, she had even discovered how best to stand so the skirts of her gown shielded her weakness. It was only too much walking, standing, and dancing that made the old injury flare.

"My leg does not pain me," she said finally, forcing herself to speak. Her eyes remained trained to his, lost in those dark, emerald depths. But something else pained her. Rather, it was an ache. An emptiness. A longing. "But I do thank you for your concern for my wellbeing, my lord."

Suddenly, she could no longer bear the detachment of staring into their reflections. While its novelty inspired a certain hunger within her, she was also tormented by a persistent longing for something more, for something deeper. Perhaps, she thought, this was his way of once more putting a distance between them. After all, it was emotion he did not want—her caring for him, any tender feelings she may possess, were shunned with equal vigor.

"If your leg does not pain you, then why…"

His query trailed off when she abruptly spun in his arms.

"Why what, my lord?" she asked.

"Why did your breath catch?" His question was issued in a deliciously deep timbre that sluiced down her spine, spreading tingles in its wake.

She swallowed. Excellent question, and how to answer without betraying herself? Without making her susceptibility to him apparent?

"My breath did nothing of the sort," she lied, gazing into the glorious vibrancy of his eyes. How unusual it was for a man to have been blessed with such loveliness. She was sure she had never seen another gentleman with eyes that could compare. Or perhaps it was merely that she had not cared to look closely enough before now.

Which was rather an arresting—and astounding—realization.

"It did," he countered, sounding pleased with himself. "Your breath caught in your throat, and you seemed to tense." He kissed the bare swath of her neck. Once, twice, thrice. His tongue darted over her flesh, and then he sucked. Gently at first, then with greater pressure.

Until she knew without question his fervor would leave yet another mark to join the rest he had already visited upon her flesh, a constellation of the ways in which he was her greatest weakness. All of it rendering her so painfully vulnerable to his touch.

To *him*.

She swallowed as he continued to devour her neck. "Is there a danger, then, in wanting one's husband?"

He inhaled deeply, and then he kissed her throat again, open mouthed. Ravenous. She tilted her head back, enjoying his consumption. Reveling in it, in fact.

"There is every danger when I am the husband in question," he said, startling her. His mouth continued its stinging path. Down her throat, straight to her collarbone. "Do you dare trust me, Leonie?"

Nay, she did not.

But something else inside her, something deep and elemental, said she did. And it was that voice which answered him now, rather than her own. "Yes. I trust you, Morgan."

He tugged her dressing gown with one hand, and she helped him, shrugging it to the carpet. His other hand slid from her throat, his fingers tunneling into her nape where her hair hung in heavy waves.

"Sweet fool," he said without heat, and then his mouth was upon hers.

SHE TRUSTED HIM.

He had heard the honesty in her dulcet voice. And he tasted it now in her kiss, felt it in her responsiveness, the way all the tension and fight drained from her in his arms. He wanted to thank her, and he wanted to punish her all at once for being so naïve, for believing in him so easily when he was the last man she ought to gift with her unconditional faith.

His fingers tightened in her hair as he kissed her, his tongue plundering her mouth, hoping she would whimper, beg to be set free, push him away. Instead, she only clutched him closer, a moan of surrender coming from her. He swallowed the sound as he consumed her mouth, telling her his secrets with every movement of his lips on hers.

You should not trust me.

I am your enemy, my sweet.

But see how prettily you let me own you...

Damnation, her capitulation, her willingness to submit to whatever he wished of her, stoked the white-hot fires of desire burning within him. His cock was ready for her, the need to be inside her an almost palpable thing.

Still kissing her, he guided them both in the direction of her bed. He had kept her in his bed all night the first time, but he recognized the precedent was a dangerous one to set for himself, as much as for her. He could ill afford to develop a fondness for her beyond his need for her body. Tonight, he would have her in her own bed, and he could discreetly leave after he had his fill of her.

He whisked away her nightdress, and discarded his own robe. They fell onto the mattress as one, mouths joined, hands everywhere. Her heady, floral scent enveloped him as he filled his hands with her voluptuous curves.

He told himself he would make love to her more slowly this time. He would savor her. Torture her with pleasure until she was screaming for him, pleading for her release. And when the Earl of Rayne finally arrived back in London once more, Morgan would relish every moment of informing the bastard how easy it had been to make his innocent sister beg for his cock.

He tore his mouth from hers and kissed down her body, stopping to admire her creamy flesh beneath him. Her breasts were so damn beautiful. Her belly was soft, and the thought of planting his seed within her, of watching her swell with his child, made his cock twitch.

Damn. He was meant to prolong the pleasure. To make this last.

He cupped her breasts and then lowered his head to suck a nipple into his mouth, earning a moan from her. He wanted his name on her lips as she cried out her release. He wanted her to spend on his tongue.

Morgan suckled her other nipple, giving her another gentle nip. She was more decadent than any dessert. His to pleasure. His to torture.

Down her belly he went, trailing kisses, worshiping her with his mouth. He did not stop until he reached the prize he sought, the apex of her thighs. He kissed the top of her mound, his hands on her thighs, urging them apart.

"My lord," she protested breathlessly.

"Hush," he told her gently, soothing her with slow caresses as she opened for him. Her cunny was glistening, pink and perfect. "I want to kiss you."

"Where?" she almost yelped. "Surely not..."

He would not argue the point with her, for he could not go another heartbeat without having the taste of her in his mouth. Instead, he dipped his head, showing her. He traced his tongue over her seam, up and down, slowly and tantalizingly. She tasted musky with a hint of sweetness. He found her pearl and flicked his tongue over it, gratified when she jolted beneath him.

Yes, there was his wanton wife.

So wicked for him.

He would take great pleasure in making her come this way.

She whimpered something indistinguishable. Perhaps it was his name. He could not be certain over the rushing of blood in his own ears. She was closer now, he could sense it, the need in her building to a towering crescendo.

Damnation, she was slick, her heat bathing him, her muscles gripping him. She came on a deep, husky moan, her release pouring from her. For a moment, he reveled in it, glorying in her complete helplessness to her pleasure. He felt her splinter into pieces, and he knew how delirious she must feel, as if the brilliance of the sun shone within her. He had made her body tremble and sing for him. And he felt a thrilling surge of triumph, as if he had just conquered his enemy upon the field of battle. Followed swiftly by a crippling bolt of lust. He had to be inside her.

Now.

Morgan rose over her as the last of her tremors subsided, taking in the decadent sight of her, at his mercy and wearing nothing save the gold and ruby necklace around her throat. Here was his revenge, and how delicious it was. How intoxicating *she* was.

He positioned himself at her entrance and then sank home in one full thrust. She cried out at the suddenness of his invasion, and for a moment, he feared he had hurt her, but then she moved, rolling her hips, urging him onward. Morgan kissed her as he surged inside her again and again, making her taste herself on his lips and tongue.

How good it felt to debauch her. To introduce her to all the sinful pleasures of the flesh. He would enjoy having her as his prize. He would make her come a thousand different ways. Surely this—she— was the relief granted him after the suffering he had endured in captivity, all the days when he had wished he would die rather than to endure one more minute of degradation.

But he would not think of those dark times now. Not when he was here, Leonora beneath him. Not when he had come so far to where he stood on the precipice of gaining everything he wanted.

He reached between their bodies, finding her pearl and working it until she came again, tightening on him so violently, he could not keep his own release at bay any longer. He spent inside her, his lips never leaving hers, and he knew in that instant not even vengeance would be more satisfying than making this woman his.

CHAPTER NINE

"**Y**OU CERTAINLY LOOK a great deal happier than when last you paid me a call," Freddy observed with a teasing smile, as Leonora settled herself on the settee in her friend's gold salon.

Leonora's face was surely as scarlet as the color of Freddy's bold day gown. Even with child and suffering from wretched bouts of sickness each morning as she had confided to Leonora in her daily missives, Freddy was as beautiful and bold as a butterfly. Nothing could detract from her loveliness, even if she did appear a trifle pale.

"I am..." she paused, searching for the correct word to describe the feelings that had burst forth within her over the sennight since she had last seen her. *Happy* seemed too mundane, woefully inadequate. Surely there was a word more apt, more precise?

"Besotted," Freddy concluded for her, clapping her hands with girlish delight. "Oh, my darling. You must tell me everything."

"I am not besotted," she denied, her flush growing hotter still, even though it was true. She *was* besotted with Searle. That had been precisely the word she was searching for.

"Your countenance suggests otherwise," her friend noted wisely. "You have been wearing the smile of a woman who has newly fallen in love ever since you crossed the threshold. Even now, though you try to dispel it, the smile remains."

Drat her observant friend. Of course, Leonora might have guessed that someone as adept at conveying the emotions of her fictional characters would also be gifted at observing them in those around her. Freddy, in addition to being blindingly lovely, steadfast of heart, giving and caring and all things wonderful, was also a talented author. Her novel, *The Silent Duke*, had recently been published to a whirlwind of praise and clamor.

"I am sure you must know such a smile better than I," she said then, hoping to deflect Freddy's attention from herself. "After all, each time I see you, you appear even more overjoyed than the last. If Mr. Kirkwood is such a commendable husband, perhaps you ought to consider hiring him to train all the gentlemen in town."

Freddy grinned. "Mr. Kirkwood is an incredibly ideal husband, but I dare not share my time with him in such a fashion. I am not nearly generous enough. Need I remind you, however, that we were discussing you and not myself? I daresay you are attempting to distract me from my course."

Because her course was making Leonora distinctly uncomfortable.

Because she was afraid her friend's assertions were true.

She had spent the days since she had last visited Freddy with Searle never far from her side. He took her to the opera, escorted her to a ball. They spent drowsy evenings sharing brandy from a snifter, his head in her lap and Caesar cuddled up to them both whilst she read him poetry. Their nights were devoted to blazing passion, and sometimes their mornings and even their afternoons, too. Only yesterday, he had caught her in the music room whilst she played on the pianoforte. He had sunk to his knees and lifted her skirts, pleasuring her with his mouth as she sat upon the bench.

It is my fondest wish to make love to you in every chamber of this house, he had said afterward.

Even now, the memory of his frank, wicked statement sent a trill down her spine, and a fresh spark of want lit within her.

"Leonora, darling?" Freddy's voice cut through her musings once more. "You look as if you need a chocolate biscuit. Tea, as well?"

"I fear no chocolate biscuit, regardless of how decadent, can cure what ails me," she said, comprehension hitting her like a stone.

"And now your silly smile has fled at last, but you look quite pale. Do I need to send for hartshorn?" Freddy quipped.

If the weight upon her chest had not been so heavy, she would have laughed. But this—her heart—was no laughing matter. And she feared it was very much in grave peril.

"How did you know you were in love with Mr. Kirkwood?" she asked, feeling vaguely ill.

Freddy's expression softened. "It was not one act or one word. It was sudden, a rush, all at once. A deep, complex gale of emotion and the understanding that I loved him more than I had ever fathomed possible. And when I realized how I felt for him, I also could not recall a time when I had not loved him. I know that sounds strange, but I feel as if he were my fate. Perhaps you think me foolish—indeed, I would not blame you if you did—but I cannot help but to feel he was always the one who would win my heart. We had to travel our separate roads to find each other, but once we met on the same road..."

Her words trailed off and she smiled, her eyes going glassy.

"Once you met on the same road, you knew," Leonora finished for her friend, who had begun sniffing in an effort to stifle the tears threatening to break free. "And now perhaps I must send for the hartshorn for you. Or at the very least, a handkerchief."

"Oh, my darling friend!" Freddy emitted a decidedly unladylike sound that was one-part laugh, one-part sob, and one-part snort. "It is my emotions, torn asunder, ever since I have found myself in this delicate condition. I tell you, I am either a watering pot or casting up my accounts or near delirious with longing for Mr. Kirkwood."

Leonora laughed, her heart bursting with joy for her friend. Such love, such contentedness. She could only pray she would find the same with Searle. That his ice would melt enough beneath the blazing persistence of her sun.

"I hope to one day aspire to such a condition, dearest Freddy," she said in a voice gone thick with emotion of her own.

Freddy's brows rose, and she scooted to the edge of her seat, clasping her hands together. "Perhaps you need not aspire?"

She flushed. "It is too soon to tell."

"Did you seduce the marquess, then?" Freddy asked, eyes going wide.

She winced. "I am afraid I made an abysmal effort at doing so, but somehow, our marriage was finally...consummated."

"And?" Freddy asked, waggling her brows in an animated manner that did not fail to draw a giggle from Leonora.

"And...you were correct about the pleasures to be had in such an endeavor," she said stiffly, aware her cheeks were once more aflame. Perhaps beet-red would be her permanent complexion from this moment forward.

"Wonderful." Freddy beamed at her. "This means I shall not be forced to box Searle's ears on your behalf."

Leonora laughed again, partially at the thought of her feisty friend attempting to box her stoic husband's ears, and partially because she knew it was no sally. "Pray leave his ears untouched. The marquess is a complicated man, but the last sennight has been rather a revelation to me. Where I once feared he would forever remain a mystery, I do have hope. He has walls built around his heart, it is certain, but I now feel as if I may be capable of scaling them."

"To the devil with scaling them, darling," Leonora said with a grin. "Burst right through them. Tear them down, stone by stone."

"One way or another, I am determined to find my way beyond them," she said. "And when I do..."

Once more, she allowed her words to fall away.

For she had realized in the breath before she would have spoken the remainder of the sentence that she had been about to say... *And when I do, I will see that he surrenders his heart to me just as surely as I have already ceded my heart to him.*

"And when you do," Freddy persisted, being Freddy and wanting more, a full confession if she could have it.

But just then, they were interrupted by a knock at the salon door and an announcement from the butler that the Duchess of Whitley and Lady Sarah Bolingbroke wished to call upon Mrs. Kirkwood.

"I am at home," Freddy announced, turning back to Leonora when the butler had disappeared. "Do not think I shall not expect to hear more, though if you do not give it freely, I shall not force you. The Duchess of Whitley and Lady Sarah should prove just the distraction you're seeking."

Her lips tightened at the recollection of Searle whirling about the dancefloor with the incomparable Lady Sarah. "How is Lady Sarah a familiar of yours now, Freddy?"

"She is friends with the Duchess of Whitley, and I have spoken with her at length at several events now. The Whitley ball, the Yardley musicale, and Wrotham's ball. She is a very talented poet. Duncan is going to publish a volume of her work at my recommendation. You will love her, darling, I promise."

Leonora pursed her lips, unconvinced. "Any friend of yours is a friend of mine, Freddy. Just as long as she never again dances with my husband, I shall never have a problem with her, I vow."

Freddy gave her a knowing look. "I understand your feelings of possessiveness all too well, my dear. I feel precisely the same way about Duncan. But do trust me on this score. Lady Sarah's sole interest is in bringing justice to the gentleman responsible for her sister's death. Her volume of poetry will create a tremendous stir."

Leonora recalled Lady Amelia Bolingbroke, who had been presented at court when Leonora had. Lady Amelia had been every bit as beautiful as Lady Sarah, but hers had been a dark beauty where Lady Sarah's was golden.

"Are you saying Lady Amelia was murdered?" Leonora asked, a shiver going through her at the notion. She did not recall precisely what the gossip had been at the time of Lady Amelia's death—something to do with an abrupt illness of the lungs, she thought—but there had never been one whisper of something as nefarious as murder.

"Not precisely," Freddy said enigmatically. "I have promised Lady Sarah my confidence, but all will become known soon enough, with the publication of her poems."

Though Freddy looked as if she had been about to say more, the arrival of the duchess and Lady Sarah precluded further conversation on the subject. How very mysterious it all was. As the two new additions settled themselves in the gold salon, Leonora found herself easily charmed by Lady Sarah and glad for the distraction of some female companionship.

Anything to help her to ignore the restless stirrings of her heart and the dreadfully inconvenient feelings she continued to develop for him. After all, it was too soon, far too soon for love.

Was it not?

"SEARLE."

Of all the ill-timed interruptions, Morgan could think of none more vexing than the appearance of his old war friend the Duke of Whitley whilst he was at The Duke's Bastard in the midst of attempting to drink himself to oblivion. Duncan Kirkwood's smuggled Scottish whisky had one hell of an effect upon the senses. At the moment, he was not certain he could stand without swaying.

"Whitley," he greeted curtly, not bothering to rise from his chair because…well, it simply would not do to fall upon one's face before half the peers in London.

"You have been avoiding me," Whitley observed, seating himself in the empty chair at Morgan's left.

He skewered the duke with a pointed glare. "Unsuccessfully, it would seem."

"You appear to be enjoying far greater success at giving the bottle a black eye." Whitley's drawl was acidic.

"If you sought me ought to cast judgment, you can go to the devil, Cris," he slurred. "I am not in the bloody mood for company."

No indeed, he was in the mood for drinking copious amounts of whisky to deaden the troubling emotions burgeoning within him. Emotions which had everything to do with the woman he had married. Emotions which would only serve to make him weak and undermine everything he had set out to do.

He could not bear to lose sight of his plans, to stray from the path he had settled upon. Not when vengeance was almost within his grasp. If the thought of betraying the woman who surrendered herself to him so sweetly each night—and morning and afternoon, at that—made him ill, he would simply drown his compunction with more spirits.

Whitley sniffed, raising a sardonic brow. "You are more soused than a drunkard who fell into a barrel of blue ruin."

"Precisely the judgment I am speaking of," he growled, lifting his nearly empty glass to his lips for another draught. "Have you a point to make, or did you sit here with the sole intent of causing me unnecessary irritation?"

"Perhaps causing you irritation brings me pleasure," Whitley quipped.

Morgan drained the rest of his glass. "If it is pleasure you seek, you ought to be looking to your wife."

"Speaking of wives, tell me, why are you here in the club, in your cups, when you are a man newly wed?" the duke asked with deceptive calm.

Morgan stiffened at the mentioning of Leonora. Sweet, delectable Leonie, as he had come to think of her. *Hellfire*, why were these maudlin sentiments inescapable? For that matter, why was Whitley inescapable? He should have known Cris would come sniffing about for the truth, undeterred by Morgan's efforts to rebuff him at the Kirkwood ball.

"I fail to see why the ordinary pursuit of my daily activities should be of such interest to you." Though he strived to affect a tone of boredom, Morgan could not deny that Whitley's continual probing set him on edge.

"Because I know you, Morgan," Whitley countered. "I know you do not take any action before careful planning and consideration. We were at war together, after all."

"Yes." He busied himself by splashing some more whisky into his glass. Thank Christ he had managed to cozen an entire bottle for himself. It rendered getting soused so much easier. "But we are at war no longer, and I fail to see what you are after."

"The truth," Cris persisted.

"The truth is I wish to get drunk." He took another leisurely swallow of liquor. "And I wish for you to leave me in peace."

"You compromised her intentionally," Whitley bit out.

Damn him. Morgan's hand shook, sloshing a splash of amber liquid over his fawn breeches. "I did nothing of the sort. Cannot a gentleman seek to aid a lady in distress without possessing motives that are less than noble?"

"You made certain you would be found alone with her," the duke persisted.

Morgan thought briefly about smashing his friend in that straight, even row of white. It would serve him right for his bloody meddling. Could he not see his interference was neither wanted nor needed?

"I did not," he lied calmly.

"Why prevaricate with me, old friend?" Whitley asked in a tone that was deceptively soft. "You told me you were concerned for Lady Leonora's wellbeing, and then you set off in search of her. When you did not return to the ballroom and neither did she, what was I to think? I had no choice but to seek you out, and to involve the lady's mother, which you anticipated I would do. There was no look of surprise on your face when we entered that chamber, Searle. Not even a blink."

Very well. He could hardly argue the point. Nor did he have the time or the inclination. He had a very alluring half-bottle of whisky awaiting him, along with the promises of silence and numbness.

He raised his shoulders in an indolent shrug. "I wanted her as my wife, and now I have her. Go play hazard or tup a whore, Whitley. I care not what you do, so long as it does not involve me."

But Whitley's expression only grew more determined. "Why did you want her, specifically?"

"Why not?" He forced a smile he little felt, raising his glass toward the duke in a mock salute. "My bride is beautiful, and I could not be more pleased with her."

Which was the truth and the reason for his inner torment. He could not want her and use her at the same time. He could not need her as much as he did, with a ferocity that threatened to tear him in two, if he was also using her to lure Rayne back to England. He could not spend all the hours in his day either fucking her or thinking about fucking her if he also meant to make her his weapon of revenge upon her heartless bastard of a brother.

"Lady Leonora is indeed beautiful," Whitley agreed. "And a very kind, gentle-natured sort, as vulnerable as a kitten, which makes your choice all the more intriguing."

"She is the Marchioness of Searle now," he reminded his friend, sending another damning gulp of spirits down his gullet. By God, for a moment, there was not one Whitley exuding ferocious disapproval but two. He closed his eyes, collecting himself as a wave of dizziness assailed him.

If he passed out in the midst of the public rooms, would Kirkwood have his arse hauled to a private room? Perhaps Whitley could help him to his carriage. It may be time to execrate—er, *extricate* himself—from The Duke's Bastard.

"You look hideously cup-shot, Morgan. Let me get you to your carriage before you pass out on the floor and piss yourself."

How like Whitley to couch a friendly request with an insult. Morgan thought about consuming more whisky, but his gut roiled at the notion. The familiar sights and sounds of the club swirled at the edges of his vision. Perhaps he ought to have spent the day at Gentleman Jackson's saloon with Monty, beating him to a pulp. Violence was a restorative where drink was a curse.

"I can get myssself to m'bloody carriage, Cris," he slurred, attempting to stand and falling back on his arse in an undignified heap.

Well, this had certainly taken a turn for the best. *Er*, the worst.

His mind was muddled, as if it had been stuffed with cotton. The warm glow of oblivion that had been tingling within him now felt like the heat of the sun, burning him, making him sweat. Or perhaps that was his newfound sense of guilt, eating him alive. *Damnation*, he had taken up the whisky to avoid such unpleasant emotions, not to wallow in them further.

He blamed this entire cratastrop-catastero…*eternal hellfire*, why had even his brain ceased functioning? This entire *catastrophe*, he blamed upon the Duke of Whitley. Without his presence, Morgan never would have consumed so much whisky in such a short amount of time. Never mind that he had already been well on his way to becoming drunk as an emperor before Whitley's arrival.

"I shall have Duncan prepare a private chamber for you," the duke said coolly. "I am not certain you can travel in this state. Whatever has happened to you, Morgan, I can assure you that playing the toss pot at one's club is decidedly not the rage."

"I do not need a private chamber, and nor do I give a proper goddamn what is the rage," he snarled, growing angry with the duke for his cursed persistence.

Kirkwood appeared at his elbow then, and it should hardly come as a surprise, for Morgan had learned quickly that the man presided over his club like a king seated upon his throne.

"Lord Searle, allow me to direct you to a private chamber for your comfort," Kirkwood offered, his tone convivial but with an underlying edge even Morgan could discern, in his cups though he was.

Kirkwood was not making a polite request of him but making an order.

Christ, he had not imagined the day when the Duke of Whitley and the bastard son of a duke would become his bloody jailers. He stood, and this time managed to keep his balance, grinding his jaw as he allowed the two men to flank him and lead him into a side door which led to a series of interior halls Kirkwood no doubt used to manage the club.

In icy silence, the three of them traveled to a private chamber that was comfortably appointed. The door had scarcely closed before Kirkwood was upon him. "See here, Searle, as you are the husband of Mrs. Kirkwood's most beloved friend, I am choosing not to toss you on your arse or ban you from my club. But by God, if you dishonor or embarrass Lady Leonora in any fashion, I will not hesitate to cut you to size and lay you low. Am I understood?"

"It seems to me you are too fond of my wife, Kirkwood," he countered, a sharp pang of possessiveness shooting through him. "I will remind you she is now the Marchioness of Searle and Lady Leonora no longer."

"Consider yourself warned, Searle." Kirkwood bowed, and then exchanged a look with Whitley before leaving.

Whitley turned to him then, his gaze frank and assessing. "What happened to you, Morgan? In Spain, the day you were taken captive?"

The mere word *Spain* was enough to make the snake coiled within him strike. He could not control himself, not his rage, not his tongue, not his fists when such moods came upon him. "What happened to me is that I was savaged, Whitley. I was taken captive first by a cutthroat band of Spaniards and then by an even more cutthroat and vicious group of Boney's forces. They tortured me until I bled. They made me scream so they could laugh. Is that what you want to hear?"

Whitley had paled, his nostrils flaring. "No. Christ, no, Morgan. You are my friend. I have carried with me for so long the guilt of that day, knowing I failed you, wishing it had been me instead."

"It never would have been you," he said, stopping himself when he realized he had revealed too much.

Whitley did not miss the revelation. "Why do you say that?"

"Because..." He swayed as the chamber spun about him.

Because it had been planned by their superior officers. Because *El Corazón Oscuro* was the alias of the Earl of Rayne, and because Rayne had been given orders to secret Morgan behind enemy lines in what would have been a highly dangerous mission. He had known the mission was coming, but he had not known *El Corazón Oscuro* was actually one of his own forces. That knowledge had only come much, much later, and even then, purely by accident during his recovery.

One eavesdropped conversation. The shuffle through some encoded correspondence. And the truth had been his. So, too, the need for revenge. Rayne's ineptitude had been the cause of his imprisonment. Rayne deserved to suffer.

But for now, Morgan was the one suffering as the room continued to spin. His gut protested. His stomach clenched. Remembrance crashed down on him, the sound of the whip cracking upon his flesh, the searing pain. Being forced to his knees, bound and gagged. One of the French soldiers, a grim-faced little fellow with an ugly scar marring his right cheek, had taken excessive pleasure in his torture. The scent of his own flesh burning would never leave him, and it returned now, as if it were real, making him gag with a violence he could not suppress.

"Chamber pot?" Whitley asked grimly.

A fresh, crashing wave of sickness overtook him. He forced the bile back down his throat. He could persevere. He always had. "Perhaps I just require a rest. A wink of sleep."

The duke guided him to the neatly made bed, watching with ill-concealed disgust as Morgan fell back upon it. "You need to sleep this off, Searle. When you wake, go home to your marchioness. It is where you belong now, at her side. Whatever lies in your past, you must look to the future. *She* is your future. Let the past die. Let it go, or it may well kill you."

"Go to hell," he muttered weakly, passing a weary hand over his face.

Whitley did not know what he had endured. Whitley had been in London, finding a wife, making himself happy, transforming himself into the forbidding sot who cast judgment upon a man clearly in need of consuming a bottle of whisky. He was about to say as much when he glanced about him and realized the chamber was empty.

The duke had gone.

Heaving a sigh of self-loathing, Morgan lay on his back on the bed, staring up at the orgy depicted on the ceiling's fresco. None of the ladies could hold a candle to his sweet Leonie. His eyes were heavy, his stomach a sea of sick.

Perhaps he could rest, just for a bit.

When he slept, he dreamt of his wife. And when he woke at last, he was covered in sweat, stomach protesting, mouth dry and tasting as if he had licked the floorboards of the public rooms.

He rose, found the chamber pot not a moment too soon, and dropped to his knees. It was, he thought, a fitting end to the day.

CHAPTER TEN

SEARLE HAD FAILED to join her for dinner that evening, as had become their customary routine. Nor had he sent word of a delay or when she might expect him. Leonora had waited, postponing dinner and agitating Monsieur Talleyrand before finally relenting and dining in silence. The courses had been customarily exquisite, but they may as well have been crafted of ash for all Leonora tasted them.

After dinner, she had withdrawn to the drawing room where she sat in miserable silence, contemplating the pastoral oil scenes depicted upon the walls and stabbing her needlework more viciously than necessary as her ire climbed. Even poor little Caesar, who had cuddled up next to her, whined every few minutes, staring at her askance with his chocolate eyes, as if to ask where Searle was.

Finally, she had retreated to her chamber, requesting a bath to soothe her troubles away. It had proved a pleasant enough diversion but hardly restorative, and now, she was pacing the floor, dressed for bed but unable to rest for even a moment as her dudgeon increased with each tick of the mantle clock. Her hair was unbound, falling in heavy waves down her back, completely dry now, and still, her husband had yet to return.

Where had he gone?

And why had he not come back?

She completed what seemed her eightieth circumnavigation of the chamber, heedless of the ache in her leg, and at long last, she heard it, the soft closing of a chamber door. *His* chamber door, to be precise. Then footfalls, familiar in their cadence.

Her husband was home. Relief swelled within her, for in truth, she had begun to worry. But left with no knowledge of his whereabouts, she had precious little recourse. Not to mention her sudden, frenzied need for him to return to her side, coupled with the troubling realization she had made during her call to Freddy, had left her in an odd state of bemusement. She had not been certain if her apprehension sprang from her overzealous emotions where he was concerned or from a true need.

But now he had returned at last, her disquiet over his absence dashed, and in its place, the monster of her inner misery grew like a weed in a summer garden. Questions swirled, ones she almost dared not ask. Questions, perhaps, she did not have the right to ask.

Questions she could withhold no longer.

She knocked at the door joining their chambers, and when the familiar, deep rasp of his voice bid her to enter, she did, crossing the threshold into his domain. It occurred to her then that for the last week, he had been coming to her chamber rather than bringing her to his. Each night, he made love to her before returning to his own bed. A customary habit, she had reassured herself. No need to fret.

She stopped when she saw him, icy tendrils of dread curling around her heart and squeezing. He was the picture of the dissolute rakehell, wavy, dark hair mussed, his cravat hastily tied, as if by his own hand rather than a valet's, his coat rumpled.

"Madam," he greeted her, a chill in his voice she did not like. "You are yet awake. What is the hour?"

"I do not know," she lied, for somehow, her religious study of the time seemed a detail she ought to keep to herself. "Where have you been, my lord? I expected you at dinner."

His lips tightened. "I was otherwise occupied."

A horrid thought occurred to her then. What if he had been *occu-*

pied with another woman? He had told her he did not have a mistress, but that had been a fortnight ago. He could have changed. She had never demanded fidelity of him, foolishly not thinking it a necessity.

"Occupied in what manner?" she asked, dread burning a destructive path through her.

"Does it truly matter? I am tired, and I would like nothing more than to call for my valet and go to bed. So, unless you wish to quarrel with me, or unless you want to play valet for me, I suggest you return to your chamber." His tone was flat, emotionless.

The man standing before her little resembled the bold lover who had wooed her for the last week. He seemed, instead, incredibly weary. Had the demons of his days at war returned to haunt him? She had not heard him crying out in the night, but she was a sound sleeper, and with him in another chamber, it was possible she would not hear him.

Instead of retreating as he had encouraged her to do, she moved forward. The strong smell of spirits assailed her. Had he spent the entirety of his day drinking, then? She studied him with new eyes, noting he did not appear soused now.

"It matters to me," she said quietly. "When you failed to appear at dinner, I was concerned."

He closed his eyes briefly, a faint wince crossing his features. "Forgive me. I was otherwise detained. You would be wise to accustom yourself to the notion I will not always be available to you. I have many matters that require my attention."

She did not appreciate his condescension. "I understand you are a busy man with estates to run. However, I do not think it unfair of me to ask you to send a note home if you find yourself delayed. I kept dinner waiting for over an hour, and Monsieur Talleyrand was quite displeased."

"Monsieur Talleyrand can go to the devil. He gets handsome recompense for the indignity of keeping his dinner warm."

Mama had warned her that most gentlemen kept mistresses. That it was to be expected and ignored. A matter of course. Was that what had happened? Had his interest so easily strayed? A man like the Marquess of Searle—handsome, tall, dashing, a national hero—had to have any number of ladies falling at his feet. Particularly ladies of a certain ilk.

"If you have grown bored of me, you need only say so, my lord," she told him quietly, a surge of humiliation making her throat threaten to close.

She had never felt more foolish than she did now, her heart all but pinned to her sleeve for him to savage while he stood before her in the evidence of the dissolution in which he had wallowed. Had the last week meant nothing to him? Why did he face her now with the cold, stark countenance of a stranger?

"There is no place for maudlin sentiment in our union, madam." He remained aloof as ever.

Why should she be surprised? He had warned her, had he not?

This is all I need from you, he had told her so crudely, referring to their lovemaking.

It is not your duty to concern yourself with me. Your sole duty is to bear my children and refrain from cuckolding or embarrassing me publicly.

Yes, she was the worst sort of fool, because she had entered into a marriage with a man who had never claimed a tender feeling toward her. A man who was hard and dangerous, haunted by the horrors of his past. A man who had abandoned her on the day of their wedding. Who was cool and remote whenever he was not setting her aflame with his mouth and his touch. Who had married her out of necessity and duty rather than out of need or want.

And she had spent the last sennight falling in love with that man.

"Forgive me," she told him stiffly, the need to flee rising within her lest she further embarrass herself before him. "I was foolish enough to think you may have had a care for my feelings as your wife. I will not be so foolish again. Good evening, my lord. I leave you to your valet."

Attempting a curtsy that ended in a searing ache of pain in her leg, she turned and made great haste in her exit.

"My lady," he called after her.

But she closed and latched the door at her back. For the first time, the ache in her heart eclipsed the ache in her limb.

HE HAD MUDDLED things badly.

Morgan woke the next morning to a throbbing head, a dry mouth, and the rampant high tide of guilt washing over him. He dressed with the aid of his valet, Carr, who had been considerate enough to bring him a vile concoction he swore would cure Morgan's maladies. He had gagged the bitter potion down, but noted no lessening in his headache when he reached the breakfast table and discovered his wife was absent.

When he inquired after his marchioness with Huell, his butler informed him that her ladyship had requested a tray and her correspondence taken to her chamber as she was feeling ill. An illness he was the cause of, no doubt. Perhaps she could not bear to see him after he had been such an ass last night.

Grimly, he settled in to his customary plate of sausages, coffee, hothouse fruit, and eggs. *The Times* was laid out for his perusal. The food smelled as delicious as always. His stomach had begun to feel—at bloody last—as if he had not just spent the last week tossing about on the ocean in a small, unseaworthy vessel. Never again would he attempt to numb himself with a bottle of Duncan Kirkwood's smuggled whisky. The devil's own elixir, that rot.

Indeed, all was as it should be. The morning sunlight shone in the mullioned windows with a brightness that should have instilled him with cheer rather than dread. But all he could see was the empty table setting where his wife should be seated. All he could think about was the naked expression of hurt on her lovely face when he had all but sent her running from his chamber the night before.

She had done nothing to earn his scorn, and he knew it. His beautiful wife was everything he had told her she was—good and sweet and innocent. She deserved far better than to be his plaything, the dangled bait of his revenge, nothing more than his leverage against her brother.

He had lashed out at himself first, then his old friend Whitley, and then Leonie herself. And he had done so in an effort to maintain the distance he needed between the two of them. For so long, he had lived on nothing but determination and the desire to exact vengeance. For too long, it was true, for they alone had sustained him through the darkest nights of his captivity. He did not know what manner of man he was, stripped of those twin motivations.

He was terrified of discovering it.

Terrified of losing the will to treat the Earl of Rayne to the pain and suffering he so richly deserved because Morgan had developed a weakness for his own wife. But something else burned within him, brighter and hotter than that terror, overwhelming it. Overwhelming him.

And the longer he sat here, a steaming plate laden with food he had no desire to eat before him, Leonie's empty chair mocking him, the more demanding it became, roaring into an insistent life of its own. Until it could no longer be ignored.

He stood with such sudden force, his chair upended and toppled backward. Huell, ever the mask of polite indifference, allowed a brief flicker of alarm to cross his countenance before stifling the rare slip.

"I have finished my breakfast," he announced. "Have it cleared away, Huell."

"Of course, my lord," the butler said in calm accents. "Did you not find it to your liking? Shall I have Monsieur Talleyrand send something more agreeable to your lordship this morning?"

A memory flashed before him then, the cruelest of his captors spitting in a tin cup of water before holding it to Morgan's lips and forcing him to drink. Forcing him to drink until he choked and could scarcely catch a breath. Such disparity between the life he had lived in captivity and the charmed existence he inhabited now. He could not help but feel as if he were split in two, halves but never whole.

"My lord?" Huell prompted.

Morgan realized he must appear the Bedlamite, knocking over furniture, refusing to break his fast, and then staring into the abyss of his past until his hands shook and his skin broke into a fine sheen of cold sweat.

The Duke of Whitley's unsolicited advice returned to him then. *Let the past die. Let it go, or it may well kill you.*

He knew what he had to do now, in this moment of desperate uncertainty. He muttered something to his perplexed butler, but he could not say what. His feet were already carrying him to where he needed to be, as if his body knew better than his mind.

Or perhaps not just his body but whatever shadowy remnants he yet possessed of his heart.

LEONORA HAD NOT consumed much of her breakfast. And neither could she seem to concentrate upon her second reading of Freddy's *The Silent Duke*, regardless of how moving her friend's prose was or how much she adored the novel. Though she had dressed and Hill had artfully arranged her hair, Leonora had no desire to leave her chamber.

By the bright light of the morning, she felt just as foolish as she had the evening before for awaiting a man who had no intention of returning home, and then seeking him out only to receive the equivalent of a crushing set down. Her stomach felt queasy. Her eyes felt as if they may erupt in tears at any moment. And overall, she did not recall ever being beset with such a grim mood.

She was stretched comfortably upon a lounge in her chamber, her leg—paining her this morning as a result of all the agitated pacing she had indulged in the previous evening—propped up on a soft pillow. Her favorite tea was cooling at her side, and she even had Caesar for company, having decided to thieve him from Searle by way of Hill, who had been only too happy to fetch the puppy for her.

Caesar had greeted her by launching himself into her lap and delivering a lusty series of licks to her chin before promptly settling and beginning to snore. On a distracted sigh, she set the book aside and ran her hand along the puppy's spine. His fur was short yet silken, and when she petted him, he made a satisfied sound in his throat and rolled to his back, baring his belly to her.

She rubbed his belly and smiled down at the sweetly slumbering pup. "He does not deserve you, Caesar. What do you say to being my companion instead? Searle can find another dog. Or perhaps a barrel of whisky."

"I had not realized you had an interest in the fine art of talking to one's self."

The deep, delicious resonance of Searle's baritone settled somewhere between her thighs even as she jumped and tossed a startled look over her shoulder to find him hovering on the threshold between their chambers, staring at her. Though there was a teasing lilt to his words and tone, his expression remained inscrutable.

"What are you doing here, my lord?" she asked coolly.

"Eavesdropping upon your decision to steal my dog," he quipped.

She frowned at him, trying to make sense of the latest version of the Marquess of Searle. He seemed a man perpetually torn, uncertain of who he was, or at least who he wanted to be. "I thought you did not want him."

Just as you do not want me. The words hung, unsaid between them.

His green eyes seared her. "Of course I do."

She wondered if they were still talking about Caesar. But it was too much to hope he may have heard her unspoken words and answered them. "That still does not explain your presence in my chamber."

He glanced down. "I have not yet crossed the threshold, my lady, as I am awaiting your permission to enter."

How silly. Her lips flattened as she considered him. This entire house and all its contents were his, right down to the slippers upon her feet. He did not require her permission for anything, much as he had already demonstrated.

But she was getting a cramp in her neck from gazing at him over her shoulder, so she supposed she may as well acquiesce.

"Please, Leonie," he added before she could respond.

This request, so raw and soft, sounding as if it had been torn from him, along with the use of the diminutive he had given her, found its way to her heart. Why did he have to chase the bitterness of last night with such light?

She swallowed against an unwanted rush of emotion. "Very well. You may enter, but I cannot make any promises where Caesar is concerned."

"Merciless as a highwayman," he said, owning the chamber with his long strides and stopping to bow before her with a poignant elegance. His handsome countenance remained still, stark. "You did not join me for breakfast this morning."

It was not what she had anticipated he would say. Caesar shifted on her lap, prodded into wakefulness by the presence of his master. She gave him a reassuring scratch on his velvety head, staring up at her husband.

"I was not feeling myself," she said coolly.

His gaze traveled over her, lingering upon the pillow beneath her leg before snapping back to hers. "Your leg is hurting?"

His concern seemed unfeigned, and it, too, pricked her heart. "It is aching a little more than ordinary after I spent a great deal of yesterday upon my feet."

Searle's frown deepened. "Why were you upon your feet?"

She stared at him, unwilling to make the admission. "Will you not seat yourself for this interview, my lord? I little wish to continue looking up at you."

Her voice was sharper than she intended, but she was feeling sharper today, rather like a knife which had just been honed. Perhaps it was what she needed to gird herself. To defend herself and her heart, both. Why, oh why, did this man have the power to affect her as no other before him ever had?

He sat on the fainting couch in the seating area of her apartments, opposite her, looking distinctly out of place amidst the gilt and femininity of her chamber. "You did not answer my question. Why were you upon your feet so much?"

For a moment, Leonora considered fabricating a less mortifying answer, but in the end, what could she say? That she had been dancing all evening?

"I was worried about you," she admitted. "I was pacing, awaiting your return, my silly imagination conjuring up all manner of unfortunate incidents which could have kept you from returning."

The harsh lines of his face relaxed, softening into an expression she had only seen on his face during their times of intimacy in the past, tenderness. He cocked his head, considering her solemnly. "And what manner of nefarious ends did you imagine for me, Leonie?"

Again, the sound of his name for her, uttered in his sinful voice, performed untold feats upon her ability to resist him. "A carriage accident, or a fire at your club. A pickpocket attempting to rob you and then delivering a mortal wound when you resisted, as of course you would."

"Ah, Leonie. Once again, you prove I am not worthy of you." He paused before issuing a self-condemning sigh. "The truth is far worse than any of those fictional scenes, though I must say, I take offense you do not think me capable of defending myself against being murdered by a lowly London street thief. But I shall tell you what delayed me just the same."

Here it was. She braced herself, wondering if he was about to admit he had taken on a paramour. Leonora stroked Caesar's fur with more vigor than necessary, causing him to rise, give his body a solid shake, and leap to the floor. He strode over to Searle, sniffing his calves and shoes. "Little traitor," she grumbled at the canine.

"Good fellow," Searle murmured, patting his head. "Although indeed, I, too, must question your judgment." He paused, glancing back at Leonora and wincing. "I was at my club."

"Mr. Kirkwood's club?" she queried, sitting up straighter at the revelation. She had been at home, worrying over him, fretting for hours, and he had been *at his club*? The scoundrel.

"The same." He inclined his head. "I am afraid I partook of too much of Mr. Kirkwood's fine Scottish whisky, and I...devil take it, Leonie, I got thoroughly soused, and Mr. Kirkwood lent me a room to restore myself to some semblance of order before returning home. I am not proud of my actions, but there is the truth for you, plainly and simply."

Her dudgeon had returned in spades. Fury lanced through her, making her spine stiffen. "Why would you do such a thing? Is it the source of your nightmares? Does the part of your past at war that haunts you drive you to drink?"

He went rigid at her reference to his nightmares, which he refused to acknowledge. She had been hoping having Caesar would soothe him as the Duchess of Whitley claimed the pup she had given her husband had done for him. Not a panacea, but a means of ameliorating the anguish, at least.

But instead, he had spent the entirety of the day drinking spirits in such a great quantity, Freddy's beleaguered husband had been forced to give him a chamber to compose himself. And even upon his return, he had still smelled of liquor.

"I do not wish to speak of my time at war," he said slowly, as if he fought to keep his voice even and calm. "I *will not* speak of it. Not with you, not with anyone. But I can promise you that what occurred yesterday will not happen again. And I can also do my best to earn your forgiveness, beginning now."

Leonora watched as Caesar huddled ever closer to Searle, pressing his snout into the marquess's open palm and sniffing deeply, then licking. She noted her husband had not stopped stroking the pup's fur or scratching his head ever since Caesar had defected to him.

Of course, she could not force Searle to share the painful details of his time at war with her. She could not fathom what he must have endured, and she had no doubt his suffering informed the man he was now, complex and enigmatic, hot then cold, always somehow beyond her comprehension.

"Why yesterday?" she could not help asking, the words leaving her before she could think better of them. They had spent an almost enchanted sennight together, and then he had disappeared. She could not help but to wonder if it was something she had done, something she had said, which had driven him from her side, propelling him to seek mindlessness at the bottom of a whisky bottle.

He swallowed, and she saw the dip of his Adam's apple before it disappeared beneath his cravat. She loved his throat, such a place of vulnerability, laden with his masculine scent, and the urge to bury her face there and inhale deeply hit her with a pang. Angry as she was with him, she nevertheless found resisting him difficult. He was her weakness, and her heart knew it. So, too, did her traitorous body.

This man was hers, and she was his. Sometimes, it seemed as if a deeper, heretofore undiscovered part of herself had always understood she belonged to this man. Fate. Destiny. Whatever the word, whatever the name, the effect he had upon her was unlike anyone and anything else. She could not deny it. Could not deny him, for that matter.

"The way I desire you, Leonie," he rasped. His vibrant gaze met hers, verdant with flecks of cinnamon and gold. "It terrifies me. Makes me weak. I have never felt for another woman even an inkling of the feelings you inspire within me. And I...I thought I had lost my ability to feel anything a long time ago."

She bit her lower lip, stifling a sob that had risen within her. A sob for his pain. Her fingers knew the ridges of the scars marking his back. He had been brutally flogged, burned, and only the Lord and Searle knew what other excruciating indignities had befallen him.

"I am your wife now, Searle." She paused, summoning her courage for what she truly wished to say. "If you seek anything, let it be me."

His jaw tensed, his expression freezing over, and she knew she had said too much. He was proud, untouchable. He did not want her aid or her sympathy.

"You know what I want from you, wife." His voice, too, had gone as cold and remote as the rest of him.

He was telling her, once more, all he desired from her was her body beneath his, pliant and ready, his to take. All he wanted from her was physicality. Not her heart, not her mind, not her caring. He did not want her to be his comfort or his source of strength.

Disappointment stung her, but she was not surprised. What truly shocked her was his willingness to seek her out after she had eschewed breakfast, and not just that but his quiet, pensive demeanor as he had approached her, the lightness of his darkness shining through until he had ruthlessly squelched it once more.

"I am yours," she told him, refusing to be the first to break the connection of their gazes. "It is you who sent me away last night."

His gaze became shuttered, his lips firming into a forbidding line. "I will be brutally honest with you, Leonie. I am not myself, or at least,

I am not the man I was before I purchased my commission and left for the Continent. I will never again be the lighthearted, careless gentleman of my youth, quick to love and slow to hate. It is not in me to be the husband you deserve."

She disagreed, for there were glimpses of the husband she wanted. But thus far, their connection had been physical. She wanted more from him than mindless pleasure. She longed to be his source of solace and comfort, his joy and hope. She longed for him to be the sort of husband who would allow her to love him.

Because she did.

Love him, that was.

The realization hit her with a blinding, terrifying bolt of clarity tinged with undeniable finality. She loved the Marquess of Searle, the austere, cold, damaged man she had married. The veritable stranger who made her body come to life and kissed her with such tenderness, the man who called her Leonie and massaged her strained muscles when she was in pain.

And because she loved him, she had to believe it *was* in him to be the husband she deserved.

"I understand better than most how something horrific can change a person," she said quietly. She did not often speak of her accident—for years, she had been terrorized by nightmares of her own, in which she fell all over again from the banister—but time had given her both distance and perspective. "I did not know you before you left for war, and I scarcely know you now. But I would like the opportunity to know you better, my lord, for this is the only *you* I have."

He stared at her, his countenance inscrutable, for an indeterminate span of time. It could have been seconds or minutes, and yet it seemed somehow like forever, rife with a meaning she could not even yet comprehend.

"We never had a honeymoon," he said at last, startling her with the abrupt statement, seemingly unrelated to what she had just said. "I wish to rectify that. I want to take you to my country seat, Westmore Manor. Surrey is not far from town, and we can remain there a sennight, if not longer. What say you, Leonie?"

When he called her Leonie, there was only one answer she could give him.

Doing her best to tamp down the hopeful smile longing to break free, she inclined her head. "I say yes."

CHAPTER ELEVEN

MORGAN HAD TO have taken leave of his senses.

Madness was the only explanation for why he had seized upon the foolish notion to bring his wife on a honeymoon, why he had swept her away from London and returned to his ancestral home for the first time in years. Sheer lunacy was the only explanation for his presence at a bloody picnic on the bank of the gently meandering stream that curved its way through Westmore Manor's immense park.

He was seated on a spread blanket, opposite Leonie, clusters of Forget-me-nots sprouting from between lush grasses surrounding them, the sweet cadence of the gently gurgling stream the only sound in the stillness of the exquisitely sunny day. She was smiling at him as if he had personally requested today's sunshine and gorgeous white clouds.

It was a smile that could make a man happily attempt to conquer nations for her.

It was a smile that made *him* catch his breath and forget why he was such a fool for entertaining the weakness he possessed for her, this accursed vulnerability within him which made him want to be the source of her every happiness rather than her every disappointment. *By God*, how had this rare beauty with the heart of an angel remained unwed long enough for him to snap her up in his vindictive, lecherous claws?

Whatever the reason, he was grateful for it.

"Thank you," she told him softly then, echoing his sentiments of appreciation and tearing him from his warring ruminations.

He neither wanted nor deserved her gratitude. One day soon, she would discover the truth behind his reasons for wedding her, and when that day came, he doubted he would ever see another willing smile from her beautiful lips. The notion should not send a pang of extreme sadness cutting through him, and yet it somehow did. By the time they returned to London, Rayne would have most certainly returned, and from that moment onward, Morgan's plan would unfold.

He cleared his throat. "I have done nothing which requires gratitude, my lady."

Her smile deepened, her eyes a shade to rival the sky above them. She wore a fetching bonnet he had been fantasizing about plucking off ever since he had first handed her into the carriage that brought them to this secluded, serene area of the Westmore Manor park. But it was the softness, the unguarded intimacy and admiration in her expression that stole his breath.

"Nevertheless," she said, "I appreciate your efforts to make amends with me."

Was that what this was? Had he decided to bring her here on a honeymoon to do penance for the manner in which he had treated her the evening he had returned from The Duke's Bastard? He did not want to believe himself capable of such consideration. He wanted to believe he had brought her here so he would be removed from the temptations of town, so he could ravish her as often as possible and preferably get her with child before Rayne returned.

That had been his course of action, all along. Ruin the Earl of Rayne in every possible way before ending him.

What had changed?

Him. He had changed, and he answered his internally posed question with ease. Something inside him was shifting, altering, much as it had upon his initial days as a soldier.

Morgan needed to distract her, to distract himself. The picnic had been his idea, a means to enjoy the fresh country air and the beautiful day, to take sustenance, and for Leonie to experience Westmore Manor all at once. But he had never intended to find himself so besieged by troubling feelings for his wife.

He plucked a strawberry from one of the dessert plates arranged upon the spread coverlet—small mountains of sugar biscuits, macaroons, bonbons, and fruits—then held it to her lips. "Berry, my dear?"

She pursed her lips, watching him with close regard, the stare that made him feel as if she could see within him to all the ugliness and deceit and bitterness he hid. Those feelings continued to make him experience a crushing combination of guilt and shame.

And here was another acknowledgment he did not like...

Her. She was the reason why he was feeling so torn, why the notion of gaining his revenge upon the Earl of Rayne no longer seemed the panacea it once had.

Regarding him solemnly, she nodded. "Yes, please."

He held out the berry like a flag of surrender. She parted her lips to accept his offering, and then her teeth nipped a bite from the end. The berry was warm beneath his bare fingers, kissed by the sun, freshly ripened and picked that morning from one of the teeming plants in the Westmore Manor conservatory for their consumption. The strawberry itself, while vibrantly red and large, was nothing special. Furthermore, he had previously been in the presence of many females who had dined, and he had never once succumbed to lust.

Watching his wife take a bite of the succulent fruit should not have an effect upon him. It ought not to make his cock go rigid in his breeches, so hard he had to shift the manner in which he sat upon the cursed blanket. It most certainly should not make him think far more sinful thoughts, such as guiding the berry between her legs and...

Damnation.

His cock twitched, and he barely suppressed a moan. Leonie ate the rest of the strawberry, nipping the large fruit cleanly at the base where Cook had removed the stem, her lips brushing the pads of his fingers as she did so, sending a fresh surge of need to his groin.

The fruit was the conclusion of their picnic luncheon. Already, they had shared wine and consumed cold meats, cheese, and bread. One appetite had been sated, but another had been roused.

His gaze never straying from hers, Morgan popped the base of the strawberry into his mouth, chewing slowly. Thoughtfully. He swallowed. "Delicious."

And he was not talking about the bloody berry. He was referring to his wife, specifically. She looked so proper, her bonnet in place, her gloves neatly folded at her side, her skirts fussed into place so that nary a hint of her ankle was visible to him.

And yet, she also looked lush. Delectable. Riper than the sweet fruit he had just consumed. Roses bloomed in her cheeks. A gentle wind blew, freeing a tendril of white-blonde hair from her careful coiffure and sending it curling over her face.

She was perfection. The most beautiful being he had ever seen. She was everything he wanted, nothing he should have. Before him, sat a rare creature, someone who cared for everyone else around her far more than she cared for herself. Leonie was so giving, so sweet. She was his lamb more than his lioness. His sweet, darling lamb.

And one day soon, she would be his willing sacrifice. He would be the lion who took her into his maws and shook her until those sweet and innocent and caring parts of her were dead. He was the predator, and she was the prey. Destruction was the inevitable, unenviable end to their story.

The man who would pay for it all with his life would be her soulless brother.

But Morgan did not like to think of any of those things. His mind balked. So, too, another part of him he preferred not to acknowledge, until he could not bear it any longer. Distraction was what he required. The ability to silence his conscience, which had somehow grown in size from nonexistent to a small seed.

"Tell me something," he told her, desperate to fill the silence with something other than the feverish workings of his mind.

She was being so quiet, after all, and quite unlike herself. His past at war had taught him he ought to fear silence, for great upheaval tended to follow it. Specifically, violence. But he could not fathom his wife, so diminutive of stature and kind of heart, would wish to abuse him.

If she did, Christ knew he would allow it on principle, for no one deserved her wrath more than he did.

Leonie smiled at him, one of her rarer smiles, the sort that brought out the dimple in her right cheek and hit him in his chest like a blow. "I confess, I was hoping *you* might tell *me* something. After all, this is your ancestral home. You must have memories of this place. I wish to know them. Indeed, I wish to know *you*."

Here, again, this woman stole his breath. She cared so much. Cared when she ought not to care. Cared because she could, because it was in her nature. Because she was *Leonie*, part angel, part goddess, and all his.

His burden, his pleasure, his pain, his guilt, his *wife*.

He wanted her so much, so desperately, not just to take her, but to assure himself of her allegiance to him forever. As he sat here with her, basking in her presence, knowing he would destroy her when he killed Rayne, he wanted nothing more than to find a way to avoid hurting her. And perhaps it was not so inevitable after all, nor so hopeless. He wanted their end to be different than what he had foreseen before he had married her.

That was how much she had come to mean to him. That was how much he needed her.

It struck him like a lightning bolt. Like a blow to the chin.

He did not just desire the woman he had married. Leonie had ceased being a duty from the moment he had first danced with her, and from then on, she had only ever been a pleasure. He *felt* something for her, far more for her than he should.

Good. Sweet. Christ in heaven.

Morgan could not afford to feel emotions for this woman. If he allowed himself to care for her too much, he would never be capable of using her to torment Rayne. He knew that, just as surely as he knew he could not banish these thoroughly unwanted feelings which had broken free within him.

He turned his mind instead to her request. She wanted to know more about him, about Westmore Manor, about his past. He could grant her that much of himself. Even if it, too, was incredibly difficult, tangled up in the webs of the past and the painful memories of a life he no longer lived.

He searched his mind, and then he began to speak, locking out the demons at war within him. "My mother and father both, along with my brother, George, are buried in the family plot here. I spent summers here with George. Father largely ignored us. Mother was forbidden by Father to come here. In truth, I harbor few fond memories of visiting. The land and its forbidding, sixteenth-century architecture can go rot for all I care. The precious few memories I do harbor, racing my horse, fishing with George, and throwing darts at the game heads mounted in the great hall until the butler caught us. Father was utterly livid. That is all I can recall, nothing of import, I fear. Only a handful of melancholy memories. Is that what you wanted, Leonie?"

His wife, who was everything he needed and nothing he deserved, watched him. That bright gaze of hers saw far more than he would have preferred, and he damn well knew it.

"I am sorry you do not have many happy memories here," she said quietly, her full lips compressing. "But if it would please you, I should like to make new memories with you here. Right now. What would make you happy, my lord?"

So many things. So many wrong, wicked things.

He would not begin with any of those.

Instead, he chose something infinitely safer. "My name upon your lips. You have said it before, but I cannot help but to feel I am forever relegated to either 'Searle' or 'my lord' out of an infinite supply of displeasure. I would have you call me Morgan, at least for today, if not beyond. Hearing my Christian name upon your lips would please me greatly."

In truth, she had not called him by his given name since the night he had bedded her for the first time. He wanted to return to that tender intimacy, even if the longing was deuced stupid of him.

And it *was* deuced stupid, there was no question of it.

Her smile deepened, her lips so soft and pink and decadent, promising. Tantalizing. "Morgan," she said.

His name, nothing revolutionary. Nothing special, *by God*. And yet...

And yet, all the blood in his body diverted to his cock in that instant.

His erection was so fierce, so demanding, he sucked in a breath and hoped his wife did not take note of his sudden, amorous state of discomfort. "Thank you, Leonie."

A wicked glint entered her eyes. Her hands clenched in the fabric of her prim day gown, dragging the sprigged muslin upward to reveal her trim ankles and shapely calves. "I was hoping we might make a new memory here. A happier one. Together. What do you think, Morgan?"

What did he think? His mouth went dry as she raised her skirts a bit higher to reveal her stockinged knees. Quickly, he calculated the distance of the waiting carriage—quite beyond sight and hearing distance—and servants, who had been given orders not to disturb their picnic luncheon. This dreamy, verdant area of the park was concealed by ancient oaks and the gentle swells of the land, giving the area a sense of intimacy, which had been his reason for choosing it for their picnic.

"Morgan?" she persisted, raising the hems of her gown and petticoats even higher, revealing her garters and the mouthwatering expanse of bare skin where her stockings ended. Pale, milky thighs taunted him.

"I think I may have to finish my dessert in a different fashion," he told her, a wicked idea taking hold as he thought of the discarded plate of strawberries.

"Oh?" A flirtatious smile tipped up the corners of her lush mouth. Her hem moved farther north. "And what shall your dessert be?"

He closed the distance between them and sealed his lips to hers, kissing her long and hard and deep, unable to resist licking into her mouth, tasting her. She was sweet, so sweet, a heady blend of sugary confections and ripe strawberries and *Leonie*.

And he was lost. He nipped her lower lip, ravenous for her, wanting to mark her, to eat her whole. "My dessert will be you, darling," he muttered against her beautiful lips.

LEONORA SWALLOWED AS a frisson of anticipation trilled down her spine and settled deep in her womb where she ached for him most. Her fingers were in his hair, threading through the long dark waves, his hat knocked aside. Need for him roared through her as she kissed him back.

Since they had relocated to the countryside, she had been treated to a gentler version of her husband. He was attentive and charming. He made her laugh with clever sallies. Upon their arrival at Westmore Manor, the full staff of domestics had been assembled. He had introduced her to them himself, and then he had personally shown her each chamber in the astonishingly large home, from its cavernous great hall to the library and the gardens.

They had been in residence for three blissful days, and Searle had been not just attentive but...almost sweet, though the word hardly seemed an appropriate descriptor for the forbidding man she had married. But this moment, this picnic upon the idyllic bank of a stream, where they were surrounded by the abundance of nature at her most munificent, where he fed her strawberries and the tiny faces of Forget-me-nots bobbed around them in the gentle, sweet-smelling breeze and the water cascaded in a relaxing gurgle.

He groaned, then broke the kiss. His gaze burned into hers, seeming to devour her as if he were committing her to memory, or as if he were seeing her for the first time. His intensity poured into her soul, and it remained there. She knew she could not remove it now, not even if she wished to do so. The Marquess of Searle was a part of her, so deep and so true he could never be removed. Not from her heart, not from her memories, and not from her life.

Nor did she want him to be.

"Delicious, my lady," he said, and then he kissed her again slowly, lingeringly, deliciously. He kissed her as if she was beloved to him, as if she was necessary.

She kissed him back in the same fashion, because he *was* to her. In such a short amount of time, he had become essential. He had become a part of her she had not known she so desperately needed. His large body settled between her legs, and he angled himself over her, feeding her kisses until pleasure was once more licking through her like fire.

Her fingers traveled happily over his broad shoulders, investigating his hardness, his strength. How difficult it was to believe anyone had been capable of containing this man. One day, she would ask him. One day, perhaps he would trust her enough to share the parts of himself he kept locked away, the parts he refused to speak about.

But today was not that day, and it did not seem to matter, with his warmth burning into her body, his scent surrounding her, the sun shining upon them, and the pretty gurgle of the stream in the background as he kissed her with such voracious possession a fresh ache blossomed between her legs. They were in an enchanted realm, no one but the two of them, and the rest of their lives could be spent learning each other's secrets.

For now, there was nothing she wanted more than him.

Because she loved him.

How she loved this man.

He tore his mouth from hers, almost as if he had somehow heard her thoughts, then gazed down at her, his lips swollen from kissing her, his eyes glazed over with passion. "Leonie, darling. If we carry on as we are, I will take you right here."

"Then do it," she dared him.

"Leonie." He kissed her, almost as if he could not resist, then broke free once more, his countenance a study in need and repression. "You make me forget where I am and what I am about. Make me forget all the reasons why making love to you wherever I wish is not always a good idea"

She smiled up at him, her heart giving a pang. How tender he seemed, how softened. How very different from the unyielding, cold Searle she had come to expect. "Good." She caught his handsome face in her hands. "Because if you ask me, making love to me here and now is a most excellent idea."

"Leonie," he protested on a groan, but as he said her name, he also dipped his head to feather another kiss over her lips as if he was starved for her.

As if he could not resist.

She did not want him to resist. She wanted him to lose control. To fling his caution to the wind. And so, she held him to her when he would withdraw, deepening their kiss herself for the first time by sliding her tongue past the seam of his lips. His response was molten. On a growl, he kissed her harder, his tongue licking against hers almost as if they fought a battle.

But this was not a battle. Rather, it was a homecoming.

Her heart had found the place where it belonged: *him*.

"Leonie," he said again, her name on his lips a prayer. An exhalation. A warning.

"Morgan," she returned, kissing him again, once, twice. *God help her*, thrice because she could not resist. "Make love to me."

She did not have to beg, though she felt certain she would have. He dragged his mouth down her neck, sucking and biting all the tender flesh available to him. Her throat would be evidence of what they had been about, and she did not care. She would cover it with fichus and powder. She would wear the mark of his lovemaking sooner than she would don the Searle rubies.

His hands were on her gown and petticoats, dragging them to her waist. Leonora kissed the top of his head, reveling in the silken thickness of his wavy dark hair. How beautiful he was, how perfectly imperfect, how *hers*. His fingers dipped with expert precision between her thighs, and then he was kissing her once more, his mouth fused to hers, their tongues tangling. His fingers left her to undo the fall of his breeches.

"I want you more than I want my next breath," he said.

Dear God, what his words did to her.

"Yes, Morgan. I feel the same way." She pulled his mouth to hers, and he entered her in one swift thrust.

Their lips met in a furious joining. Their bodies moved together in elemental mimicry. He withdrew from her almost entirely, only to slide home inside her once more. Their mouths clung, tongues tangling, and he made love to her with such sweet ferocity she feared she would weep.

In the aftermath, she held him against her, and it was only then that the words she intended to keep to herself escaped her.

Quite involuntarily.

"I love you, Morgan."

But once they had left her lips, there was no recalling them, regardless of how much she wished she could.

MORGAN HAD FOUND a new use for the library at Westmore Manor. As a lad, he and George had often found their way to the old, cavernous room with its walls of ancient tomes to escape from their father's wrath. As a man, he was finding solace in the same space all over again, albeit in a different manner and with a different companion.

Each evening following dinner, he and Caesar had lately made a habit of joining Leonora there. The first night Morgan had accompanied her, he had seated himself upon a winged-back chair, listening to her read from *The Silent Duke*. The second night, she had invited him to join her on the divan. This night, he stretched comfortably across the oversized piece of furniture, his head in Leonora's lap, Caesar cuddled up to his side.

She was once more reading from her book, and he was luxuriating in her attentions, much like a cat lying in the sun, allowing himself to be pet. Her fingers tenderly stroked his hair as she read, her mellifluous voice filling the room with warmth.

But though he basked in her touch and the opportunity to be so near to her—the soft fabric of her gown and her luscious thighs an ideal, floral scented pillow for his head—he was also distracted once more. More than distracted, even, he was haunted by the words she had spoken several days before. The novel she read was doubtlessly riveting, but one sound echoed above the din in his mind, and though it was hers, the words were different.

All wrong.

I love you, Morgan.

The words his wife had sweetly and innocently whispered to him by the stream after he had made love to her would simply not bloody well leave him. They were a litany, repeating in his mind.

A devastating and unwanted litany, running without end. Making him wonder whether or not the path he had chosen was wise. Lodging a stone of guilt within him that had begun as a pebble and turned into a veritable boulder as the days had passed.

Yes, damnation and holy Hell. His wife had fallen in love with him. Ordinarily, such a discovery would no doubt please a husband. Perhaps even be cause for celebration. For Morgan, however, it only filled him with dread, misgiving, and doubt.

Because he wanted her love. He wanted her love with a selfish savagery that left him ashamed of himself, because he knew he was not worthy of that love. He knew he had done nothing to deserve it. He also knew his ultimate goal of dueling with Rayne would destroy the way Leonie felt for him. Especially when the duel ended, as it must, in her half-brother's death.

He did not want to destroy the way she felt for him. He was a heartless scoundrel because he liked the sound of her voice, lilting and lovely, husky and feminine as she read to him. He liked her fingers in his hair, the manner in which she gave herself and her caring to him so freely, so willingly. He liked the way she kissed him as if he were beloved to her, the way she held him in her arms after they made love. He even liked the little mongrel she had bought him. At the thought, he gave Caesar's silky head a scratch.

He liked the life they had begun, tentatively, to build together. For a man who had spent so much of his recent life in darkness, Leonie was a source of great, blinding brightness. She made him long for that which he ought not. She made him never want this false idyll he had begun with her to end.

For a moment, the most absurd notion occurred to him. They

need never return to London. He had no wish to take his seat in Parliament. Instead, they could remain here, tucked away in the country. He could become a country gentleman, and she would be at his side, and he would never have to watch as the naked adoration in her gaze withered and turned to hatred. He could allow the Lord to mete out justice to the Earl of Rayne one day instead of himself...

He knew he could not. He could not abandon his plans for retribution. His unexpected feelings for his wife had rendered him maudlin, but they could not erase the determination that had seen him through the long days of his imprisonment and torture. He owed it to himself to see Rayne punished for his misdeeds.

"Morgan?" Leonie's dulcet voice cut through the bitterness of his musings. "You are growing tense. Is something amiss?"

Damnation. This too rocked him, the manner in which she knew him almost better than he knew himself. Everything is amiss, he wanted to say. The urge to unburden himself to her rose within him, but he brutally forced it down.

"I was thinking of George," he said instead, and it was not a lie, for he had been reminded of the times he and his brother had hidden here in the library.

"Your brother." She closed the book and set it aside, using both of her hands to gently massage his scalp. "You must miss him very much."

"I do." This too was honesty, torn from him. "Sometimes I feel lost without him. This life—becoming the Marquess of Searle—was never meant to be mine. He died when I was away, while I was at war. Part of me still expected to find him waiting for me when I finally returned home."

"But he was not."

"No one was," he said, bitterness lacing his voice, curdling his gut. "I am the only family I have left. But I do miss him. Returning to Westmore Manor has been more difficult than I supposed it would be, for my memories of him are everywhere."

"Even here?" she asked carefully.

"Even here." He swallowed against a sudden, unwanted sting of tears. "We hid here from our father when he was in a rage. Our mother adored reading, and he loathed books. He could not abide by this library, which made it an excellent place of escape, especially since there were so many books to be read here...though most of them boring old Latin tomes."

"It is fortunate indeed I brought my own books to entertain you, though I fear The Silent Duke was rather disturbing you this evening instead of distracting you."

He sighed. What could he say without revealing himself to her? "I am beholden to you, wife."

And in more ways than she knew.

"You have me now, Morgan," she told him suddenly, continuing her tender ministrations, soothing him with her touch, her nearness, her compassion. Soothing him in the way only Leonie could. "You need not feel as if you are the only family you have left. I am your wife, and it is my dearest wish for us to have children of our own."

Children with Leonie.

The notion sent a fresh burst of warmth unfurling within him. He swallowed against a rush of emotion, some of it foreign, all of it wild. "You want to have children?"

"I have always wished to be a mother," she admitted.

He turned his head in her lap so he could see her, having been too long deprived of her countenance. She was smiling, her eyes glistening, and she looked...happy. There was no other word to describe it. The way she looked made him feel so small. So wrong.

Morgan caught one of her hands in his and brought it to his lips for a reverent kiss. "You will make a wonderful mother, Leonie."

And he had no doubt she would. She was the most giving woman he had ever known. Selfless and courageous, bursting with love. How no one had snatched her up before him was a mystery. A mystery for which he was grateful anew.

"It was a silly hope for a spinster wallflower," she said then. "I am grateful to you for giving me that chance now."

He could not bear to dwell upon her misplaced gratitude, for it made him ill.

"I am grateful to you for allowing me to be your husband." Here too were words he meant with everything in him, but they made him sick as well, for his intentions were not pure, and the angel holding him in her lap, hands, and heart deserved so much more than what he could give her.

He prayed she would not hate him when the truth was revealed.

"Well, you rather ruined me, did you not?" she asked lightly, clearly striving to brighten the mood.

"Yes." His tone was grim, for he felt grim at this reminder of the man he had become.

She pressed a kiss to the crown of his head. "I am glad you did, Morgan. More and more with each day."

And his guilt grew, along with his need for her.

CHAPTER TWELVE

MORGAN CHANCED A glance at Leonie as she rode with effortless grace at his side. The boulder of guilt that had been growing inside him since their arrival at Westmore Manor a sennight earlier, had grown to the size of a mountain by now. Just then, the insistent roar of thunder broke through the countryside, spooking Leonie and Morgan's mounts.

Bloody hell.

A cursory glance at their surroundings filled him with dread. He had been so caught up in his thoughts, he'd failed to realize how far they had traveled, and neither had he noticed the ominous portent of the darkening clouds on the horizon. They had traveled too far to risk returning to Westmore Manor before the storm unleashed its rage upon them.

"A storm is brewing," he called out to his wife above another rumble of thunder in the distance.

"Shall we return to Westmore Manor?" she asked, clutching her smart hat against a sudden gust of wind that threatened to tear it from its jaunty perch atop her head.

"I fear we do not have the time to make it there before the rains soak us." He cast another glance toward the darkening sky. This particular storm appeared to be fast moving. He judged it would hit them within minutes, soaking them to the skin. "Fortunately, we are not far from a gamekeeper's cottage. It has been abandoned for some years now, but I do believe it will provide us the shelter we need until the storms pass."

She nodded. "Lead the way."

Damnation, she was beautiful. He drank in the sight of her sitting sidesaddle on her mount. He would not have guessed she was as fine a horsewoman as she was, more than capable of controlling her mount and galloping alongside him, or slowing to a trot and keeping pace. But of course, he supposed nothing this woman was capable of should ever surprise him. She was nothing like what he had expected her to be, and nothing like any other lady he had ever known.

She was Leonie, and that was all. He could not help but to admire her determination, strength, and poise yet again.

"Morgan," she said then. "Shall you lead the way?"

He realized he had reigned in his mare and had been content to remain there admiring her whilst the clouds drew nearer and a bolt of lightning lit the sky. What the devil ailed him?

"Of course." He guided his mount in the direction of a copse of trees not far from where they rode, knowing the way to the cottage even though so many years had passed since he had last seen it.

He supposed that was the way of things at Westmore Manor. The land was in his blood, in his memory. And he would always belong here, regardless of where in the world he traveled and how far he wandered, or how greatly he'd changed.

As he rode toward their new destination, he could not help but feel his connection to Leonie could be the same. That she could always be his home, no matter how far he roamed from her.

But then, the skies opened and a torrent of rain fell upon them. He told himself what a fool he was for entertaining such a ludicrous notion. Westmore Manor was a piece of land that had existed before him and would become the burden of another Marquess of Searle after him, and that was all. There was nothing special about it, and only the accident of his birth made him belong here. And his marchioness was only his because her brother had nearly seen him killed. She was the tool of his vengeance, nothing more.

By the time they reached their destination, they were thoroughly soaked from the downpour. He delivered Leonie inside the door after securing the key from its old hiding place, then led their mounts to the dilapidated stable on his own, tethering the horses and tending to them before rushing back to the cottage.

In his absence, Leonie had thrown back the window dressings, allowing some meager light in, and she was on her knees before the hearth, attempting to spark some dry kindling she had scavenged.

On her knees, though surely such a position pained her.

"Leonie." He stalked forward, water running in rivulets from his hat and coat, sloshing all over the bare floor. "You ought not to risk injuring yourself in such a fashion. Allow me to light the fire."

The unseasonable warmth of their first few days at Westmore Manor had given way to more temperate weather, and the storm had brought an even stronger chill to the air. His sodden garments heightened the cold, and he had no doubt hers did as well.

She had removed her hat, and her glorious hair was a beautiful jumble of wet curls. "I cannot injure myself by remaining in one place upon the floor, Morgan," she told him, continuing her task as she flicked a glance in his direction. "This cottage is damp, and I knew you would be cold after tending to the horses for so long. I must have a contribution of my own, else I shall feel most useless."

He understood her pride, and a ferocious streak of that same emotion went through him as he stood there watching her. She was more than capable, and she continued to impress him with her calm resilience and perseverance. Her life had not been an easy one, he would wager. She had suffered the effects of her injury since she had been a girl, and for that same reason, she had been relegated to the periphery of society. Then, he had come along and ruined her, forcing her into marrying a man she scarcely knew. A man who had proceeded to treat her coolly. A man who had abandoned her on the day of her wedding.

And what had she done? She had given him a bloody dog.

Then, he had taken her body, made love to her time and again, knowing he was misleading her, withholding truths from her that would perhaps affect the manner in which she regarded him forever. He had done it anyway, because he was a jackanapes.

And what had she done? She had told him she loved him.

He got them tangled in a storm because he was so consumed by his own thoughts, he failed to notice the sky, and what had she done? Attempted to light a fire to bring *him* warmth.

Not a thought for herself. Never a thought for her own needs. She was selfless. For the hundredth time, he realized just how unworthy of her he was. How much he did not deserve her. How much he would never deserve her, and how damn lucky he was to call her his wife.

He tossed aside his dripping hat and coat and went to her, dropping to his knees at her side. "Leonie."

She paused in striking a tinderbox, the contents of which likely dated back at least five years, perhaps more. "Yes?"

He took the tinderbox from her gently, setting it aside. "You have no need of this. I daresay it will not light, having been abandoned all these years, and is most assuredly damp, having been kept within this closed up cottage. I do not think anyone has been within to air it out since my father."

"Oh," she said, biting her lower lip. "I had not realized how long it had been since someone had occupied the space, though I did have my suspicions. Still, I am determined, Morgan. If anyone can manage a spark to form, it shall be me. Are you cold? Surely you must be, drenched to the bone as you are."

She was still thinking of him, more concerned for his wellbeing than for her own, and it humbled him mightily. "I have not known you long, my dear, but I feel quite certain if anyone could force an old tinderbox to produce a spark, it would be you. Your determination knows no bounds, nor does your willingness to attempt to make a difference for the betterment of all those around you."

Her head jerked toward his, a smile stealing over her lips. "Thank you, husband. I shall consider that a vote in favor of my capability."

And thus said, she took up the tinderbox from where he had placed it on the floor, set upon her course.

AT LONG LAST, the spark ignited, and Leonora quickly held it to the stack of dry kindling she had arranged within the fireplace. Fire licked the edges of rough-hewn wood, and gradually, steadily, a fire ignited. Flames flickered to life. Crackles rose in the air, along with the sweet scent of burning wood, as her hard work came to fruition.

She could not deny the joy, nor the sense of accomplishment, warm and pleasant, washing over her. She felt at once as if she was capable of anything. Capable of everything.

"A spark from an old tinderbox, my lord," she told him triumphantly, unable to suppress the grin wreathing her face. "There you have it."

"I should never have doubted you, Leonie," he told her softly with one of his rarer smiles. "Your ability to perform the miraculous never ceases to amaze."

His words made the warmth inside her blossom and spread. "And what miracles have I performed, my lord? I confess, I cannot think of one."

He took her hand in his and brought it to his lips for a kiss that could only be described as reverent. "You have made me feel again."

Her heart thudded at his admission. She had foolishly confessed her love to him that day by the stream, and he had not remarked upon it since, though they had spent each day in each other's company, laughing, making love, and getting better acquainted. Part of her had been convinced he had not heard her. Part of her had been terrified he had.

"What have I made you feel, my lord?" she dared to ask, cursing herself for the breathlessness in her voice.

He took her hand—bare since she had shed her gloves to avoid soiling them in her toils—and pressed it flat against his chest, over his heart. His hand was large and cool atop hers as she absorbed the steady thumps through her fingertips. Though his waistcoat was damp, the heat of his body radiated through.

"You made me realize I still have a heart, Leonie." His gaze seared hers, holding her immobile, sending a fresh surge of tenderness for him straight through her. "Do you feel it?"

"Yes," she whispered, and though her leg had begun to ache, she would not move from this position, nor would she look away from him. She would fashion herself into a statue if she must, just for the chance to have him look at her with such unguarded warmth.

"It has always been there," he continued. "But now you give my heart a reason to beat."

"Oh, Morgan." She knew how much this revelation cost him. "I feel the same way. I was waiting for you all my life."

"Jesus, Leonie," he rasped, his expression changing, turning hungry and fierce. "I do not deserve you."

"Yes," she countered, bringing her other hand to his beloved face to cup his jaw, "you do."

With a sound that was half growl, half groan, he pulled her to his chest, settling his mouth over hers in a voracious kiss. She kissed him back with all the emotions bursting inside her, new and strange and overwhelming. Love, need, admiration, longing. It didn't matter that her riding habit was sodden or that the air of the cabin was damp and musty. The heat from the fledgling fire and the way Morgan made her feel combined to set her aflame.

On another groan, he pulled away at last, his breathing harsh as it coasted over her lips. He touched his forehead to hers, and their gazes held. She felt as if he could stare into the deepest recesses of her, as if he saw her, all of her, better than anyone else ever had.

"You are soaked from the rain," he said, then kissed her again, this time nothing more than a slow brush of his mouth over hers. "You need to get out of this wet gown. I have no wish for you to take ill."

"But—"

"Hush." He kissed her again, and then he stood, scooping her into his arms and lifting her as he did so. "Let me take care of you, my sweet."

She clung to his neck while he carried her to a chair not far from the fireplace and then settled her gingerly upon it. "I am perfectly capable of seeing to myself," her pride compelled her to protest.

"You are more than capable, as you have proven again and again." He smiled at her as he dropped to his knees on the floor before her, and then kissed the tip of her nose. "Allow me."

Perhaps it was the gesture, so tender and so unlike him, perhaps it was the underlying affection in his tone, she could not be certain. But she sat still and permitted him to play lady's maid. He unbuttoned her and whisked away the outer layer of her soaked garments. She shivered as his touch skimmed over her bare arms, sending a bolt of want straight to her core.

The flesh between her legs was slick and pulsing, and she pressed her thighs together in an effort to stay the almost unbearable need. This dusty cottage, abandoned for years, in the midst of a violent thunderstorm, was not the place for lovemaking. As if nature had heard her thoughts, a large crack of thunder rent the silence between them.

"It is fortunate we found this shelter," he murmured before dipping his face into the crook of her neck and kissing her.

She could not suppress the weak sigh that slid from her lips. Nor could she resist tilting her head to grant him greater access to her sensitive skin. "Fortunate indeed."

He trailed a path of open-mouthed kisses over her throat, making his way to the hollow at the base where her pulse galloped. Her heart hammered with such insistence she was amazed the sound of it did not ring through the air, loud as the thunder. His hands cupped her breasts through the linen of her chemise.

"So responsive," he murmured. "So beautiful. Are you cold, darling?"

She was on fire. Indeed, she did not think she could ever be cold again. Not with this man as her husband. "No. I could never be anything other than warm with you near."

"Good. It is my duty to keep you..." he paused and kissed along the protrusion of her collarbone..."safe..." He nipped her skin. "And warm."

Her breaths were ragged, her heart beating even faster. She clutched his broad shoulders, marveling at the strength and muscle of him. She could not resist burying her face in the dark, tousled waves of his hair and kissing the top of his head. It hardly seemed possible to have fallen in love with him so deeply and thoroughly, to feel as strongly for him as she did.

"You are doing an excellent job, my lord," she said, her words ending on a helpless moan when his lips closed over one hardened nipple, sucking the peak into his mouth.

He released her nipple and moved to her other breast. "I could do better," he said, his voice gruff and even deeper than ordinary, before his lips closed over this stiffened bud, too.

She arched into his relentless suction, unable to resist. "Morgan," she whispered. "I love you."

The confession sprung from her, as naturally as her next breath and every bit as true. And this time, she did not mind. She felt neither embarrassment nor anxiety, but instead a deep sense of release mingled with rightness. Why withhold her feelings from him? Why contain her love for him within herself? He was her husband, in word and deed, and she would be his wife for the rest of her life. Where a fortnight ago, she had possessed little hope they would ever share more than a physical attraction, she could not help but to feel differently now.

They locked gazes as he kissed a path down her stomach. What she saw reflected in his glittering eyes made her go weak. "I am not worthy of your love," he said, kissing the curve of her belly, caressing her with his big, strong hands. "But I am a greedy bastard when it comes to you, Leonie, for I cannot get enough of your love or you. I want it all, and I want it forever."

She did not know why he insisted he did not deserve her or was somehow unworthy, though she suspected it related to the dark days he had spent in captivity. He had yet to share even the slightest crumb of information about that part of his past with her, but she would not press. She would be patient and wait for him to unburden himself, in his own time, in his own manner.

"You have it," she promised him, her heart breaking for him. He was so proud and stoic, and she knew now why he had seemed so dangerous to her before she had grown to know him. He was always a solitary figure, forever seeming so alone, so harsh, all rigidity and angles and bleakness. But he was so much more than she had ever supposed. "You have me and my love forever."

"Nothing is forever." An indefinable emotion flitted across his face, but it was gone before she could study it. His countenance was once more unreadable, his jaw hard.

How beautiful he was, soaked to the skin, on his knees before her, handsome and fervent and hers. One month ago, she had been a maiden. How quickly everything had changed. How quickly she had changed. And she was grateful for those changes, grateful for this man. Grateful to be his.

"My love is forever," she promised him, and she meant those words. She meant them with everything in her. "I do not give it lightly. And I have not ever given it to another before you."

He did not respond in kind, and neither did she expect him to. This was a man who had made it painfully obvious to her that all he wanted was her body. But she longed for his love. Her feelings for him did not require reciprocation, though her heart certainly hoped for it. She would wait for him, give him all the patience he required.

"Thank you, darling," he told her solemnly.

His hands had lowered to her calves, and he caressed the silk of her stockings, his touch gliding maddeningly upward, beneath her chemise and petticoats, over her knees, past her garters until his bare flesh met hers. A breath hissed from her at the contact, the raw sensation. He had touched her so many times before, but each time felt more potent than the last.

Wordlessly, he guided her legs apart, and she let him. His thumbs traced slow, wicked circles on her inner thighs. And still, he pushed her skirts higher, all the way to her waist. Until she was nothing but riding boots, stockings, and splayed limbs. Until she was open to him, on display for him, his for the taking.

"Ah, Leonie." He trailed his kisses lower, his hands moving over her bare skin, soothing, inciting. His head dipped.

Her boots skidded over the uneven floorboards. Her thighs fell completely open, and cool air kissed her cunny in the moment before her husband did. His tongue traced her first, licking over her seam, parting her folds, finding the aching bud at her center, and sucking. Her hips bucked. White-hot pleasure seared her.

"Morgan." His name left her lips. This time, her fingers found purchase in his thick, wavy locks, sinking into them.

He licked her, his tongue flitting over her in disparate tempos. Slow and sure, long and fast, hard then soft, quick, a nip of his teeth. "Mmm." He sucked, then released her, his words spoken into her hungry flesh in yet another form of delicious torture. "So sweet, my Leonie. All of you. Everywhere."

Her ability to speak or think vanished. All she could do was feel and surrender to him utterly. His mouth upon her was glorious. She arched toward him, her body leaving the chair, seeking more of him, his pleasure, his sustenance, the release only he could give her. And then, as his mouth worked over her, he sank a finger deep inside her.

She bucked, taking him deeper.

"Yes, my darling," he murmured against her, his tongue flicking over her once more.

Another finger slid inside her. She was so slick, the wet sounds of him pleasuring her filled the cottage, above the din of the storm outside.

Leonora's head fell back, her eyes closing, and she lost herself. Need built within her, tightening into a knot, threatening to break.

She gave in. Felt her last grip upon her control break free. She reached her pinnacle, tightening around his fingers, thrusting herself shamelessly toward his mouth, seeking, seeking...

Him.

Seeking him as if he were all she needed.

Because he had become that to her, this man she loved. Her husband, the grim, cold stranger. The beautiful, giving lover. He was an enigma, a beautiful mystery, but he was hers, on his knees for her.

He kissed her inner thigh. "I love watching you spend, Leonie. You take my breath."

Just as he took hers. She opened her eyes to find his intense gaze upon her.

They had the rest of their lives for her to win his heart. And win it, she would.

"I AM WHOLEHEARTEDLY glad to see you managed to weather the storm unscathed, my lord," Huell Senior greeted Morgan and Leonie at the door upon their return to Westmore Manor.

"I am not so certain we emerged entirely unscathed," Leonie said with a secret smile, meeting Morgan's gaze.

He could not argue, for it was true. She was wet, her jaunty hat still soaked, her white-gold hair curling in damp tendrils about her beautiful face, her riding habit hopelessly wrinkled and damp, the hem muddied. He was no better, it was certain, in his own wet riding attire. But they had returned from their ride different than they had been when they had left. There was no denying it. Leonie was changing him. Had changed him already.

And he...he liked it.

He liked *her.*

"I beg your pardon, my lady, were either of you injured?" Huell Senior asked his marchioness.

"No, but I do thank you for your concern, Huell." Her cheeks flushing, she tore her gaze from Morgan's and settled it instead upon the hoary-haired domestic. "I was referring to the cloud that opened up overhead and drowned the both of us. I am certain I must look a fright."

"And I am equally certain a lady as lovely as you could never look a fright, even if she emerged dripping from a dip in the River Thames," Morgan quipped, flirting brazenly with his wife before a domestic and not giving a bloody damn. The boulder had not been removed from his chest, but it felt lighter after the time they had spent together in the old gamekeeper's cottage.

A new sensation, strange and bright, laden with possibilities, rose within him.

It had a name, he thought.

Hope.

For the first time in as long as he could recall, he had hope. Perhaps all was not lost for him yet. *Yes*, perhaps there was a way he could alter his plans. Mayhap he could deliver his vengeance upon the Earl of Rayne in a different fashion than the one he had originally settled upon.

The smile Leonie sent his way only served to buoy that sensation. He found himself grinning back at her.

"You flatter me, my lord." Her tone was sweet and low, and it sent an arrow of heat straight to his groin, which was deuced uncomfortable given he stood in the entry hall of Westmore Manor with his elderly butler as an audience.

He cleared his throat and attempted to count to twenty in Latin to distract himself.

Fortunately, Huell Senior dispelled the silence. "I took the liberty of seeing the earl settled in the amber chamber, my lord. He arrived whilst you and her ladyship were off on your ride."

The feeling within him froze and withered like a plant beneath the blight of an early winter frost. "I beg your pardon, Huell. Who might be the earl to whom you refer?"

Huell blinked, a slight furrow creasing his weathered brow. "The Earl of Rayne, my lord, her ladyship's brother, of course. He did mention he was expected, and weary after a long journey from abroad. Forgive me if I have acted in haste in his placement."

The boulder rolled back into place upon his chest, threatening to crush him.

Rayne was here. Beneath this very roof.

El Corazón Oscuro.

"Alessandro?" Leonie asked, her voice ringing with her shock. A shock that matched his. "But how can it be? He is on the Continent."

Yes indeed, how could it be? But of course, Morgan knew precisely how. He also knew why. The message he had sent Rayne had reached him. So, too, had the warning, just as he had planned.

Too soon, he thought. *Far too soon.*

The hairs on the back of Morgan's neck stood on end. His mouth went dry. In a blink, he returned to that horrible day when he had been taken captive by Rayne's guerrillas. He had been helpless on that day. And helpless on all the days that had come after until he had escaped at last.

He would not be helpless today.

A chill settled over him. The boulder was immovable, just as he must be.

The day of reckoning had arrived.

CHAPTER THIRTEEN

MORGAN PACED THE length of the Westmore Manor study yet again, irritation surging. His quarry had arrived, and he did not like to be kept waiting. Upon learning of their unexpected guest, Morgan had convinced Leonie to return to her chamber and change from her wet garments. She had reluctantly agreed, though her excitement at the prospect of seeing her brother was evident in her expression.

He, however, had not bothered to return to his chamber, instead, sending for Rayne and awaiting him in his father's old study. But though the earl had hunted Morgan down, it would appear he was in no hurry for their confrontation to occur, because he had yet to materialize in the flesh. Leaving Morgan with nothing to do save tramp up and down the faded Aubusson and grit his teeth whilst contemplating storming to the amber chamber and forcing the fox from his den.

In his next tour of the chamber, he noted a pair of dreary oil paintings depicting the hunt. The former Marquess of Searle had reveled in the sport of killing creatures smaller than himself. Here was one more part of the past that required removal. Morgan would need to replace the carpets and the wallcoverings. Even the desk, an ornate French affair, could go.

He had no wish for reminders of the man who had sired him. What he did wish for, was the opportunity to face Rayne. He had planned this moment so meticulously, but now that it had at last arrived, he felt oddly uncertain of how to proceed, what he would say first. Indeed, he felt...numb.

Because when he had first begun to lay the foundation for his revenge, he had never guessed the day would come when he would develop tender feelings for his wife, the woman who was meant to be his instrument of vengeance and nothing more. He had never even imagined Leonie would become so precious to him, nor that she would be so giving and beautiful and sweet.

He had never supposed she would fall in love with him.

Christ, what a mess he had made for himself.

A hell of his own making.

"Searle."

He spun about at the low, accented voice, the same voice that visited him occasionally in nightmares. There stood his nemesis, the Earl of Rayne. Dark-haired, dark-eyed, and soulless, his face an expressionless mask.

"We meet again, *El Corazón Oscuro*," he bit out grimly.

Rayne bared his teeth, but the snarl on his lips could hardly be called a smile. "Where the hell is my sister?"

His façade had slipped, and Morgan saw beneath it clearly. The earl was furious. A violent surge of satisfaction tore through him. "Do you refer to my marchioness, Rayne?"

The earl's jaw tightened as he stalked forward, fists clenched. Rayne was a large man, and Morgan knew the violence he was capable of, having seen him in action on the Peninsula. But Morgan matched him in size and viciousness. He stood his ground, unafraid.

"What have you done to her, *cerdo inglés*?" Rayne demanded.

English pig, he had called him. Morgan might remind the earl he, too, was half-English. But here was further evidence of how shaken the earl was, allowing his anger and his concern for Leonie—his only vulnerabilities—to show.

Morgan grinned. "Have you traveled all this way just to wish us happy? What a loving brother you are, my lord. Or shall I call you *Brother* now that we are family?"

"You had no right to include Leonora in this," Rayne spat.

"The Marchioness of Searle, I believe you meant to say." He could not resist the jibe. "She is mine now, after all. I took great pleasure in making certain of that."

A dull, angry flush crept over Rayne's face. "If you have hurt her, I will skin you alive, and then I will feed your mangled carcass to my swine."

"Your threats mean nothing to me," he countered, fairly vibrating with a rage of his own. "I am the dangerous one here on English soil, not you."

"It was you who had me removed from my post, was it not?" His accent grew even more pronounced.

Ah, victory. It did not feel as satisfying as he had supposed it would, but here, at last, was his opportunity to gloat. To know he alone had the upper hand. All the power.

"Did you truly believe I would not notify our superiors of your failure after I learned your true identity?" he countered.

"I am surprised you learned my identity at all, Searle." Rayne sneered. "You were always rather *estúpido*, no? Dull-witted."

Despite being the heir to an English earldom, Rayne had spent much of his life in his mother's homeland, and it showed in his speech. Morgan had conducted his research well, and he knew the strained relationship Rayne had shared with the former earl. He also knew Rayne had allowed his estates to be managed in his absence by an inept steward who was perhaps even swindling him, and that the entail was suffering badly. But above all, he knew Rayne's infrequent trips back to English shores had been for the sole purpose of seeing to his sister's wellbeing, the one duty in England which meant enough to him to force his return.

Leonie.

And that was where Morgan had decided to strike first.

"If I am stupid, what does that make you, Rayne?" Morgan countered coldly. "You jeopardized an entire mission by having me taken captive by your own forces."

At the time of his capture, Morgan had been leading a network of spies throughout the Peninsula. His mission on the day of his capture by Rayne's guerrillas had been to make his way behind enemy forces and ascertain their movements and positioning. Because of the danger of capture and the secretive nature of his mission, he had not been told who he was meeting in the Spanish countryside, only that his contact would appear following his and Crispin's meeting with *El Corazón Oscuro.*

"My men were meant to take you captive," Rayne countered. "I do not suppose Chapin told you that, did the spineless weasel?"

This information gave him pause. "Chapin told me nothing. I uncovered the information on my own. I know you were meant to escort me to the rendezvous point that day. But instead, in some foolish show of force, you had your men take me prisoner."

"It was not a show of force. I am feared enough without needing to take one English lord prisoner." Rayne's expression turned mocking. "I was carrying out orders. My men were to take you behind French lines."

Morgan thought of the cutthroats who had taken him captive. They had fought back against the French soldiers. Two of them had been killed, the others taken captive along with him. He had never seen them again. It had never occurred to him Rayne had acted in accordance with orders.

But there was also the very real—indeed, likely—possibility Rayne was lying to him now in order to allay the repercussions of his actions. Even if Chapin had somehow misled him about the true nature of the mission, however, the fact remained that Rayne's men had failed. And Morgan had been taken prisoner, tortured, and would have swung on the gallows if not for his desperate escape.

One man and one man alone had sent Morgan to what would have been his bloody, vicious death. One man was responsible for the scars on his back, the demons in his blood, the rage in his soul. And that man was the Earl of Rayne. That man deserved the retribution Morgan would feed him. That man deserved to know suffering, agony, and guilt.

"I do not give one good bloody goddamn what your orders were that day," he growled, a fresh tide of anger swelling within him. "You are responsible for what they did to me, and you must pay for your sins."

"If I must pay for my sins, then why the hell did you marry my sister?" Rayne growled.

He thought of the beatings, the lash of the whip upon his flesh, the smell of his own flesh burning, bitter and acrid. Of his fingers clawing through the soil, tunneling himself free, the darkness and the terror, the fear his tunnel would collapse, burying him alive, the realization spending his last moments breathing in dirt would be better than enduring another day of torment.

"So I could destroy you," Morgan answered with grim and brutal honesty. "If I make her miserable, her misery will be your misery. I will keep you from seeing her and any offspring we have together. She is completely in my control now, and you have no rights where she is concerned. I will do everything in my power to make certain you have no contact with her for the rest of your life. I want nothing more than your suffering. I was tortured and nearly killed by the French because of you, and if I must sacrifice your sister to bring you low, so help me God, I will."

A gasp tore through the chamber in the silence following his impassioned decree. Not his own, but female.

Familiar.

This time, the boulder crushed him as he met the gaze of his wife, who stood on the threshold of the study, freshly changed in a sprigged muslin afternoon gown that was as pale as her lovely face.

She had overheard his exchange with Rayne. He knew not how much, but he knew it was enough. *Jesus*, the hurt in her eyes. The accusation, the disbelief. It made him ill.

"Leonie," he said, moving toward her instinctively. He needed to explain. The words he had spoken had been meant for her brother. Not for her. Never for her. "It is not precisely as it seems."

She held up a staying hand. "No. Do not come any nearer to me, Searle. I demand an explanation."

"The explanation is simple, *hermanita*," Rayne said before Morgan could begin. "He married you to have his revenge upon me."

LEONORA FELT AS if she had received a blow to her midsection. As if all the air had been knocked from her lungs. She felt, for one sickening moment, the same way she had years ago as a girl during her fall from the banister at Marchmont Hall. Plummeting, the realization she could not save herself, the inevitable end awaiting her with all its horrible pain...the knowledge later, when she had wakened with the splint on her leg, knowing she would never again be the same. But now, she was more broken this time than she had been after that fall.

He married you to have his revenge upon me.

Her brother's words echoed in her mind, adding to her mounting misery. She would not have even believed them had she not just walked into the words of the man she loved, overhearing the vitriol in his tone, bitter as poison.

She is completely in my control now, and you have no rights where she is concerned... I want nothing more than your suffering...

It was almost as if another man had spoken those words, as if another man stood before her now. The Marquess of Searle was even more of a stranger than she had supposed. Colder and more dangerous than she had feared. Vicious, just as she had always known.

And she was a fool. A hopeless, wallflower spinster, so green in the ways of men and women, she had fallen quickly beneath his spell. He had kissed her and touched her, held her, made love to her. He had made her feel wanted for the first time.

But he had not wanted her at all, had he? No, he had wanted to use her. He had wanted her only to gain some sort of vengeance upon Alessandro. He had used her and manipulated her, and she had given him her heart.

She pressed a hand to her stomach, the sudden urge to retch so strong and so violent she nearly lost control of herself. There was only one question she wished to ask her husband, for it would answer all the others, and it would tell her what she must do.

Leonora inhaled slowly, then exhaled, looking only at Searle. His green gaze was dark. Impervious as ever. "Did you marry me with the intention of gaining some sort of revenge upon my brother?"

He did not hesitate. "Yes."

She cried out, unable to contain the sound of her own anguish even though she could not bear to appear weak before him. Or at least, not any weaker than he already supposed her to be.

"Leonie," he said softly, stepping closer.

The mere sound of her name on his lips—*nay*, she reminded herself, not her name, but the one he had given her, the one that had begun to feel like hers—filled her with disgust, with rage.

With a crippling sadness.

"No." She took a step in retreat, making certain she was beyond his reach. "I do not want you to touch me. Not now, and not ever again."

"Leonie, you are my wife," he persisted, his jaw going rigid. "I can offer an explanation."

As she saw it, there was not one explanation he could offer which would not break her heart into tiny shards before grinding them beneath his boot heel for good measure. She swallowed against a humiliating rush of tears. "I do not wish to hear it, Searle."

"Leonora, come back to London with me," Alessandro urged.

She turned to her brother, a fresh ache in her heart. It had been too long since she had last seen him, far too long. He looked older, more lines bracketing his dark eyes and his mouth. His countenance was harsh and grim. He looked like a man who had stared into hell and could not forget what he had seen. Much the same as Searle did. But then he moved toward her as well, his brown eyes glittering with sympathy, his arm extended, and she found comfort in that gesture. Comfort in the familiar warmth of the brother she had always known and loved.

She nodded, thinking of nothing but her need to escape. To put distance between herself and Searle. "Yes, Alessandro. Take me back to London, if you please. I cannot remain here with him."

"No," Searle denied, his tone cold. Flat. "You will not leave me, Leonie."

Her gaze went back to him as a horrible realization hit her. "You planned this all along, did you not?"

Dear God, she was an even greater fool than she had supposed. So easily led astray by a handsome man paying her court. It would seem she had learned nothing from all the years she had spent as a wallflower, living her life on the periphery. Handsome war hero marquesses did not dance with crippled spinsters, did they? Nor did they ruin them and then marry them.

He stared back at her, a muscle ticking in his jaw, before he responded at last. "I planned to wed you, yes. But everything that came afterward, Leonie, I did not plan. I could never have planned that."

She felt as if she were seeing him for the first time. He was a monster. She had married a heartless, cruel, bitter man. "You ruined me intentionally."

It was not a question but an accusation, though she need not have said it aloud, for she already knew the answer.

He inclined his head, his sensual lips flattened into a thin, grim line. "Yes. I did."

Alessandro clutched Searle by his rain-flattened cravat. "What the hell did you do to her?"

Searle smiled grimly, calmly, almost as if he took pleasure in Alessandro's lack of control, as if it was what he wanted. "What do you think I did to her, Rayne?"

Alessandro growled deep in his throat. "I will see you on the field of honor for that, *cerdo.*"

"No," Leonora cried out, hastening forward in an effort to separate her husband and her brother, to defuse the situation before Searle could accept her brother's challenge. She had no wish for a duel to be fought between the two men, regardless of how much hurt and humiliation she had endured at the marquess's hands. "You will not fight a duel in my name. The two of you will settle whatever rancor lies between you in some other fashion."

"Name your second," Searle said, ignoring her.

There was a fire in his eyes she had never seen before, a finality to his tone. He had planned this as well, she realized. The satisfaction in his voice could not be mistaken, for she had heard it often enough to recognize. There was no question. Searle *wanted* to fight her brother in a duel.

Her desperation reached a new crescendo, and as she increased her pace, determined to break up their glaring match and standoff before it was too late, her injured leg gave out on her. She fell to the carpet in a mortified heap of muslin and petticoats, her humiliation complete. Pain radiated from the old break, shooting up her leg.

"Leonie."

"Leonora."

Two men fell at her side, and she had to choose which one of them to seek for aid. Which one she dared to trust. She turned away from Searle, arms reaching toward her brother instead.

CHAPTER FOURTEEN

HIS OPPORTUNITY FOR revenge had arrived sooner and swifter than he had anticipated. Morgan should have been well-pleased. Rayne had challenged him to a duel. They would meet on the field of honor. Morgan could put his bullet between Rayne's eyes, precisely where it belonged. He could end his quest for vengeance.

But as he sat alone in the study that still looked as if his hateful father may walk over the threshold at any moment and demand Morgan vacate his chair, he felt none of the satisfaction he ought to feel. Instead, he stared at a half-drained brandy snifter, still wearing his riding clothes though they had long since dried upon his person. No, he did not celebrate the achievement of his goal, success so close.

He should be thinking of the return trip to London on the morrow, the duel he would fight several days hence. He should be sending word to Monty, who would act as his second, asking him to prepare his pistols. He should be happy, envisioning the look of surprise on Rayne's face as he took his last, halting breath.

But all he could think about was the sight of Leonie in a heap of skirts upon the floor. Her leg had given out on her, and she had collapsed, had been in physical pain to rival the emotional pain he had already inflicted upon her, and he had wanted nothing more than to soothe those aches. Of course, she had not turned to him for aid. He had not been the one whose hands she clasped. He had not been the man who gently helped her to her feet and escorted her from the chamber.

No, that honor had gone to the Earl of Rayne. Her brother. His nemesis. The man he was going to kill.

He lifted the brandy to his lips and took a long, satisfying draught. His plans continued to unfold with flawless, almost effortless precision. Forcing Rayne into challenging him had always been his plan. In truth, he had supposed such an accomplishment may have required a more extensive foundation to be laid by him. He had not imagined the earl would be so easily manipulated into taking action.

Nor had he imagined how badly it would hurt to see his wife's reaction as her facile mind quickly and cleverly surmised the ugly truth he had done his best to avoid since wedding her. He had not married her with good intentions. He had sought her out, hunted her down much as his hated father had done with countless game. And how easily he had routed her. How effortlessly.

She had danced with him, been alone with him, and with her reputation at risk, she had capitulated instantly, agreeing to become his wife. What had happened after their vows had taken him by surprise, however. He had never intended for her to develop tender feelings for him, and nor had he intended to become so besotted by her that the sight of her hurt caused him a physical pain, as if someone had gutted him with a bayonet.

Their earlier ride and subsequent idyll in the gamekeeper's cottage seemed a world away now. She had told him, once again, that she loved him. He had never wanted to hear those words. Nor did he wish for those words to affect him as they did, settling deep inside him, finding their home in a place he had no longer believed capable of emotion.

He drained the remnants of his brandy and rose from his desk, stalking across the Aubusson to pour himself another. After securing the next futile attempt at abating the guilt threatening to drown him, he grasped the ormolu bell pull—crafted in the likeness of a fox, also chosen by the former Marquess of Searle, naturally—and rang for Huell Senior.

The faithful retainer appeared promptly. "How may I be of service, my lord?"

"Did Lady Searle accept the tray I sent to her chamber?" he asked.

Leonie had refused to dine with him, and he had been forced to share a demoralizing meal with no one but himself for company. Rayne, too, had eschewed the meal, but Morgan did not give a damn if the bastard perished from starvation. His only thoughts were for his wife. When he had inquired after her welfare, he had been told she had not wished for sustenance, that her ladyship was feeling ill.

An illness he had caused.

He wondered if her love for him had already withered and died, turning into hatred. Should Rayne somehow get lucky with his aim when they met on the field of honor, she would likely not even mourn his death.

"It was declined, my lord," Huell Senior replied.

Damn it. Surely, furious with him though she was, she must possess some hunger.

"See that another tray is taken to the marchioness's chamber, and this time make certain the servant who delivers it insists that it is taken inside."

She needed to eat, and he refused to allow her to make herself ill because she was being stubborn. She could already be carrying his babe, and if she was, she needed to keep her strength. An idea occurred to him then. "And Huell? See to it that strawberries are delivered with the meal, if you please."

"Of course, my lord. Will there be anything else, sir?" Huell Senior was expressionless as ever. If he noted a disparity between the flushed, happy marchioness who had returned with Morgan from their ride earlier and the pale, joyless woman who had retreated to her chamber as if it were a shield behind which she could hide, he did not show it.

"That will be all, thank you," he forced himself to say, waiting until the domestic had gone once more to drain the remainder of his brandy.

Let the fruit be a reminder to her of all they had shared. It was the only gesture he dared, and even this symbolic offering he knew he should avoid, but he could not help himself. Before she had left his study in the company of the odious Rayne, she had told him she never wanted to see him or speak to him again.

The coldness of her voice still shook him now. She had not yelled, had not railed against him. Instead, she had been passionless, as though all the life and vibrancy had been stolen from her.

And he was the one who had stolen it, he supposed. He had taken what was not his, her love, her trust, her innocence. Everything she possessed. Even her dowry, meager though it had been, was his.

He had manipulated and used her. He had also deceived her.

Her whispered words from their moment of tender passion in the gamekeeper's cottage earlier returned to him, mocking, reminding him of all he had lost.

Morgan, I love you.

But he had destroyed that love. Just as he had destroyed her. She had been the only light in his darkness. The best damn thing to have ever happened to him. And he had ruined her. Ruined whatever tender feelings she once possessed for him.

He poured another brandy, took a sip, and then he hurled his full snifter into the fireplace, savoring the crash as glass collided with brick. It shattered into a thousand jagged slivers. All the glittering pieces that remained were useless and dangerous.

Just like him.

LEONORA TOLD HERSELF she was prepared for siege.

She had locked the door between her chamber and Searle's. She had refused to descend to dinner and sit at her husband's side as if nothing had occurred. She had also refused the tray which had been sent to her following her polite—and disingenuous—refusal. The supper tray had almost certainly been *his* doing, and she did not wish to eat a morsel of food if her husband was the source of its offering.

She was not ill as she had claimed, but she felt as if she were. Her heart ached. Her stomach was a sea of sickness. Her head pounded, and in all, she had never felt more miserable than she did now. She could blame it on getting caught in the unexpected thunderstorms during her ride. She could claim a lung infection had settled upon her, and it would do as an excuse.

For the moment, at least. She would not feel guilty for the deception she was perpetrating upon the household. After all, the Marquess of Searle had never known a moment of guilt for the deception he had perpetrated upon her.

The uncomfortable settee in the sitting area had become her haven in the last few hours. A place she had eschewed altogether, for its outmoded and rigid furnishings—from thirty years prior or more, unless she missed her guess—had been uninviting in the extreme. The old and faded wall coverings, the worn rugs, the tired pictures on the walls, and grim furniture had not been worthy of her concern before, because she had never intended to spend her evenings trapped within the confines of the chambers.

But they bothered her now, for they were pointed reminders. Reminders she did not belong here. Reminders that everything she had experienced as the Marchioness of Searle thus far, had been a lie.

A carefully cultivated, horrible lie.

The breath left her once more, and she sat, fully dressed in the sprigged muslin afternoon gown she had changed into upon her earlier return from riding with her husband. *Nay*, not her husband, for that title seemed far too intimate for what the Marquess of Searle was to her.

In truth, he was a stranger. Perhaps even an enemy. How easily and fluently he had crafted his deception, making her believe he was honorable enough to wed her after he had ruined her. In truth, he had not been concerned for her wellbeing at all. He had ruined her quite intentionally, knowing who she was, knowing how he would use her to incite her brother's reaction.

At least she had Caesar for companionship, his warm little body curled against her in feline fashion, gently snoring whilst she fretted away and absentmindedly scratched his silken head. She had reclaimed the dog, taking back the gift she had given him, for he did not deserve the loyal adoration of the pup. His machinations deserved suffering and loneliness. Machinations that still confused her and left her reeling from her untenable position in the morass he had fashioned for her.

There remained much she needed to decipher.

Pieces of her past interactions with him returned to haunt her now. How foolish she had been to think him honest. To think him a good man suffering from the scars of his past.

In truth, the scars she had seen and felt upon his flesh were only a small part of the story.

And it all made horrible, disgusting sense. She was a spinster wall-flower who suffered from an unfortunate limp, the laughingstock of her peers. Her only suitor prior to Searle, was a lord who intended to win a handful of notes in a wager. How stupid she had been. How shamefully, embarrassingly easy to manipulate.

She felt silly now. And stupid. So very stupid for falling prey to his handsome face and knowing hands and skillful lips. An intelligent woman such as herself ought to have known the difference. She should have deciphered his true motivation. If she had, she could have avoided all of this…

Suffering.

Yes, that was the only manner in which one could reasonably explain the sad state in which she found herself. She was suffering. Lonely and miserable and mortified, ashamed of herself, hungry because her pride had not allowed her to consume dinner, and—

A knock sounded upon her door just then, interrupting the ragged meanderings of her mind. Caesar started into wakefulness, letting out a sharp yip of disapproval. Leonora calmed him with some gentle, reassuring pats.

"You may enter," she called, not wishing to cross the chamber, and open the door herself. Her leg was paining her more than ordinary after her fall earlier. As if realizing she had been deceived and manipulated by Searle had not been humiliating enough, her graceless plummet to the floor had heightened the indignity.

She supposed her visitor was another servant bearing a tray or perhaps her lady's maid. But she was startled when Alessandro entered the chamber, closing the door softly at his back. Her half-brother was tall, far taller than she, bearing the dark hair and eyes of his mother. His stubborn jaw, high cheekbones, and the blade of his nose were all their father, however.

"Rayne," she greeted warmly, her heart singing with gratitude that he had returned to check upon her.

When he had delivered her to her chamber earlier, she had been too distraught to give him a proper greeting. After several hours of solitude, she had calmed herself enough to allow happiness to overtake her at this unexpected reunion with him, even if it had occurred for all the wrong reasons. She loved Alessandro very much, and she was pleased to see him once more, though this new version of him appeared harder, harsher, and gaunter than the brother who had last departed for Spain.

"Forgive me, am I intruding, *hermanita?*" he asked, his accent less pronounced now than it had been earlier during his angry confrontation with Searle.

"Of course not. You could never intrude," she assured him.

"Come, sit with me."

Caesar growled, his hackles raising. She patted the pug, calming him, wishing the little fellow had exhibited the same protective instinct whenever she had been in Searle's presence. Perhaps she would have taken a hint from his instincts and guarded her heart better.

Alessandro seated himself opposite her, looking brooding and dark and very much out of place in the faded femininity of the marchioness's apartments. "Are you in much pain, my dear?"

Only the most excruciating pain she had ever experienced. A broken heart hurt more than a broken bone, the agony blossoming from within, radiating throughout her entire body. Not even falling from the staircase as a girl had been so traumatic. Or perhaps it was that too much time had elapsed, and her memories had begun to fade. She could not be certain.

All she *was* certain of was that she hurt. *Dear God*, did she hurt. Everywhere.

She swallowed down another rush of tears, brought on by the combination of her brother's concern, and her inner self-loathing. "I shall be fine." The smile she managed for Alessandro's benefit was tremulous at best. She wondered if her nose was red and swollen.

His countenance gentled with sympathy. "Is it the old break in your bone, or is it your pride?"

"Both." She sniffed. "But, also, my heart, I am afraid."

Her brother's jaw clenched. "You have feelings for Searle, *hermanita?*"

She nodded grimly, unable to form the words lest she once more burst into tears.

"I will kill him," he vowed savagely. Rage vibrated in his voice, darkening his expression. "I was going to shoot to maim him on the field of honor, but by God, I shall kill him for you, Leonora. No one in the world would mourn such a vile excuse for a man."

"No," she implored, finding her voice at last. "I do not want the two of you to duel. I beg of you, cry off. Do not go."

She feared for her brother, and in truth, she feared for Searle as well. She had witnessed the virulence of the enmity between the two men with her own eyes, and she did not know what each was capable of. As angry and hurt as she was, as deeply entrenched in despair over Searle's betrayal, she did not wish for anything ill to befall him. And neither did she want Alessandro to be injured or worse on her behalf.

Alessandro's expression tightened even further, his mouth flattening into a pinched line. "I must go. He had no right to use you as a pawn in his quarrel against me. You are my family, my sister. Can you truly believe I would allow him to ruin you without making him answer for his sins?"

She flinched, for here was the answer she feared. While Alessandro had spent much of her life abroad where he felt more at home than within the stifling constraints of English ballrooms, he was her brother, and she loved him fiercely. Like her, he was an outsider, laughed at behind fans because his mother had been a Spanish tavern wench when she had wed Leonora and Alessandro's father. From all accounts, Alessandro's mother had been miserable as a countess until her untimely death, even though her match with the former earl had been one founded in love.

"I was not ruined, Alessandro," she said, using his given name for effect. "Searle and I were alone in a salon when Mama and some of my friends happened upon us."

"Ruined," her brother repeated grimly. "Precisely as that bastard intended."

"What happened between the two of you?" she asked then, needing to know. She had overheard fragments of his conversation with Searle, but not enough for her to know for certain what had occurred between them.

Alessandro's lip curled. "What happened is none of your concern."

Irritation surged within her, momentarily supplanting her inner torment. "How dare you say such a thing? The bad blood between you is the reason I now find myself here, the Marchioness of Searle, with a husband who has spent the entirety of our acquaintance lying to me."

Her brother made a low sound of disgust. "All the more reason for me to aim with the intention of killing."

"Alessandro," she bit out, the ferocity of her response making Caesar stir uneasily at her side. "Please."

His nostrils flared. He resembled nothing so much as a horse about to bolt. But at last, he appeared to calm himself, relenting. "It is not done to speak of war before a lady."

"I do not care," she countered. "We are not in a drawing room, and the laws of propriety do not govern us here, not with so much at stake. Tell me, Alessandro. I deserve to know, do I not?"

A guttural, vicious oath escaped him, but it was in his mother's tongue and not hers, so its definition was lost upon Leonora, and she deemed her ignorance just as well. For the expression upon her brother's face was murderous.

"You wish to know? Very well," he growled. "I shall tell you. I have been aiding our army in my mother's homeland. Because I have spent so much time there, because I have a reputation amongst the people, I am able to move freely there. Unlike here, I am trusted there, treated with honor and respect. When the war came to us, I decided I needed to do my part."

Of course he would. His most recent, lengthy absence from home made perfect sense now.

"Oh, Alessandro," she said softly, her heart aching for him. All this time, she had imagined him simply gone, and he had been at war. "What have you done?"

He shook his head. "You need not worry yourself with it, *hermanita*. I am here when many other good men are not. I was working with our army, using my men to pierce enemy lines and obtain important information about their positions. I was meant to aid Searle, but the detail I sent with him was ambushed by French troops and he was taken captive. My men were either slain or taken prisoner and then sent to the gallows."

Leonora pressed a hand over her mouth to stifle a sudden sob that threatened to break free. She had not imagined. Had not even begun to guess at the true nature of Searle's hatred for her brother or the reason for it.

"He believes you are responsible for his capture," she concluded at last.

"Yes, the fool does," Alessandro acknowledged, his tone grim. "And not just that, but that I somehow arranged it. He thinks I personally arranged for my men to capture him to make myself seem more fearsome. In truth, I was acting upon the orders of our superior, who felt Searle would be better served in the event of his capture to be viewed as the prisoner of Spanish guerrilla soldiers rather than being complicit with them. Napoleon's army executes spies. If Searle had been considered a spy…"

"He never would have escaped," Leonora finished for her brother. Even though Searle had hurt her badly, and even though he was safe and presumably somewhere in the vicinity of his study, entertaining himself with drink and his own bitterness for company, the notion of Searle facing execution sent a shiver down her spine.

Alessandro inclined his head. "He would have been hanged on the gallows, without question. Dozens of better men than the Marquess of Searle have already been captured and met their fates at the end of the hangman's noose."

Another thought occurred to her then. Or rather, another question she wanted to know the answer to. "Was Searle a spy?"

Her brother did not hesitate. "One of the best. His capture was a tremendous blow, and I have taken the blame for it."

"From others, beyond Searle?" she probed.

"Yes, *hermanita*. From my superior officers. From everyone who is important." Alessandro's lip curled. "When Searle escaped, he made certain everyone was aware I was responsible for his confinement, at least in his version of events. He made a campaign of undermining my credibility. I lost my position on the same day I received word my sister was being forced to marry the Marquess of Searle. Information which was kindly sent by your bastard-of-a-husband."

She struggled to make sense of the information he had just divulged. "I do not understand, Alessandro. How could Searle make you lose your position?"

"Easily." Her brother's smile was bleak. "I never purchased a commission, and my involvement with the army was informal, at best. When I was no longer useful to them, they turned their backs upon me. But not before letting me know my sister had become the means by which Searle intended to gain his vengeance upon me."

"Searle wanted you to know he had compromised me," she said, her mind frantically working.

"The message was sent by him, and it was received by me." Her brother paused, the frown on his brow deepening. "It is the reason I left Spain and returned to England with as much haste as possible. It is also the reason why I followed the two of you here rather than awaiting your return to London. I could not bear to think of another day of you being at his mercy. Has he harmed you physically? If he has, I will call the devil out this very night, our seconds be damned."

It had not occurred to her until that very moment just how badly a part of her had been hoping Searle's deceptions had not been as egregious as she had initially supposed. Just how badly she had longed for evidence of his innocence rather than his guilt, proof he had not intended to use her against her brother, proof he had not been so reckless or careless with her love for him.

But it would seem she was doomed for disappointment, because the Marquess of Searle had not only planned to use her against Alessandro; he had laid the foundation with the efficiency of a master builder. Stone by stone, beam by beam, he had raised the testament to his hatred from the ground. And he had built that hatred into a thing of awful, ugly beauty. He had built it until it festered and ruined everything in its wake.

Her tongue felt as numb as the rest of her at this latest realization of the depths of her husband's betrayal. But she forced herself to speak anyway, because she knew her brother expected an answer and because she could not bear for any more violence or upset this evening.

She wanted peace.

She was tired.

And sad.

So very, very sad.

"Searle has never raised a hand against me." Her voice was flat and dull, even to her own ears. A testament to the turmoil raging through her. Her brother had revealed so much, and she had so many questions. She required so many answers. "He would not harm me physically."

Of that much, she was certain. The marquess was a confusing and complicated man. But she did not fear him. His touch had only ever brought her pleasure. Though Searle had savaged her heart, she would not pretend he had harmed her otherwise when her brother posed the question.

"I will spare him for another day, then," her brother growled.

"You will not face him in a duel," she insisted. Even after everything she had heard, she did not wish for her brother and her husband to face each other with pistols at dawn.

"I must, *hermanita*."

Her brother's voice was tinged with a sad acceptance, as if he, too, did not wish to fight a duel but somehow found it necessary.

"You must not," she countered, and at last, all the fragments in her mind came together, settling into awful, ruinous place. "Only think of it, Alessandro. A duel is precisely what he wants from you. Why else would Searle have conducted such a concerted campaign here in England, making every effort to reach you abroad? Why would he have made certain word of his compromising me reached you? He wanted you to leave Spain, and he wanted you to come back to England to avenge my honor. He wants to duel you."

Because he wants to kill you.

The last sentence hung unsaid in the air between Leonora and her half-brother. But it was true, nonetheless. She saw it all so clearly now, for though her husband had done his best to hide his true intentions from her, she knew precisely what they were now. She realized, too, why he had acted as he had.

"I understand Searle," Alessandro said then, his tone bitter. "Perhaps better than he knows himself. In Spanish, we have a way to describe men who are forever changed by the horrors they have seen at war, *estar roto*. He is a man broken, and he blames me for whatever he faced at the hands of the French. He will not give in until he has what he wants. Nothing has stopped him yet."

Estar roto.

The unfamiliar phrase turned itself over in her mind. Yes, the Marquess of Searle was a man who was broken on the inside, where he wore even more scars than he did on his skin. Little wonder he had never confided in her. That he had never shared anything more than the physical with her. Caring for her was beyond his capacity. His quest for vengeance had overtaken him, until nothing remained for her.

"I do not believe in this duel," she persisted. For the more she thought about it, the more terrified she became.

No good could come from Searle and Alessandro meeting each other with pistols at dawn. The past had already shaped them, made them who they were, left them scarred. Sins had already been committed which could not be undone.

"I love you, *hermanita*, and I will make him pay for what he has done to you," her brother told her, rising to his feet. "See that you get some rest this evening. Tomorrow will be a long journey back to London, and I hate to see you in pain."

"Alessandro." She gripped his coat sleeve when he leaned down to buss a brotherly kiss over the crown of her head. "If you love me, you will not do this."

"Rest now." His mouth was once more compressed into a harsh line. "My love for you is the reason I am meeting him on the field of honor."

Leonora watched her brother take his leave, a true feeling of helplessness swelling within her like a river after heavy rains.

Sometime later, a second supper tray arrived. She did not miss the brilliant red strawberries in their fine porcelain bowl, in stark contrast to the muted colors of the rest of the meal.

And she knew without question Searle had sent them to her.

Why? To mock her, or as a reminder? She could not be certain. All she did know was that, despite her growling stomach, she could not bear to eat a single bite of food from him.

"Tell his lordship the thought of strawberries makes me want to retch," she relayed to the maid who bore the tray.

If only it did.

CHAPTER FIFTEEN

MORGAN TOLD HIMSELF it was just as well his idyll at Westmore Manor—a false happiness, not meant to last—had come to an abrupt end. He told himself he did not miss her delicate floral scent or the soft, seductive sounds his wife made when she spent. He told himself he was on the precipice of garnering what he had wanted ever since he had burrowed his way out of the old stone barn in which he had been kept during his imprisonment, revenge.

And then, he told himself to finish his claret and pour another.

So, he did.

What else was there to do, after all, awaiting the appearance of his scapegrace cousin, who was presently not at home according to the disapproving butler? If Monty was *not at home*, it meant he was probably still abed, even though it was nearly four o'clock in the afternoon. Not much had changed in Morgan's absence while he was away at war, at least not where his cousin was concerned. Monty had become a duke early in life, and, blessed with the sort of looks that made the fairer sex swoon, he spent his days drinking and fucking his way through the demireps and dissatisfied wives of London.

Morgan was halfway through his second claret when Monty appeared at the threshold, clad in what appeared to be the previous day's evening wear. His breeches were rumpled, and he wore no coat, only shirtsleeves, waistcoat, and flattened cravat. His hair was mussed, and beneath his eyes, he sported the telltale bruises of a man who had spent the night carousing.

"Seated upon my throne," drawled Monty, raising a brow. "Drinking my bloody claret. What is next, Searle? Tupping my mistresses?"

Mistresses. Naturally, Monty possessed more than one.

But there was only one female he wished to tup, and it was the same female who had refused to dine with him, speak to him, and subsequently, ride in a carriage with him for the lengthy return trip to London the day before. Nor had she deigned to acknowledge him this morning, so he had promptly left Linley House in search of his errant cousin. He chased those thoughts from his mind, because he had not ferreted out Monty so he might pine over Leonie.

Morgan stood, vacating his cousin's chair. "You look as if you spent the evening swilling blue ruin and slept in your clothes," he told Monty.

Monty's dissipation was an old story, but Morgan had spent the last few years staring into the face of not just his own mortality but that of everyone around him. As he traded places with his cousin, he could not help but to think Monty was getting older. Three-and-thirty now. Surely far too old to still be playing the young buck about town.

"You sound like my mother," Monty quipped, grinning unrepentantly. "She pecks me like a hen. *Montrose, you need a wife. Montrose, you need an heir. Montrose, you must stop drinking to excess. Montrose, if you insist upon keeping company with slatterns, you will get the pox.* It's all deadly boring. I do not regret sending her to Scotland with my sister for a moment."

Morgan had just taken a healthy gulp of his claret when his cousin had begun his impersonation of Aunt Letitia. The falsetto, combined with the bit about the pox, nearly made him choke. "Good God, please tell me Aunt did not say anything so untoward."

"She did," Monty confirmed, splashing some claret into a glass for himself and settling into his chair with an undignified plop. "Now tell me why you have come, daring to rouse me from my much-needed slumber. As you mentioned, I had not even the time to prepare myself, and I have been forced to greet you in the garments in which I slept. Dreadfully *de trop*, I am afraid."

Under other circumstances, Morgan would have laughed at Monty's lighthearted dismissal of his indulgences the night before. But there was too much turmoil roiling within him. Too many important matters weighing upon his mind.

"I need you to act as my second," he blurted.

Monty sobered instantly—as much as his cousin could ever sober, that was. "Your second?"

"I am facing the Earl of Rayne on the field of honor. Will you stand with me?" he asked.

His cousin frowned. "The Earl of Rayne is your wife's brother, Searle."

He did not flinch. "Yes."

"You are facing him in a duel? Why? I thought you hadn't even lifted the Forsythe chit's skirts."

His blood boiled at Monty's casual reference to Leonie. "You are speaking of my marchioness, Montrose."

"Erm, of course. Do forgive me." Monty took a gulp of his claret and closed his eyes. "Ah, yes. Beginning to feel more like a gentleman than a dog again. Claret in the morning is just the thing."

"No amount of claret can turn you into a gentleman," he could not resist pointing out. After all, it was true. He loved his cousin, but Monty was...*Monty*. "And I do hate to relay this information to you, but we are, in fact, in the midst of the afternoon."

"The devil it is. I've only just woken up." Outrage tinged Monty's voice.

"Christ," he muttered, raking a hand through his hair. "Will you be my second for the bloody duel, or do I need to find a substitute?"

"Of course I shall, but you never answered me." Monty paused, raking him with a searching glance. "Why Rayne? And since when is he returned to London? I thought the strange fellow did not like our cold and rainy shores."

Morgan downed the content of his glass and then held it out for Monty to replenish. "Rayne is responsible for my capture in Spain. I mean to kill him."

"Christ!" Monty's hands shook in the act of pouring, sending claret running all over the desk. "You cannot mean to kill the man. You will be jailed for committing murder."

Morgan watched the red liquid spreading over the polished surface of his cousin's desk, much like pooling blood, and he could not shake the feeling it was an omen of sorts. Blood would be spilled. His or Rayne's. Either way, their duel would be to the death.

The thought set his jaw on edge. Where once the thought of his vengeance costing him his life had seemed a paltry price to pay, he could not deny how much Leonie had changed him.

"Are you prepared for such an eventuality, Cousin?" Monty pressed, surprisingly insightful.

He thought of Leonie's beautiful face. Her voice. Long waves of white-blonde hair, kisses that stole his breath, a touch that was so tender he could not help but to feel it in the deepest recesses of his black soul. He thought of picnics by the stream at Westmore Manor, of flowers and strawberries, of pleasure and passion.

I love you, Morgan.

She could be carrying his babe. Could he leave a child behind in the world? Could he leave Leonie?

And then cold realization intruded. None of that mattered, for she would not forgive him for his betrayal. He thought of the manner in which she had looked upon him, as if he were a stranger. As if he had broken her heart. And perhaps he had.

The words of the servant who had sent her the second dinner tray returned to him, just as vicious now as they had been then.

Forgive me, my lord, but her ladyship says to tell his lordship the thought of strawberries makes her want to retch.

209

"I am prepared," he said grimly.

"I AM PREPARED to put a stop to it however I must," Leonora told Freddy.

Shock rendered her dear friend's expression slack. "Rayne and Searle cannot truly intend to duel."

"I am afraid they do." She took a deep, calming breath lest her upset once more take control of her. After having relayed the entirety of her sad tale to Freddy upon her return to London, she was desperate for her friend's advice. "I have asked my brother to reconsider, and he will not."

"What of Searle? Have you confronted him?" Freddy asked, anger coloring her voice. "How dare the rotter ruin you, my best friend, at my very own ball, with the intention of using you in such a nefarious manner? Why, I would like to duel him myself for hurting you."

"Oh, Freddy." Tears welled in her eyes on a sudden, fresh wave of emotion. But she refused to allow them to fall, and so she furiously blinked them into submission. "You cannot duel on my behalf, though I do appreciate the vehemence of your affections. Would that others would feel so inclined to care for me."

"Surely Searle cares for you, at least in some fashion," Freddy argued then. "You seemed so happy on your last visit, and then you left for your honeymoon. I had such high hopes for you."

"As did I," she admitted, dejected. "I am hopelessly confused, for I have lost my heart to him...or at least, to the side of him he showed me in the last fortnight. It was a different Searle, Freddy. He was tender and sweet, as if his only task in the world was to please me. I felt as if I had come to life for the first time in his arms. Does that sound foolish?"

"Not at all, darling." Freddy shook her head. "It sounds like what a wife ought to feel for her husband. Indeed, it sounds *precisely* like the way I feel whenever I am with Mr. Kirkwood."

Somehow, her friend's revelation only increased her sense of dejection. "But what you and Mr. Kirkwood share is a true and real love. What I shared with Searle was one-sided, built upon lies and manipulations. He only married me so he could provoke Alessandro into dueling with him and gain his revenge."

"Revenge is an ugly and dark beast, is it not?" Freddy asked quietly, her expression pensive now. "But if you will recall, Duncan and I fell in love under similar circumstances."

That much was true. Mr. Kirkwood had been determined to gain vengeance against the father who had abandoned him in his youth, and in so doing, he had used Freddy to gain what he wanted. In the end, he had done everything in his power to win Freddy back.

Leonora swallowed thickly. "But you and Mr. Kirkwood were in love. Searle does not love me. I am not even certain he cares for me."

"Angry as I am at him for his mistreatment of you, I cannot help but to wonder, Leonora," Freddy surprised her by saying. "I think back to the manner in which he was aiding you at the ball. He seemed genuinely concerned for your comfort. And knowing you as I do, I am certain you would not have fallen in love with a man who never showed you any kindness or affection. Surely you had inklings that he cared?"

Her friend's words gave her pause, made her search through her mind for a re-visitation of all her interactions with her husband. He had made love to her for the first time with gentle care and beautiful consideration. He had gifted her the Searle rubies and told her she was an angel. He called her Leonie, and his kisses melted her. When he made love to her, he worshiped her—there was no other word for the glorious manner in which he made her body come to life.

How could the Searle she had come to know in the last few weeks be the same man who planned to destroy her?

"I…" she allowed her words to trail away, realizing she had no idea of the manner in which she ought to answer Freddy. Had Searle given her reasons to believe he cared for her? *Yes.* Had he also betrayed her brutally? *Yes.* "I do not know what to think or believe or trust, Freddy. As terrified as I am that he fooled me, I am more afraid I fooled myself. That I was so desperate for the husband and family I have longed for, I was too blind to see what was plainly before me."

"No." Freddy's response was as instant as her frown. "You are not to blame for the situation in which you find yourself. Searle is."

"But I am a fool, am I not?" This time Leonora could not contain her tears. "Because I love him still, even after realizing what he has done. I cannot simply stop my heart from feeling."

Her misery rolled through her, pouring out as sobs. How could she love him after his betrayal? How did he retain the power to make her so weak? Why did she long for him, even now? It made no sense. Her heart was a confused, hopeless mess.

Freddy sat beside her on the settee, drawing her into an embrace. "You are not a fool, darling. Searle is. Shall I box his ears for you now?"

She hugged her friend tightly, sniffling into Freddy's shoulder. "No."

"Are you certain? I would like nothing better."

A laugh bubbled up inside her. Ridiculous, but there it was, levity in the midst of great sadness. Only true friends could accomplish such a feat. "Thank you, but no. If anyone shall box Searle's ears, it will be me."

Freddy's hand moved over her back in a soothing circle. "Very well, I shan't box his ears. But I do have a different tactic in mind. One that, if Searle feels for you the way I suspect he does, will put an end to this duel nonsense. Do you want to hear it?"

"Yes." She sniffled. "Oh dear, Freddy. I do believe I am leaving an indecorous stain of tears and, well, perhaps even snot upon your sleeve."

"I do not mind, my darling," her friend assured her. "That is what friends and sleeves are for. Now, do listen to my plan…"

MORGAN RETURNED TO Linley House just in time to dress for dinner.

He had gotten thoroughly sotted with Monty, and then the two of them had engaged in a bout of sparring in Monty's ballroom rather than Gentleman Jackson's, which left him in possession of a bruised jaw. Monty had fists like great, meaty ham bones. Morgan was not nearly as quick-witted and responsive when he was in his cups. The result had been disastrous.

But, as his valet Carr shaved him—Morgan winced when the man's razor skated over his freshly bruised flesh—and then helped him to slip into evening wear before tying a cravat at his neck. He had to admit he felt strangely numb. Almost as if he were trapped within the body of a stranger, going about his day, no inkling of what he ought to do or where he should be.

Because all he wanted to do was seek out Leonie. It was a dreadful impulse; one he would be wise to banish with as much haste as possible. But there it was. He was at home, and somehow, home had come to mean his wife. His body ached for hers. His heart thrummed for her. His eyes had looked for her everywhere.

He did not even know if she was at home, for his pride had not allowed him to inquire with Huell. And if she was, he knew without a doubt she would not deign to dine with him. But he had nowhere else to go. No social engagements, for he had begun summarily refusing all invitations sent him following his marriage to Leonie. The social whirl was not for him, and he had only suffered the various balls and musicales he had endured because he needed her as his bride.

He did not wish to go to the club, for Kirkwood would likely have heard of his actions by now. Morgan did not doubt his wife had instantly run to Mrs. Kirkwood's side upon her return to town, divulging everything. Which meant Kirkwood would either toss him out on his arse or challenge him to a second duel.

Both of which he deserved.

He thanked Carr and dismissed him, lingering for a few moments in the dressing room of his chamber, staring at himself in the looking glass. He scarcely recognized the man looking back at him. Jaded, harsh, all ugly angles and tired skin, he looked weary. And angry.

He looked like the man who had hurt Leonie, and he hated that man. He hated himself. The Duke of Whitley's words returned to him suddenly, echoing in his mind, landing somewhere in the vicinity of his chest.

Let the past die. Let it go, or it may well kill you.

He thought of Leonie, of how alive he felt whenever he held her in his arms. When he touched her. When he kissed her and made love to her. And he wanted that feeling, wanted it more than the hollowness of vengeance.

But if he let go of his need to exact revenge upon Rayne, what did he have left? Retribution had been his driving force, the only emotion to propel him forward. He had been raised by two strangers who hated each other, and then he had spent the last few years mired in the hell of war. He did not have gentleness in him. He could not be the man Leonie needed. The man she deserved. She loved him, and he...he did not believe in love.

Did he?

Of course, he had most certainly killed whatever it was she felt for him. Lust, longing, desire, regardless of the name, he was sure he had replaced it with hatred instead. How fitting. Perhaps the son was forever doomed to repeat the mistakes of his father.

Disgusted with himself, he left his chamber and descended to the dining room. His head was aching with the after-effects of the claret he'd consumed with Monty, and no doubt the blow he'd received as well. He needed some of Monsieur Talleyrand's rich French cuisine to take away the edge, or else he needed more claret. Whichever he could get his hands on first.

But as he reached the main floor, he forgot about sustenance and drink, and his pounding head altogether. Because there stood his wife, dressed in a blue evening gown with gossamer net, Forget-me-nots woven through her white-blonde curls, and she had never been more lovely than she was in that moment.

"My lady," he said, his tone roughened by the burst of longing shooting through him.

Did the flowers in her hair hold a deeper meaning? Something within him dared to hope. Two days had passed since their picnic by the stream at Westmore Manor, but it may as well have been a lifetime.

"My lord." She dipped into a formal curtsy as he reached her.

He bowed, her sweet scent overwhelming him. Her expression was guarded, her lovely pink lips compressed. "You are a most welcome sight this evening."

And she was. He could not deny it, regardless of how impenetrable he wished to be. She melted the hardness inside him, purified the ugly, jagged shards into something better. Something worthwhile. Replaced the darkness with her brightness, even though he did not wish the transformation.

"Thank you, Searle." Her gaze traveled over his face, lingering on his jaw. "Have you been engaged in a bout of fisticuffs? I do believe you have a bruise."

He rubbed the sore area gingerly. "A bit of sport with my cousin, Monty, nothing more."

She surprised him by raising her hand and gently tracing his jaw with a tender touch. "It looks as if it must hurt."

Morgan swallowed against a sudden knot in his throat at the caress of her fingers over his skin. Longing slammed into him. He had not allowed himself to admit how shaken her defection had left him. Without thought, he clasped her hand in his, holding it to his freshly shaven skin.

He turned his head and then pressed a kiss to her palm. "Not when you touch me, it doesn't."

A shadow passed over her features. "Why, Morgan?"

"Because you are an angel, Leonie, just as I've always said. Of course you would have the power to heal as well." Though he deliberately misunderstood her, he meant the words he spoke.

Her eyes glittered with unshed tears. "I am not an angel. Just a flesh and blood woman. But you know very well I wasn't speaking of your bruise. I am talking about this horrible need for vengeance against my brother."

He released her hand. "I will not speak of it."

Indeed, he could not, for the mere question made bile rise in his throat. It restored to him the memory of every lash he had suffered, every burn. It took him back to the beatings, to the dark nights when he had been convinced he would die, when he had been sure he had been broken at last, body and mind and spirit crushed by his enemies.

A sweat broke out on his brow, and the pounding in his head returned, intensified a hundredfold. He was back in the dirt, burrowing with his bare hands, tunneling for his life, listening for the slightest hint of sound, heart hammering from the knowledge that at any moment he would be caught and hanged.

"Searle." Leonie's face was before him, dispelling the bleak reveries that threatened to consume him. "You are pale. Do you need to sit? Shall I fetch you something?"

He shook his head. He did not often suffer such a crippling return to those dark days whilst he was lucid. Only his dreams were ordinarily haunted.

"Searle?" she repeated, concern in her mellifluous voice.

"I require a moment." He forced out the words, his tongue feeling thick and dry in his mouth.

"Come." She led him to the drawing room, stopping before a striped divan. "Sit, my lord."

He stood, unmoving before the piece of furniture. He wanted to sit, and yet, he didn't. He desired his wife's attentions, her calming presence, her soothing touch, and yet he wanted to push her away. His head throbbed. His skin was cold. All he could think about was the darkness, tunneling through the earth, scrabbling for his life, what he had done just before making his desperate bid for freedom...

Her small palms found his shoulders, guiding him downward, and he allowed it. The action took him back to the day he had come upon her in the salon at the Kirkwood ball, and their roles had been reversed. That day, he had been the one to see she was suffering and in need of aid.

She sat beside him, one arm going around him as her other hand found his, and she laced their fingers together. "Take slow, deep breaths, Morgan."

He did as she ordered, inhaling through his nose and exhaling from his mouth. His grip on her fingers tightened. He did not want to need her. Did not want to take comfort from her. And yet, he was helpless. If he had needed further proof she was an angel, here it was. She alone could calm him. She alone could force the violence and the memories and the madness away.

She alone could save him.

But did he want to be saved? *Could* he be saved? Or was it too late?

"Will you tell me?" she asked softly. "I want to know what happened to you so I can help you."

"I do not want your help," he forced himself to say. "The only thing that will help me is facing Rayne on the field of honor and putting my bullet in him."

She flinched.

He ought to be ashamed of the virulence within him, the hatred festering and seething for the Earl of Rayne. The man was Leonie's half-brother, after all. But it was how he felt. He hated Rayne with the scorching intensity of a thousand blistering suns. Bloodlust surged inside him, replacing the sick sense of anxiety.

"How can you truly believe harming anyone will make you whole?" Leonie demanded.

Her hand still clasped his, and her arm was still around him, holding him to her. And damn it if he did not take comfort in it. In *her*.

"Nothing can make me whole," he told her truthfully. "What happened to me...it changed me. I will never again be the man I was. You saw the evidence of what they did to me, Leonie, and that is not nearly the half of it."

"Tell me," she urged.

He forced himself to look down into her upturned face. She was so trusting. So bloody caring, even when he did not deserve it. He could not be certain which was worse, her silence or her nearness. Both were torture in equal measure.

"I killed a man," he found himself saying, lost in the depths of her gaze. Lost in her.

"Death is a part of war." Her hand clasped his more tightly in reassurance. "You were a soldier, Morgan."

"You misunderstand, Leonie." He paused, a violent surge of nausea stealing his breath for a moment. "The night I escaped from the enemy soldiers holding me captive, I killed my guard with my bare hands. He had come to do violence upon me, the sort you cannot imagine, the sort I have no wish for you to ever know...and I could not bear it. I choked him, and I watched the life leave him. I faced many soldiers on the field of battle but this was different. They broke me that night. I became a monster."

"You did what you needed to do to survive." Her tone was fierce, and a tear clung to her long, golden lashes. "There is no shame in any of your actions, Morgan. You were brave, so very brave to free yourself."

He caught the tear on his forefinger. "Do not weep for me. I am not worthy of your sadness."

He had hurt her. Lied to her. Manipulated her. He had married her with the intention of meeting her half-brother in a duel. He was plagued by demons, covered in scars. There was no good in him. And yet, Leonie looked upon him with such tenderness. No pity, no sympathy, just...

Love.

Naked and raw, pure and true, *love*. Her love for him was written on her face. So real, such a force, he almost believed in it. Almost believed love could be real, that it could heal him, and that *she* could heal him, if he only let her.

"But you are worthy, Morgan. If you would only look inside yourself, you would see that." She kissed the tip of his finger, and the wetness of her tear clung to her lips.

Something inside him snapped. His mouth was upon hers in the next breath, his tongue tracing the seam of hers, licking the saltiness of her sorrow from her lips. She opened for him without hesitation, and she tasted sweeter than she ever had. Bittersweet.

He cupped her face, angled her to where he wanted her, and deepened the kiss. Need for her burst forth, flooding him. He was helpless. He forgot about the duel. Forgot about Rayne. Forgot about the awful, ugly sins of his past. And he kissed his wife. He kissed her as if she were his last meal, laid before him, as if he could consume her.

Suddenly, he no longer wanted dinner. To hell with food. To hell with anything but Leonie. They kissed and kissed, breaths mingling. Her heartbeat was so fast and strong he felt its flutter beneath his fingertips.

Yes, this was what he had been missing for the past two days. What he had been missing all his life. Just this woman, this one incredible woman who loved so fiercely, whose heart was so good, who knew suffering well enough to understand what he needed before he knew it himself. And he wanted everything she had to give him. When he kissed her, she chased away the darkness. When he drank her in, she washed away the pain, the memories.

She shook him. Rocked him to his very core. Humbled him, too. After everything he had done to her, after everything he had said—each cold word and colder deed—she was still showing him such tender concern.

She tore her mouth from his, and he allowed it. Gave her the space she needed, respected her boundaries. "It is too much, Searle," she whispered. "Too fast."

He nodded and released her, because he understood, and he did not want to push her. The last thing he wanted was to make her feel forced into returning to his bed. He had sent her from him, and he deserved her punishment now. He deserved her silence and her reticence. *Christ*, he deserved her scorn, which she had yet to truly show him. Perhaps she was too good, incapable of experiencing the rancor which led him to the brink of madness on a daily basis.

But there was one question he dared to ask. One answer he needed to know. "Can you forgive me, Leonie?"

Her long lashes swept down, guarding her secrets, hiding everything from him for a beat. And then she glanced back up at him, the conflict within her evident in her expression. "I cannot make any promises, but I will try. In return, I ask one favor of you."

He stiffened, anticipating her question before she even asked it. "The duel will carry on, Leonie. It must."

Her face lost all its softness as she went rigid. "All I ask is that you reconsider crying off the duel. You do not have to promise me a thing."

Morgan wanted to deny her outright. His every instinct demanded that he must. He had always been a man who believed in justice. Bringing Rayne to his knees was all that mattered. The thought of standing over the earl's prone form, pistol in hand, victorious, had been carrying him through his days far longer than Leonie's sweet kisses, creamy flower-scented skin, and tight cunny had.

He did not owe her the promise he would consider walking away from his only chance to right the wrongs which had been perpetrated against him. He did not even owe her a response.

But she was awaiting his answer now, her expression grave, and she looked so fragile and delicate, as if one wrong move from him would send her toppling like a felled tree. The haunted look in her eyes troubled him in turn. He had no wish to be the cause of this woman's sadness, nor the source of any of her tears.

"I will reconsider," he allowed grudgingly, for it was the only answer he could give her, even if it was not the one she deserved. "But I promise nothing."

She smiled sadly. "That is no more and no less than you have always promised me, my lord."

In defeated silence, the boulder of dread within him swelling to the tremendous burden of a mountain once more, he led his marchioness to dinner.

CHAPTER SIXTEEN

L EONORA WOKE IN the night to a familiar sound.

Searle was suffering from nightmares again.

Her only instinct was to throw back the covers. Though she had not long been a resident of Linley House, she knew her way well enough to hesitantly step through the darkness of her chamber. His strangled scream of undeniable horror made a shiver slide down her spine.

Whatever had happened to him during his imprisonment, it was enough to terrorize him months later. He had alluded to the horrors earlier in the drawing room, sharing more with her than he ever had. She could not imagine, did not wish to imagine, the full extent.

She could only hope and pray that Freddy was right and that her plan would work. That the experience of his capture had left him so scarred and fraught it had created a beast within him, a beast which demanded Alessandro's blood as forfeit and would accept nothing less. But Freddy had suggested if Leonora could give Searle comfort, show him he need not be alone, that working through his demons at her side would be far better than making new demons and ruining lives, the duel could be avoided, and Alessandro and Searle would both be saved.

Leonora could not help but to wonder as she blindly fumbled for the latch on the door adjoining her chamber to Searle's if there was any hope at all. It seemed her husband's scars ran too deep. His bitterness and rage and helplessness had all poured from him earlier in the drawing room, and it had been heartbreaking.

But not as heartbreaking as the sounds of agony being torn from him now. As she made her way inside his chamber, she heard his breath emerging in pants. Moving as swiftly as she could, she went to his side, mindful of the violence of his response the last time she had awakened him from a nightmare.

She groped through the murk of the night, finding the edge of his bed. "Morgan," she said softly, pausing where she stood.

He stirred, groaning, then ground his teeth together with such force she shuddered at the sound. But still, he slept, trapped within the horrors of his mind, reliving the days of his imprisonment.

"Morgan."

"No! Do not touch me!" he cried out with perfect, horrible clarity.

"Oh, Morgan," she whispered, tears pricking her eyes.

She hated what he had done. She hated his intention of dueling with Alessandro. She hated that he had manipulated her and used her and made her believe theirs could be a true marriage rather than one founded in lies and his own need for revenge. But she could not hate him.

Not when she loved him so, and not when the undeniable sound of his agony over what he had endured echoed through the night.

She reached for him then, thankfully finding his hand in the bed-clothes, and holding tight. "Morgan, it is Leonie," she said again, this time with a firm voice. "You are safe. I am here. Wake up, my love."

He jerked beneath her touch, and as her eyes adjusted to the filmy moonlight filtering past the window dressings, she discerned his silhouette as he sat up in bed, breathing harshly.

"Leonie?" His fingers tangled with hers, tightening. "Is that you?"

"Yes." She squeezed back, telling herself she could not cry. She must not cry. Why, oh why, was she so easily overcome with emotions these last few days? It seemed as if she was forever on the verge of tears. But he would not appreciate her weeping all over him—his pride would not have it—and she knew it too well. "I am here, Morgan."

"Did I hurt you?" he asked hoarsely.

Yes, but not in the manner you refer to.

"No." Without thought, she brought his hand to her lips, kissing the back of it.

He was so strong, so tall and powerful, every bit of him lean and masculine, honed to perfection. And yet he was, just as Alessandro had said, a man broken. Broken on the inside. *Estar roto.* Shattered by what had happened to him. And he had attempted to paste his pieces back together with hatred instead of with love.

Could her love be enough to heal him, to make him whole? Was it possible? Or was she too late?

"Leonie?" Her name in his deep voice did not fail to have an effect upon her.

"Yes?" She kissed his hand again, unable to resist inhaling the scent of his skin. So familiar, so beloved. His hand was vital, filled with life and strength, and she clung to it, just as she clung to hope he would change his mind about facing her brother on the field of honor.

"I am sorry."

Her heart swelled.

"For waking you," he added.

The hope blossoming inside her wilted. "It was not your fault, my lord."

He was silent for a moment, and she sensed he was attempting to calm himself and gather his wits. "I am also sorry for hurting you. I did not apologize to you earlier, when I had the chance, and I should have."

The foolish hope was revitalized, like a dry flower given a much-needed drink of rain. "Thank you."

She said nothing else, simply stood there in the darkness by his bedside, clasping his hand, pressing it to her cheek to absorb the heat and the vitality of him. For an indeterminate amount of time, he held on as if letting go meant she would fall from the edge of a cliff. And she held on, too, because she felt the opposite, that releasing him meant the end.

Of them.

Of everything.

But she was also the girl who should have died when she fell from the bannister all those years ago. She believed in healing and second chances. She believed in purpose and joy and meaning where it otherwise seemed there could be none.

So, she refused to let go. She needed to believe she could change the path upon which they found themselves. That hope remained for him to find his way back to her, and for her to await him, arms open. Vengeance was not the answer, and she knew it to her soul. Love was. It always had been. Freddy was right.

"Leonie?" he asked at last.

"Yes, Morgan?"

"Thank you for coming to me and waking me. Christ knows you ought to have let me suffer in my sleep. Not even I would have blamed you."

She turned their hands as one, kissing his inner wrist, just where his heartbeat pulsed against her lips. "*I* would have blamed me."

"Angel," he said without heat.

"Not an angel," she denied. "Merely your wife."

"You do not owe me anything," he was quick to say, his tone growing cool.

But she would not allow him to build up the walls between them with such unobstructed ease. "I am here because I care about you, Morgan. Not because I feel obliged to be here. There is a difference."

"Is there?"

"Yes." Her response was instant. Perhaps too quick, and perhaps she revealed too much. But her response was already there, hovering in the thickness of the air between them. "I have never felt obligated where you are concerned. I have only ever wanted to be a good wife to you. I fear I have not."

"Of course you have. You are the best wife a man could ask for, and the only wife I want. Never doubt how selfless and inspiring and wonderful you are, Leonie." His voice was low, almost savage in its intensity. "Never let that be taken from you. You are the only good part of my life, and that is the absolute truth."

"I wish I could believe that." She could not keep the sadness from her voice, for it was there, pulsing, burning, a painful bud unfurling in her heart.

And yes, how she wished she could believe him. But she could not, could she?

"Believe what you will. I may not have always offered you the truth, but what is between us Leonie, this passion, *that* has never been a lie."

She longed to believe that as well. Good heavens, how deeply and how thoroughly and how desperately she longed for it. But he had already proven her easily influenced, and she had no wish to feel any more the fool than she already did when it came to this man.

"I want to believe you," she allowed slowly. Hesitantly.

"Believe what you must."

"If only it were as simple as that." She shook her head, swallowing against a fresh rise of tears. "Nothing in our marriage has ever been simple, has it, my lord?"

"I am not a simple man, I fear. But here is a simple question for you. Will you come to bed with me?"

His request startled her. It was not what she had expected. Ordinarily, he wooed her with kisses and heated caresses. He came to her, invading her chamber with his fierce masculine presence and bringing her to her knees with desire.

But that had been before she realized he had married her with the sole intention of inciting Alessandro to duel him. That had been before she understood how easily he had used her.

"I will not lie with you whilst you continue with this misguided need for revenge," she told him firmly. Because regardless of how much she longed for his kisses and his touches—even after everything that had happened and all she had discovered about his treachery—she could not allow herself to make love to him. Not when he wished to harm Alessandro. Not when he was hell-bent upon destroying everything they had built together over the last few weeks.

But perhaps all they had shared had meant nothing to him. And if it did...no, she could not bear to think it. She could not have been that mistaken, that foolish. Earlier, before dinner, and here now in the depth of the night, Morgan seemed to have softened, even if incrementally. He was less harsh, less cold, less rigid. More vulnerable.

"I want you in my bed, Leonie," he said then, his voice raw, his admission seemingly torn from him. "Not to make love to you—though there is nothing I long for more—but because I want you...here with me."

His words found her heart, burrowing deep. So deep, she was unable to utter a word. Emotion rushed through her in a confused, jumbled hodgepodge. It was a confession that robbed her breath, stole her ability to speak. It was the sort of confession she had never imagined she would hear from the Marquess of Searle.

She did not say a word, because she could not, and because she did not have to. Her decision was made. She slid into the bed alongside him. Instantly, his arms encircled her, pressing her against his warmth. And she embraced him in return, clutching his lean waist, nestling her face against his bare chest, just over the steady, reassuring thump of his heart. He wore nothing beneath the bedclothes, but she refused to allow herself to be tempted regardless of how very hot, firm, and enticing the feeling of his muscular body in her arms was. Her hands traveled slowly over the deep ridges of his scarred back, savoring the feeling of him.

Savoring their closeness.

Without saying a word, she clutched him, her body molding to his, and this time—for the first time—they were entwined not because of desire but because of the connection they shared. The deep, visceral bond. He needed her, and she knew it. But she also needed him. Needed him as the man he could be rather than the man he currently was. Needed him to be strong enough to choose love over hatred, to grasp the future with both hands instead of holding desperately onto the past.

It would require time, she knew, and they had so little of it.

One more full day until the duel at dawn. Shivering, she clutched him tighter, as if she could somehow protect the both of them from what was to come. If only she could.

He pressed a kiss to the crown of her head. "Cold?"

"No." She kissed his chest, the dusting of hair upon his skin tickling her lips. "Fearful."

He stilled, his entire body going tense against hers. "Of me?"

"Of what you will decide," she elaborated, kissing him once more.

"For tonight, all I have decided is that you feel at home in my arms." His pronouncement was grim but final.

And she had to agree. She *was* at home in his arms, and she could not shake the feeling, running to her marrow, that it was where she belonged. But she could not luxuriate in it either. For she knew all too well that it, like her marriage to Searle, was founded in deceptions and half-truths.

For the moment, however, nothing felt better than being in her husband's bed, his warm body pressed against hers. "For tonight, I agree," she said.

And holding tight to him, she fell into deep, dreamless slumber.

MORGAN WOKE WITH the swell of a deliciously full, warm breast in his palm. He woke with his face buried in a sea of white-blonde curls, his arms wrapped around his wife. He woke with the most painful cockstand he had sported in recent times, a feat achieved no doubt by the combination of his lust for his wife, his several days of forced celibacy, and the fact that his prick was currently nestled against the delectable curve of Leonie's rump.

Against her delectable, nightdress-covered rump.

There was a most unwanted scrap of fabric keeping him from his wife's smooth, creamy skin. But it was just as well, for he had other, far greater concerns to consider than the conundrum of waking in his own bed with his glorious wife all around him, yet still unable to roll her to her back and wake her in the manner she deserved.

With his tongue upon her cunny.

The mere thought was enough to make his mouth water.

No. He caught himself and his wayward mind, for he must not dwell on the lust for her coursing through him. He had a decision to make this morning, and last night had proven to him it would be far more difficult than he had ever supposed.

Gently disentangling himself from her, he rolled to his side, taking in the sight of her, listening to the sweet music of her gentle, deep breaths. A fierce ache tore through him as his eyes drank in her sleep-softened features, the early morning sun casting her in an ethereal glow.

This time, the ache was not just desire. It was bigger than that, stronger too, more complex. More confusing. When he looked upon her, he felt the urge to protect her, to make her happy. He felt the urge to wake every morning just as he was, with her scent in the air, her in his bed. When he looked upon Leonie, the ugliness inside him abated, drowned out by the way she made him feel.

Realization hit him with more force than one of Monty's fists.

The sensation in his chest, the lump in his throat, the dread and the guilt seizing him when he contemplated never again waking with his glorious wife in his arms, when he imagined living without her, when he thought of the babe she may be carrying in her womb this very moment…it was…it was…

"Love." He said the word aloud, testing the single syllable upon his tongue.

Such a simple, concise means of conveying an emotion more profound than he could even comprehend. An emotion he had, until this moment, believed a fiction. How impossible it seemed that four letters strung together could encompass the vastness of feelings inside him.

But somehow, it did. So, he said it again. "Love."

And again, this time louder. "Love."

Leonie stirred at his side, a sigh of contentment leaving her lips and lodging in his heart as she nestled closer to him. He gathered her to him, burying his face in the silken cloud of her hair. What a fool he had been to believe he could not forfeit his revenge, when all along the one thing he truly could not bear to lose had been right here.

Her.

He loved Leonie. His marchioness, his wife. His life.

The discovery was big, far too big to keep to himself. The need to tell her rose within him. "Leonie."

She made a kittenish sound in her throat as she nuzzled his chest. She was so damn sweet, one-half innocent, one-half seductress. Completely his.

"Leonie," he persisted, stroking her thick curls back from her face so he could see her. "I love you, Leonie."

Her eyes were still closed, but she stretched like a cat, the bedclothes sliding down to reveal her lush breasts straining against the fine fabric of her nightdress. "Mmm. Morgan?" Slowly, her lashes fluttered open, and she looked adorably befuddled to find him gazing down upon her. "Is something amiss?"

"No." He shook his head slowly, a smile he could not suppress lifting his lips. "Everything is precisely as it ought to be."

"It is?" A frown furrowed her brow. "I do not understand."

No, she would not. Neither did he, if he were brutally honest with himself, but perhaps they could make sense of things together. He cupped her face gently, staring into the vibrancy of her eyes. He saw all the answer he needed in the depths of her gaze. He saw there a woman who was strong and giving, who loved him enough to fight for him even when he did not deserve her perseverance.

And he was going to tell her the undeniable truth rising like a tide within him. He was going to unburden himself. To lay himself bare before her. His past still lived inside him, and nothing would erase it, or the scars he bore on his body. But maybe today could be the start of something new.

The beginning of his healing. Mayhap it was not impossible.

As he looked at her now, he had to hope, to believe.

The words left him. "I love you."

"You..."

He swallowed as a fresh knot threatened to climb his throat, forced down the uncertainty wrought by watching his parents tear each other to pieces with their mutual hatred, by allowing the hatred he felt toward Rayne and his captors to nearly consume him. "I love you, Leonie."

She was silent and still as his revelation hung in the air.

A wild combination of terror and elation stole through him.

Just when he thought he could not bear another moment of awaiting her response, those perfect, rosebud-pink lips of hers moved.

"You love me?"

He nodded as the terror was chased away entirely by elation. The words, the sentiment, the woman before him...it all felt right. "I love you."

Her smile was stunning. "Are you awake?"

Morgan chuckled. "Yes."

"Am I awake?" she asked next.

"I believe so." He could not resist closing the distance between their mouths, taking hers in a long and slow kiss before pulling his lips free. "It would seem you are."

"Yes," she agreed, her voice hushed. Her hands caressed his. "It would seem I am. But, this sudden change, Morgan…what brought it on? What altered between last night and this morning?"

"Nothing altered that quickly." His response was effortless. "Rather, it has occurred slowly, over time, within the last month."

Since they had been wed, he meant, and he watched as comprehension dawned on her lovely features. "Oh, Morgan. Do you mean it?"

"I have never meant anything more," he said, and he spoke the avowal with all his heart, with every conviction he had, so deep and so strong his voice shook. "I am sorry it took me this long to realize what has been before me, what has been happening every minute of each day I have spent as your husband. I could have spared you so much hurt, Leonie."

This time, it was Leonie who initiated their kiss, tugging his head back down to hers and sealing their mouths. This meeting of lips was more ravenous than the last. Tongues and teeth clashed. He bit into the plush fullness of her lower lip. They kissed longer and deeper, and this kiss was different than the rest. Different because it signified the beginning, the true beginning of their union.

Their hands moved over each other's bodies, her palms skimming over his shoulders, down the plane of his back, tightening over his buttocks. His fingers sank into her hair, trailed over the ripeness of her breasts, the hardness of her pebbled nipples still concealed beneath the nightdress. And then his hands found the generous flare of her hips, worshiping her by feel.

He rolled them as one, so that she was flat on her back beneath him, the hem of her nightdress riding high on her thighs as he parted her limbs and settled himself between them. Tearing his lips from hers, he rocked against her, his rigid length probing her wet heat through the barrier between them.

Bracing himself over her, he met her gaze. "I will not fight the duel with Rayne."

"Do you promise?" she whispered, looking thoroughly kissed and thoroughly delectable.

He wanted to devour her. Need for her raged within him, drowning out everything else. "I promise, Leonie. I am so sorry, so damned sorry for what I have done. Sorry for deceiving you, for lying to you. Sorry for ever being the cause of your pain. If you cannot forgive me for my sins, I do not blame you. I was wrong. I thought making Rayne pay for what I endured would soothe the demons within me until I met my own fate. But the truth is, you are what soothes my demons. You are what can heal me. Only you."

Tears welled in her eyes, then slid down her cheeks. "I love you, Morgan."

"And I love you." He kissed her again. "Let me show you how much."

"Yes." She kissed his lips, the corner of his mouth, his chin.

Once she started, it seemed she could not stop, and she kissed him everywhere, upon his jaw, his ear, his neck. Her tongue flicked over his skin, soft and slick, leaving a trail of fire wherever she tasted him.

Together, they divested her of her nightgown, and then no more barriers remained between them. He worshiped his way up and down her body, stopping only when he could not bear to prolong the pleasure another moment.

"Look at me," he commanded her as he stilled, on the brink of claiming her.

Her lashes lifted, and he fell into twin pools of blue as he slid inside her in one hard thrust. They were one. He took her hands in his, entwining their fingers as he began to move.

"I love you, Leonie." His mouth was upon hers once more.

He kissed her lingeringly, making love to those pretty pink lips, licking and biting and savoring as he made love to her body the same way. Slow and steady. Deep and gorgeous. The ache inside him built, his ballocks tightening, and when she cried out her second release, trembling beneath him, he could not hold himself back any longer.

A pinnacle of need and white-hot release bathed him in sensation, filling him with not just love but rightness. With the sure, unshakeable knowledge he was where he was meant to be, and that if anyone could help him to heal, it would be her, his angel.

He kissed her cheek then, her nose, any part of her his mouth could find. "I was right, darling. You do feel at home in my arms. But not just for last night. For every night that comes after, and every day, too."

And he knew precisely what he needed to do next.

CHAPTER SEVENTEEN

T HE CONVEYANCE CARRYING Leonora and Morgan arrived at Riverford House the following morning. As the phaeton came to a stop, she could not help but marvel how strange it was to return to her old home with her husband at her side. They were presenting a united front in their first visit to Alessandro since the duel had been called off, she could not help but to feel as if a massive weight had been removed from her chest.

She and Morgan had spent much of the previous day in each other's respective bedchambers, alternately making love, talking, and laughing like young sweethearts after Morgan had sent word to his cousin, the Duke of Montrose, that the duel would no longer be happening. As Morgan's second, the formal arrangements of the duel occurred between Montrose and Rayne's second, his old friend Viscount Hampstead. The moment Leonora had watched Morgan close the missive bearing his bold scrawl, her heart had sung.

Part of her could scarcely believe he loved her. It felt like a dream, almost too wonderful to be real, and she could not shake the lingering sensation that at any moment, she would wake to discover Morgan loved her only in her fanciful imagination.

Her husband alighted from the phaeton first and then reached a hand up to help her descend, as well. She met his gaze as she did so, searching. "Are you certain you wish to face Alessandro today?"

His jaw hardened, a hint of the shadows haunting him crossing over his features. "He is your half-brother, Leonie. I must face him, for your sake, and put an end to the bad blood between us. What better day to do so than the day I was meant to duel him?"

Gratitude filled her then at the effort he was making on her behalf, for she knew what it must cost him. Giving up on the vengeance that had propelled him for so long could not be easy. Nor, she suspected, was swallowing his pride before Alessandro, the man he held responsible for his captivity and torture.

"Thank you, Morgan," she said softly.

"You need not thank me for doing what is right," he said wryly. "In truth, I allowed my anger and hatred to consume me, and it is I who is thankful to you for loving me enough to see me through it."

"Always," she promised.

Arm in arm, they approached Riverford House. They had scarcely crossed the threshold and waited while the somber butler announced them. But what they found within the familiar drawing room was not Alessandro at all. Rather, it was Mama, her face pale and stained with tears.

"Oh, Leonora," her mother cried, rushing to her and throwing herself into her arms with a sob, "it is horrible news, is it not? I do not know what we shall do now."

Frowning, Leonora cast a look over Mama's shoulder at an equally perplexed looking Morgan. She patted her mother consolingly. "Whatever is the matter, Mama?"

"Did you not receive my note?" Mama's voice bordered on hysterical now as she clutched Leonora tightly. "I thought it was why you had come. Rayne has killed the Duke of Montrose."

Horror warred with disbelief. "Good heavens, Mama. What are you talking about?"

"The duel." Her mother released her and spun about suddenly, facing Morgan. "That accursed duel was your fault, and you refused to fight it. Now we must all pay the price."

Morgan's face lost color, going ashen, and she could see him shuttering himself off, the old demons inside him mingling with an onslaught of new, prompted by the news Mama had just delivered. News which, if true, would be…

Devastating, to say the least.

"Where are my smelling salts?" Mama asked weakly, the cap on her head fluttering beneath the strength of her dudgeon, as if she stood in a stiff breeze.

"Do settle down, Mama," Leonora urged, trying to remain calm herself. "There was no duel, for Searle instructed Montrose to cry off on his behalf yesterday."

"Of course there was." Mama sniffled, then held a handkerchief to her nose. "Rayne went off to Battersea Fields before dawn this morning, though I begged him to act with care for the law and for his title both. And now, he has returned with a bleeding Montrose."

Here was some information she could work with at last. "Where has the duke been taken, Mama?"

"I must sit." Mama sobbed into her handkerchief. "Oh, it is not to be born. The Duke of Montrose is a scoundrel, but Rayne shall be arrested for murder over this."

Leonora met her husband's gaze, silently urging him to remain strong. Mama was in histrionics, and surely there was more to the story than she had shoddily relayed. She led her mother to a chaise lounge, then helped her to settle herself upon it. "There now, Mama. Think, if you please. Where was the Duke of Montrose taken?"

"To your old chamber," Mama answered, her voice pale.

"I will show you the way," she told Morgan grimly. Turning back to her distraught mother, she promised, "I shall send your maid Hendricks to you at once, and bid her bring the smelling salts. We will return soon."

"Thank you, my daughter."

IT SEEMED ALMOST fitting that after Morgan had finally realized what was important in life, it was about to slip through his fingers after a mere twenty-four hours. As he followed Leonie grimly through Riverford House, one litany repeated itself in his mind, a strident chorus of denial.

It cannot be.

It cannot be.

It cannot be.

But whilst Leonie's mother seemed to have a flair for the dramatic, she did not appear to be confused about what she had seen, a bleeding Monty being carried into the townhome. Pray God he wasn't dead. Pray God Rayne, that vicious bastard, had not refused to back down from the duel and faced Monty instead. It was almost too ludicrous to believe.

Except, Morgan would believe anything of the man who had been *El Corazón Oscuro.* He had witnessed the atrocities carried out upon enemy soldiers by the guerrillas Rayne had captained. And he could not bear to lose his ne'er-do-well cousin. Could not bear to be the blame for Monty's death. For all his faults, Monty was loyal down to his marrow, and willing to do anything to aid another. *Sweet Christ,* Morgan would never forgive himself if…

Nay, he would not think it. Would not believe it. Not until he knew for certain.

By the time they reached the chamber in question, he was nearly out of his wits, frantic with worry, fear, and dread. His palms were damp with sweat, heart hammering like a blacksmith upon the anvil, as he found the latch and let himself in.

The sight that greeted him as he stood on the threshold filled him with relief and perplexed him all at once. Monty lay on a bed, Rayne hovering over him. Both men were bloodstained, Monty's coat and shirt sleeve cut away to reveal a makeshift linen bandage tied tightly around his upper arm.

"Has the physician arrived yet?" Rayne snapped, rather than offering a greeting.

"What the hell is the meaning of this?" Morgan demanded, stalking into the chamber, aware his fretting wife followed on his heels.

It was unseemly for her to be here, witnessing Monty wounded and in dishabille, but what the devil was he to do about it? Her demonic half-brother appeared to have *shot* his cousin.

"This... *son* of a whore sot me," Monty offered weakly, his speech notably slurred as he paused, apparently realizing belatedly that he had misspoken. "*Shot* me."

His first thought was thank Christ his cousin was not dead. And his second was good God, why was Monty so thoroughly sotted at this time of the morning? His third thought tore from him with the report of a pistol, echoing in the chamber.

"What the hell have you done to Montrose, you bastard?" he growled as he reached his cousin's bedside, uncertain of whether he ought to punch Rayne first and ask questions later, or wait to hear the earl's explanation.

Leonie had rushed after him, her sweet floral scent following with her, and the staying touch of her hand upon his coat sleeve leashed the savage beast within him. "Let Alessandro answer," she murmured.

Rayne's dark eyes were cold. "I defended myself on the field of honor. When you failed to arrive, your second decided to face me in your stead. As you can see, he was in no condition to wield a weapon. I attempted to tell him it was *fútil*, and that I would not face a man in his cups, but he raised his pistol and took aim at my head. It was either the fool, *el tonto*, or me, so I shot to maim. He can be grateful I did not shoot to kill."

The rage in him began to slowly dissipate as he turned to his cousin. "What the hell were you doing standing in for me? I sent word to you yesterday morning to cry off."

"You did?" Monty shifted on the bed, then let out a hiss of pain.

"*Cristo*, stay still or the bleeding will worsen," Rayne ordered Monty.

"Of course I did," Morgan charged, irritation at his drunken cousin gaining the upper hand over concern for his wellbeing. "Did you not receive it?"

"I negated my correshpondence." Monty paused, the expression on his face one of sheer befuddlement as he realized his words were once more wrong.

Morgan would have laughed if it wasn't so pitiful and if the situation his cousin's carousing had placed them all in had not been so dire. "You mean to say you neglected your correspondence. Why? What the hell were you doing, Monty?"

"What do you suppose he was doing, Searle?" Rayne growled, his tone rife with disgust.

"Not fit for the earsh of a lady…er, the *ears* of a lady," Monty offered with great effort.

Hell and damnation. He knew Monty caroused, but had he possessed an inkling his cousin would ignore his correspondence and then arrive at the predestined time at Battersea Fields, drunkenly wielding a dueling pistol on his behalf, Morgan never would have asked the fool to be his second. Nor would he have entrusted the all-important task of cancelling the duel to him.

Judging from his appearance and the strong scent of spirits wafting from Monty, mingling with the copper scent of blood, he had been drinking all night long. Likely in the company of one of his many paramours.

"Damn you, Monty, I did not want to fight Rayne, and I did not want you to face him on my behalf," he bit out, his anger returning, this time directed at a target other than his wife's half-brother. "I wanted this entire business to be at an end. I wanted peace, and now here you lie, bleeding and wounded. The dowager Countess of Rayne is downstairs weeping in the drawing room, convinced you are dead and Rayne has committed murder, and you are so drunk you cannot even string together a coherent sentence. If Rayne had not already done the honor, I would shoot you myself for being so bloody stupid."

Wordlessly, Leonie slid her gloved hand into his, her fingers tightening in reassurance. He took comfort in her presence at his side, in her calm in the face of such unnecessary upheaval. They were united, man and wife, one in love and in life, and together, they could accomplish anything, weather any storm, face anything that befell them. He felt it now with such certainty his gut clenched, and he was thankful anew, so damn thankful for the incredibly giving, wonderful woman he was privileged enough to call his.

He did not deserve her.

He never would.

But he would happily hold her in his heart and in his arms every day forward just the same.

"You did not wish to duel me?" Rayne asked then, interrupting the heaviness of Morgan's thoughts.

"No." He glanced down at Leonie, loving her so desperately, he ached with it.

She smiled back at him. "Searle has had a change of heart."

He found himself grinning into her lustrous eyes. God, she was beautiful. And good for him, so bloody good for him. The balm his soul had been missing, and he had been too prideful to accept. "That is an excellent way to describe it, my love." He paused, turning his attention to Rayne. "I want to leave the past where it belongs, in the past. I am willing to forgive the part you played in my capture if you are willing to forgive my attempts to use Leonie against you."

The earl raised a brow. "I will forgive you for using *Lady Leonora* if you promise to never again hurt her. If she sheds even a tear because of you, I will hunt you down and show you no mercy. Are we understood?"

"Perfectly," he replied through gritted teeth. "You have my oath. I will do nothing but attempt to make *my marchioness* as happy as possible for the rest of her life."

"I love my husband, Alessandro," Leonie added, her tone quiet but firm. "You need not worry for me."

"Oh, holy hell," muttered Monty from the bed, his tone notably weaker. "I'm bleeding to bloody death after shuffering a mortal enemy…er, a mortal *wound*. And the two of you are mooning like sick…lovesick…fuck, I need some whisky."

"Whisky is the last thing you need," Rayne told Monty coolly, before Morgan could say the same thing.

"You have sent for a doctor?" he confirmed with the earl, for Monty looked pale once more.

The sight of blood had made him squeamish, even as a child, and Morgan could only guess the reason for his cousin being carried into Riverford House—and the dowager's subsequent misconception he was dead—was owed to him having passed out at the sight of it.

"Of course." Rayne inclined his head. "I am not a savage, though you would like to think me one, Inglés. I have no wish to have the blood of a drunken duke upon my hands."

How odd, he thought suddenly, to face the man he had once known only as *El Corazón Oscuro*, his true identity as a peer who was one-half English, one-half Spanish, revealed. Life was strange indeed. Morgan never could have known the day he had faced the feared Spanish guerrillero that he would one day meet him again in a London townhouse under such circumstances.

Still, though he would make every attempt to move forward in deference to Leonie, Morgan could not forget the sins this man had committed, be he earl or the common Spanish peasant he had pretended to be.

"You have blood enough upon your hands," he could not resist saying.

Rayne's jaw tightened. "In that, we are well met. For so do you."

Morgan's nostrils flared, a surge of rage beating to life inside him. "And some of the blood I shed is owed to you, Rayne. I would say we have both sinned, and we are both in need of repentance and forgiveness."

"It is my fondest hope that the two of you shall one day be able to put aside your differences and become friends rather than bitter enemies," Leonie said then.

Ever hopeful, his angel. Ever too good to be true.

"She has a heart of gold, this one," Rayne said then, as if reading Morgan's thoughts. "Break it, and I will break you."

Morgan raised Leonie's hand to his lips for a reverent kiss, his gaze never leaving hers. "I will never break her heart, and you can thank her for my benevolence. For she is the only reason you are yet cursing the earth with your presence."

"Touches my heart," Monty interrupted. "Truly. But I am bleeding my life's...blood all...over...the...the..."

"*Cristo.*" Rayne muttered the oath. "Where the devil is this doctor? We had more luck finding physicians in the mountains of Spain in the midst of war than I have in London."

Monty's bandage had slipped and loosened, and a fresh pool of blood was working its way into the bedding, running down his arm. The earl swiftly put the bandage back into place and tightened it with hasty, efficient motions.

"You owe me a debt of honor for this insh-insult," Monty told Rayne, outraged but notably weakened.

"Happily," the earl clipped. "Name your price."

"Marry my sister," Monty said.

"Done," Rayne said, his voice cold.

Leonie gasped. "Alessandro?"

Lady Catriona was a hellion. Just the sort of wife a man like Rayne deserved. Morgan grinned. "Capital idea, Rayne. What better way to join the families even further?"

"If she meets my standards, I will wed her," Rayne said with as much passion as one might muster to describe a speck of lint upon one's coat sleeve. "Provided she agrees to my terms, I do not object. I am in need of a wife and an heir, and I do not wish to be encumbered with either. My home is not here, though I acknowledge I have duties to the line."

"I will...hold you to that promise," Monty warned.

"Done," Rayne said, looking imperturbable even as his hands were covered in Monty's blood.

A knock sounded at the door then, heralding the arrival of the physician at last.

"Get stitched up, Monty," Morgan told his cousin wryly. "I can hardly thrash a man who is bleeding."

"You can hardly thrash me a'tall," his cousin quipped with an attempt at a grin.

"Come, my love," Leonie urged him. "We must allow the doctor to do his work."

He let her tug him from the chamber, for he knew well enough to listen to the woman he loved.

CHAPTER EIGHTEEN

ALL WAS RIGHT and well in Leonora's world, and the sun rising over London, making its presence known in the slat of golden light it sent through the window dressings, seemed cheerful proof. A fortnight had passed since Morgan had first declared his love for her. The Duke of Montrose was on the mend. Alessandro seemed prepared to honor his promise to wed Lady Catriona, Montrose's sister. Mama's delicate constitution had recovered when she had realized Alessandro had not, in fact, committed the duke's murder.

But best of all, Leonora and Morgan had spent each day wrapped up in each other. They were not perfect, nor would they ever be. But they had each other, and together, they were stronger than they could ever be apart.

She kissed his scarred shoulder reverently. Every part of him was beautiful to her, especially here, where his flesh had healed in grooves and puckers, all evidence of his resilience and determination.

He made a deep, sleepy sound and rolled toward her so their bodies were facing, her leg still slung over his hip but instead of his arse, she now straddled a part of him that was very warm, very hard, and very much awake.

His eyes opened, a sensual smile curving his lips. "Morning, Leonie."

She found herself smiling back at him, love coursing through her. "Good morning, my darling."

He brushed some curls from her face, his touch so gentle she could have wept. "I love waking up with you in my bed. With you in my arms."

"I love it, too." She turned her head and pressed a kiss to the palm that lingered, gently cupping her face.

Since the day he had first told her he loved her, she had spent every evening in his bed, staying the whole night through. When nightmares shook him, she was there to soothe him. When he reached for her in the night, she reached back. Allowing her to see his vulnerabilities had not been easy for him, and she knew it.

"And I love *you*," he told her, his gaze intense.

She leaned into him, pressing her lips to his, unable to help herself. "I love you, my darling man."

Not a day passed that she was not grateful for him, for his love. Her life without him had been fulfilling, but it had also been a mere routine of duties and social engagements. She had spent the last few years longing for a husband, for a family of her own, and now, her waiting had proven most worthwhile. Now, she knew she had been waiting for the right time, the right man.

For this man, who was no longer broken inside.

For this man, who had proven he could be whole once more.

For this man, who made *her* whole with his love.

"Thank you," he told her, fitting his mouth to hers for a slow, lingering kiss.

When the kiss ended, she was breathless, the sweet languor of desire stealing over her. "For what?"

"For being you, my fierce little lioness." Another kiss. "For refusing to give up on me."

"In truth, you ought to thank Freddy." She kissed the corner of his lips. "It is she who convinced me you just needed more love and more persistence."

"It would seem I owe Mrs. Kirkwood a debt of gratitude." He

nibbled on her neck, the light rasp of his teeth over her skin making her pulse pound.

"I will happily accept your gratitude on her behalf," she said on a sigh when her husband's large hand found its way to her breast. "Even had Freddy not convinced me, I would have found my way back to you. I will *always* find my way back to you."

He raised his head, his gaze burning into hers. "Do you promise?"

Her answer was swift. "I promise. I am yours. My heart is yours."

"Good." A small smile flitted over his lips. "Because I am a greedy bastard when it comes to you, my love. I want you, your heart, your body, your today, and every blasted one of your tomorrows."

"You have them." Another inconvenient prick of tears stung her eyes, but this time she knew the reason for her recent susceptibility to shows of emotion. And the unsettled nature of her stomach in the mid-morning. And the tiredness and hunger which seemed to forever plague her over the last few weeks. "You have them all, Morgan, and one more thing as well."

"Oh?" He flashed her a rogue's grin, clearly thinking naughty thoughts. His thumb stroked her nipple, setting off a fresh ache between her thighs. "And what is that, darling?"

"A daughter or a son," she said simply.

He stilled. "Pardon?"

"A babe, Morgan," she explained, happiness swelling inside her again now as it had the day before when she had made the realization with Freddy's aid. They had laughed until the laughter had turned into happy tears, knowing their children would take their first steps together, just as they had wanted. All through the remainder of the day and the evening, Leonora had kept the news to herself, though she fairly burst with it. "We are going to have a babe."

"You are certain?" Awe tinged his voice. His hand slid from her breast, gliding over bare skin to settle upon the curve of her belly.

"As certain as can be," she said, resting her hand over his. "All the signs are here, and it took a chat with Freddy yesterday to make me realize."

"Another debt of gratitude to Mrs. Kirkwood for me."

She searched his gaze, a sudden bout of nervousness hitting her. "This, too, I shall accept on her behalf. You are pleased, are you not, my love? I know it is soon, but I am eager to be a mama."

"Pleased?" He kissed her, one fast, hard press of his mouth over hers. "I am bloody elated, Leonie. But do you mean to tell me you have known since yesterday and said nary a word?"

"I was waiting for the right moment," she admitted weakly.

He kissed her again. "With you, every moment is the right moment. Whitley told me once I must let go of the past or it will kill me, and I did not know then how very right he was. Letting go of the past and moving forward with you is the best decision I ever made. All I want is our future together, our family growing, our love growing every day. And now, I must thank you again, darling. Thank you for this precious gift."

She smiled at him. "How will you thank me, my lord?"

Her husband gave her a wicked grin. "I have a few ideas."

She wrapped her arms around his neck and tugged him to her for a kiss. She had a feeling she would like his ideas.

All of them.

And when he gently rolled her to her back, his lips never leaving hers, he proved her right.

EPILOGUE

FROM THE MOMENT Morgan had learned he was going to be a father, he had set three objectives.

Objective one: make his wife's confinement as comfortable as possible. *Accomplished with the aid of many kisses, back rubs, and, of course, strawberries.*

Objective two: prepare himself to be the best father he could be, for he did not want to have the same cold relationship with his children that he suffered with his own sire. *In medias res, for he knew nothing about being a father aside from the immense love he felt for his daughter or son.*

Objective three: spend the rest of his life making Leonie and their children happy. *A promise.*

Retribution had been the sole thing on his mind when Morgan first saw Lady Leonora Forsythe. Loving Leonie had been the sole thing on his mind nearly every day since. But that love was about to grow bigger.

"Bloody hell, man," Monty's exasperated voice cut through Morgan's introspection. "Your pacing is making me dizzy."

He made what must have been his two hundredth circumnavigation of his study, Caesar trailing nervously in his wake with each step, and pinned his cousin with a glare. "Are you certain it is not the port?"

Monty glared at him. "You need not be judgmental. It is not every day a man is forced to be present for a lying in. I do not mind telling you I am quite bilious over it."

"You are here to offer me support," he noted wryly. "Not to drain my wine cellar. And how do you think I feel? My wife is in pain and I can do nothing to aid her."

"Confinement is the business of females," Monty said with a sniff. "She has the physician and her mother to attend her. Our place is to sit in the study and fill our gullets with spirits."

Morgan raised a brow. "And how is that different from any of your other days, Monty?"

Monty glared back at him, unrepentant. "Other days, I would be betwixt the thighs of a woman. Instead, I have spent the last few hours coddling my ungrateful cur of a cousin as he paces a hole in the Aubusson."

Only Monty.

Morgan shook his head. "It has been a rather long time, has it not? Do you think something is amiss?"

Monty gave an inelegant snort. "I think all is well, and you would think so, too, if you would sit and drink the damned port."

The study door opened then, and Morgan spun on his heel, heart in his throat. The dowager stood at the threshold, looking weary but wearing a smile. "You have a daughter, my lord."

Happiness and love broke open inside him, and his knees actually shook from the force of his emotion. "And Leonie?"

"She is well." The dowager's smile deepened. "You may go and see her now, if you like."

He was already in motion, his strides eating up the distance between him and his beloved wife—and now—beloved daughter. Monty called something after him, and unless it was mistaken, it was something about thighs, followed by the dowager's scandalized exclamation.

But he did not care. He passed the physician, giving the man his thanks, and it was all a blur of halls and carpets and doors until at last all he saw was his wife, looking like a goddess, her white-blonde curls rioting about her flushed face, a swaddled babe in her arms, a happy smile upon her lips.

"Morgan," she greeted him. "Come and meet your daughter."

He went to her side, pressed a kiss to the crown of her head, and gazed down in wonder at the tiny, pink, utterly perfect face of his daughter. She had Leonie's nose and lips, he noted with pride. "She is beautiful, just like her mother. How are you, Leonie?"

"I am well. Tired, but well." She reached up with one hand, cupping his face. "And so very happy."

He could not resist kissing those generous lips before placing a kiss on their daughter's forehead as well. "What shall we name her?"

"What do you think of Georgina?" Leonie asked. "After your brother."

Raw, unadulterated love rose within him, an uncontrollable flood. He traced their daughter's soft cheek. "Lady Georgina. I cannot think of a name more fitting." He turned his attention once more to his wife, soaking in all the love he saw reflected back at him. "I love you, Leonie. I love you both so much it takes my breath."

Her smile made his heart sing. "We love you, too. Today, tomorrow, and every day that comes after. Forever."

Tears stung his eyes as he gazed upon his wife and the tiny life they had created. "Forever," he echoed, for he liked the sound of that.

About the Author

Bestselling author Scarlett Scott writes steamy Victorian and Regency historical romances with strong, intelligent heroines and sexy alpha heroes. She lives in Pennsylvania with her Canadian husband, their adorable identical twins, and one TV-loving dog.

A self-professed literary junkie and nerd, she loves reading anything but especially romance novels, poetry, and Middle English verse. When she's not reading, writing, wrangling toddlers, or camping, you can catch up with her on her website. Hearing from readers never fails to make her day.

LINKS:
Website: www.scarlettscottauthor.com
Facebook: facebook.com/ScarlettScottAuthor
BookBub: bookbub.com/profile/scarlett-scott
Instagram: instagram.com/scarlettscottauthor
Pinterest: pinterest.com/scarlettscott
Twitter: twitter.com/scarscoromance

Printed in Great Britain
by Amazon